THREE DIGGERS

THREE DIGGERS

Percy Clarke

NONSUCH

First published 1889
Copyright © in this edition 2005
Nonsuch Publishing Ltd

Nonsuch Publishing Limited
The Mill, Brimscombe Port, Stroud, Gloucestershire, GL5 2QG
www.nonsuch-publishing.com

British Library Cataloguing in Publication Data.
A catalogue record for this book is available from the British Library.

ISBN 1-84588-084-6

Typesetting and origination by Nonsuch Publishing Limited
Printed in Great Britain by Oaklands Book Services Limited

CONTENTS

INTRODUCTION
TO THE MODERN EDITION

MARK Twain, in attempting to convey the nature of the events which shaped Australia's natural character, declared that it 'does not read like history, but like the most beautiful lies'. Far more than simply colourful, it is, like Robert Frost's straightest course, 'a zig-zag line of a hundred tacks', where disparate cultures and perspectives have clashed and melded against the backdrop of a vast and spectacular landscape. What emerges is something very particular, deeply familiar and consistently strange. The literature of such a culture, in its role as guide and host, can only attempt to convey a sense of the essence of a time. Percy Clarke's *Three Diggers*, written in 1889, is an example of a work which succeeds in this regards.

Set against the cathartic events of the what became known as the 'Eureka Stockade of 1854', it is ostensibly a simple tale of good and bad, a 'ripping yarn' of the old-school style. Like the many thousands of others who flocked to newly-born Victoria in search of easy gold, three men come together by chance and circumstance. They are surrounded by a raggle-taggle band of prospectors and would-be millionaires, spurred on by the spectacular events in California. It is a cast made up of Irishmen, of Englishmen, Armenians, Americans and even an occasional Australian, all the 'diggers' which have become so much a part of the nation's folklore. Clarke's three central characters, the diggers of the title, are essentially representative of this heterogeneous tribe. It is the misadventures of 'Melancholy Jacques', the indomitable Irish doctor Michael O'Donoghue, and the wonderful Harry Coates that chiefly stake their claim upon our attention. Their attempts to find love, happiness and, of course, gold are the essence of the tale and it is around these men that Clarke moulds his narrative.

Three Diggers opens in the 'year of grace, 1854', in Ballarat, Victoria. The historical significance of this setting lies in the fact that in 1854, in Ballarat, a civil uprising played itself out that is regarded by many as having

fundamentally changed the course of Australian history. This uprising was
known as the 'Eureka Stockade', and was fought between the diggers of
the goldfields and the military authorities. Its first and only armed civil
uprising, it is considered to be of equal significance to Australia's history as
the storming of the Bastille was to the French and, together with Gallipoli,
is the country's most debated military action.

It began with the discovery of gold in 1851, and with the tensions
that began to mount between the prospectors and the official
authorities. The colonial government, in the form of the now infamous
Gold Commission could be brutal in its dealings, and rigorous in its
demands. Taxation came in the form of licenses, and was collected with
little delicacy. Fuel to the growing fire of the diggers grievances was
the suspicion that the local administering authorities were riddled with
corruption.

In 1854, a Scottish digger by the name of James Scobie was murdered.
Among the accused was a local publican James Bentley, who was also a
friend of the magistrate. His acquittal in the face of weighty evidence
began a fearful procession of events. Bentley's hotel was immediately
burnt to the ground. Military reinforcements were called for from Sydney,
and the diggers rallied around, raising what became the 'Eureka flag' and
building the Eureka Stockade. Talks of peace came to nothing as the
miners demands were summarily dismissed and compromise gave way
to the use of overwhelming force. The miners were massacred by the
assembled military, and became martyrs to their cause. There was public
outrage at the heavy-handed nature of the government. A enquiry began
which dismissed the magistrate, re-tried Scobie's killers, and disbanded the
Gold Commission.

It is a feature of much colonial literature that it has a tendency towards the
subversion of traditional hierarchies. This feature is notably very much a part
of the Australian tradition, particularly under the auspices of 'larrikinism',
the almost institutionalised regard for the mockery of authority, and is
something which has consistently informed both its art and its political
debate. Clarke's work is no exception in this respect. The lines that divide
the hero from the anti-hero become suitably blurred, as were the lines of
authority of the time. A cavalier attitude to the rigours of the law became
not something to condemn; rather, the author elucidates the more intuitive
and malleable sense of justice that emerges in these rough-hewn times.

The drama of Clarke's *Three Diggers* is projected upon this ruptured canvass, and draws the reader into a pivotal time of change. In terms of its place in the literary canon, *Three Diggers* deserves its position beside the work of such writers as Boldrewood and Marcus Clarke. Further, it is delivered with a wit and lightness of touch, such as Jerome K. Jerome, whose *Three Men in a Boat* first appeared in the same year, might well have written had he been more inclined to prospect his rivers than to simply drift upon them.

PREFACE

WHEN I committed my first infant to the care of its literary nurses, my parental anxiety was assuaged and I was reassured by the kind words of critics, amateur and professional. *Hinc illæ lachrymæ*; which being translated, means: If this the younger brother, which I now trust, Moses-like, upon the broad stream of public opinion, should find equal favour, not I alone, but they who thus encouraged and approved the first step must be congratulated.

Conceived in that land of the sunny South where the scene is placed, the story had originally no further motive than the somewhat unobtrusive one summed up in the old adage, "Man proposes, but God disposes."

Though

"Temptations sore long time he bore,"

the writer stood proof in his original intention, and while on the one hand it is not his desire to obtrude the moral, he trusts that some grains of amusement, if nought else, may be gathered by young and old from the following pages.

Finally, it is confidently believed that in the experiences of the three travellers "on the sands of time," whose fictitious names must shroud their personality, nothing will he found unfitting for perusal *virginibus puerisque*, whose unaffected applause would fill with delight

THE AUTHOR.

OLD CHARLTON, S.E., 1889.

CHAPTER I

INTRODUCTIONS

YEAR of grace, 1854. Month, June. Place, Ballarat, Australia. Let me carry you, my reader—critical or indulgent—back more than thirty years in the world's history, and introduce you to three men grouped in easy attitudes around the bloodshot eyes of a brush-wood fire burning in front of a canvas tent, which is pitched, with thousands of others, among the plains and thickets of Ballarat. The night is clear, and the air sharp; each of the unnumbered, shadowy tents at some distance from this camp stands out either illuminated by, or silhouetted against the glare of its own or a neighbour's fire, for the hour is past sundown, and the diggers having "knocked off" for the day, are enjoying their frugal supper of damper and mutton, washed down necessarily with copious draughts of a hot, inky liquid, which for the want of a better goes here by the name of tea. In the clear air come sounds of distant revelry—the "rational" enjoyment of some successful digger and his comrades.

"Ugh," says one of the indistinct figures at our particular bonfire. "I for one shan't be sorry when warm November is with us; better to be roasted in a hot wind, than frozen on a cold winter's night."

As he speaks he jumps up, and with the nervous energy of a thin, spare man of his class, throws a log or two from the wood-heap close by, on the fire, first drawing out his pannikin of tea from the red ashes, and draining with salamander-like impunity its scalding contents.

"Ah, me bhoy," says his *vis-à-vis*, seated almost within the door of the tent, "ye should just be clothed with a rational amount of sebaceous or fatty tissue like meself; it's such thin attinuated osseous bodies as yours that call a timperate climate bad names, and give more trouble to the undertaker than half a dozen like me own, what with wanting extra long pieces of board, wadding, and the like, to prevent your bony joints from rattling about when your friends are waking ye. What says the Melancholy

Jacques, if indade he can spare us a mouthful of that precious breath he's pulling in through his Titanic pipe; do ye find the climate so disagreeable to that very material structure of flesh and bloodh?"

The man thus addressed, turns rather Ponderously towards his cross-questioner, gravely removes the pipe from his mouth, and, with unmistakable country accent, replies,–

"Well, doctor, you're so well lined by nature that you could stand an Arctic winter, let alone a mere sharp night like this; but for Harry and me, an Australian winter night soon finds out whether our natural blankets are thick or thin."

The leaping and sparkling flames, refreshed by the last log or two, shine on the faces of all three, and for the first time we can distinguish to whom the three voices belong. The last speaker, John, or Jack Wainwright, referred to by his friend as the Melancholy Jacques is a muscular red-visaged blue-eyed and curly young Saxon of twenty years, whose quiet old-country ways, inherited from a long line of unadventurous Warwickshire farmers, have earned for him the undeserved epithet "Melancholy". His stalwart build, square face, and slow movements denote rather a heavy than a sad temperament, while his slow utterance of deep bass tone is almost as incisive as that of a lawyer arguing a heavy case, though, like the Yorkshire clod of ancient notoriety, his words are common-place enough, and his meaning clear. He and his black briar pipe are as inseparable as Damon and Pythias of old, and his two comrades realizing the privations he suffers with the pipe out of his mouth, hesitate to give him cause to remove it. His especial aversion is hurry or haste, and though his great strength allows him to get through a great deal of labour, he works as leisurely and apparently as lazily as a jobbing gardener in a suburban garden, who is paid by the hour to lean on his spade-handle.

Wainwright's—or Jack's, for he will be known throughout the book as he was those thirty years ago by his prænomen—questioner, whom he addressed as "doctor," appears by the fitful firelight to be a good-tempered, handsome, sandy-haired Irishman, over whose head thirty years have passed with as little effect upon his original child-like generosity and lightness of spirit as half that space over the heads of many now-a-day folks.

His clothing, which serves for purposes of description as a pattern of his companion's garments, consists of a once red, but now very discoloured flannel shirt, almost hidden under the rough pilot jacket and mole-skins, tucked into clumsy, but strong boots, all alike stained with clay and gravel. These, in common with his bearded face and the battered and tip-tilted wideawake hat, in the front brim of which he has ingeniously cut a hole to catch and support the bowl of a large German student's pipe, would give his old friends of Dublin medical college little chance of discovering in him the once natty, trim Michael O'Donnoghue, M.R.C.S., who, scarcely twelve months ago, walked the hospitals in very different attire and circumstances. Emigrating with the view of making a practice of his own, he had suddenly been drawn into the all-absorbing vortex of that whirlpool, whose centre was the gold-field of Ballarat, and he had but two months before this story opens, jumped down from the rumbling and grumbling coach as it pulled up opposite the Eureka Hotel, Ballarat, a carpet-bag, a few pounds sterling, and a small medical *vade-mecum* his only stock in trade beyond a clear head, a light heart, and an unalterable determination to make the best of everything, known in these days as the Mark-Tapley spirit.

He had barely finished stretching his bruised and cramped limbs after his hundred-mile ride from Melbourne, before his attention had been distracted by a disturbance, locally known as a "slosh round," taking place within the bar of the hotel. Within a second the doors of the bar swung violently open, and a mob of half-drunken diggers rushed out, hustling in their midst a couple of better-dressed men, one, the stalwart young farmer just described, the other, a spare, wiry-looking man, whose clear grey, restless eye looked fearlessly, and somewhat imperiously, at the swelling and surging crowd of bullies around him; his sallow, wrinkled cheeks were a trifle paler, his moustached lip somewhat firmer than usual, as with undaunted air he led his rosy-cheeked chum out of the circle of idlers, who, baffled of what had seemed an easy and innocent prey, surged round the two with threatening gestures. As the two pushed their way forward, these threats increased and reached that point where a spark of unfortunate comment may cause an explosion—a result precipitated by the grey-eyed man himself. It is given to few to exercise complete control over their feelings under great provocation, and Harry Coates certainly was not one of the few, for with angry looks and scathing contempt he replied to his assailants' threats.

"Why don't you show fairly, if you want to fight me for stopping my chum here being fleeced at dice?"

At once the mob closed in on them both, and these rash words might have cost Coates and Wainwright their portable property, if not their lives—for the times were lawless, and most of the mob armed—had not our little doctor, actuated by true Hibernian generosity and desire to help the weaker side, with a rapid and well-executed flank movement, turned the tables. Catching a big burly fellow from behind, he pulled him back almost suffocated by the flannel scarf he wore, let him go stumbling and crashing to the ground, and then darting into the opening thus formed, placed himself back to the other two, squaring his fists in scientific manner. The laugh which followed the discomfiture and fall of Bully Ben, as the prostrate man was courteously known among his comrades, and the diversion caused by the pluck and readiness of the doctor, half assuaged the diggers' wrath, which with ready tact the newcomer applied himself wholly to appease.

"Noo then," said he, "gentlemen in the middle, and, by me troth, larrikins outside. If any one wants to find what the material tissue of his nose or eye-lids can swell to by the application of a set of knuckles, I'll be happy to give him an example with personal experiments on himself in a couple of shakes. Maybe some of you might want a tooth drawn, shure I'm a duly qualified, first-class surgeon-dentist, though I say it meself, and as this is my first appearance among ye, I wont charge anything at all, but guarantee that ye'll be more than satisfied with the operation."

The doctor's word and quip amused even the roughest of the rough lot, though his long words were rather unintelligible to most of them, and their wrath quickly subsiding, they all, after having vainly persuaded the doctor to accompany them for "a booze," adjourned back to the bar, leaving the trio standing alone and looking at one another.

"Put it there," had said the grey-eyed man (who was none other than our friend the first speaker by the fire) holding out his hand for the doctor to shake. "My name is Coates—Harry Coates—and my chum here is Wainwright; we're camped down there at Poker Flat, and will give you a feed or a shake down any time you call round."

"There, man, don't say any more; shure I only did what any other dacent fellow would have done when he heard you speak, that is belaved ye more than I would the set of howling blay-guards around. But now I'll take it rale kind if ye'll tell me whereabouts among these grog-shops I can get a bed for to-night. I'm a sthranger in the land of Ham, as my old schoolmaster used to say, and don't know my way about town."

Coates had then urged him to take "pot and bed luck" with them for that night at any rate, and on the next day they were all three so well satisfied with one another, that they agreed to stand back to back from that time in the quest which had brought them all there, that is, the search for gold. The two months had gone quickly, and so had the doctor's pounds in the purchase of necessary stores, and though "the firm" had met with scarce any luck, they had perseveringly stuck well together and had shifted their camp from Golden Point down in the direction of Mt. Boninyon, where a tumbling creek brought the much-sought-for water, both for domestic and "business" purposes, within a couple of hundred yards of their tent. Here they had prospected with more fortune than at their last claim, and their conversation to-night had been on the "colour" which had shown during the day. The cradle and the pan had at last sifted out quite a respectable little packet of gold grains, averaging about two ounces to the ton, according to Coates, who was an experienced hand at gold-digging. So their spirits were this night above par, and the chances of making their fortunes seemed to bear more immediate hopes of realization than ever before, and set each one to counting his unhatched chickens, and building castles in the air. Coates decided, when he had accumulated enough, to return to the old country, and settle a sufficiency on his only sister, whom he had left seven years ago a shy school-girl of fifteen in the charge of an aunt. The balance he was going to invest in growing fruit in California, a venture then unheard of, but in which he expected to live a varied and pleasant life far removed from all such obnoxious adjuncts to existence as frost or fog.

"Eh, man, ye'll find the little girl a grown woman with little girls of her own by this time, I'll be thinking," says the doctor, "and as for the life on the fruit farm, ye'll find that such a dull monotony, that with your highly-strung nervous system ye'ld get chronic dyspepsia or derangement of the cerebral tissue, otherwise called monomania. Noo don't ye do that, but join me in me grand scheme for the emancipation of the down-trodden Irish from the rule of the presumptuous and haughty Saxon. Come and help Michael O'Donnoghue to rule Ireland at home, and support the great cause with your heart and money, me friend. Eh, and work for the liberation of Ireland, just as ye would to separate a tumour from your own body."

"Unfortunate illustration, old fellow," rejoins Coates; "a tumour is hardly to be compared with ould Ireland, I should think, from your point of view; and surely it can't, when separated, lead an independent existence."

"Eh, there, see noo" (the doctor always said noo for now, and took one or two other quaint little liberties with pronunciation, besides having a weakness for long terms, and, like many professional brethren, for technical illustrations), "see noo how clever the man is getting with his *argumentum ad hominem*. Why to be shure I meant Britain was the tumour, and as for being able to rule itself at all when the Irish secede, why I never said it would, me bhoy, and I don't think it ever will."

With a laugh at his friend's sophistry, Coates turned to the other, who had been silently puffing away, resting on his side, and glancing from one to the other during this dialogue. "Well, Jack, do you think you're likely to further our doctor's plans for the liberation of the Irish people from the rule of our haughty countrymen? Ha! Ha! I'm afraid, though, you are thinking more about that blue-eyed lass you've left behind you, than all the politics in creation. Now haven't I guessed aright? Ah, you young fellows, what gay times you have with your youthful likes and loves, careless of the world around you."

The gleaming gum log seemed to shed a somewhat deeper glow on the ruddy Jack, or was it that he blushed? He was saved the trouble of replying by the doctor who, with a great guffaw, cried out. "Hoot, hoot, just listen to the man with his aged querks and quips. I' faith a regular primature Daniel, a proof of the possibility of the seven ages of man all being rolled in one. Go on thou lean and slippered pantaloon. Ye're decaying us both; why ye must ralely be a wrinkled old spicimen of senility who covers up the defacing marks of time with some patent face-wash. Never ye mind, Jacques, me bhoy; shure if ye ever make that fortune, ye shant want the help of meself to unite ye in the holy bonds of matrimony to the fair lass, be she anybody from a duchess to a village girl, and whether she has eyes as blue as an Irish sky or as brown as an English fog!"

Mistaking the doctor's expression of village girl for vicar's girl, Jack protests. "Now look here, it's too bad of you two to link me up with the vicar's girl; as for blue eyes she hasn't such, they're a light brown, and it is no use talking of love and all that; she wouldn't have me if I asked her"—"Which ye have, ye know," muttered the doctor, but loud enough in the silence of the camp to be overheard by his comrade.

"Well ye-e-es, when I was quite young perhaps I did."

"Shure how old we're all getting," says the doctor. "Gentlemen, do ye see me getting a bald pate; why I feel me teeth falling out already, even my voice acquiring palsy."

"And what did she say?" says Coates, looking moodily at the fire, and raising himself on one elbow. "Didn't she treat you haughtily? Tell you that she wondered at your impertinence, although most likely she had just been making you fetch and carry for her? Was surprised you had the assurance to take such a liberty after having received no encouragement, while all the time she had been setting her cap at you until your blood ran like quicksilver? Until you felt that one word more and you must snatch her away in your arms like young Lochinvar; until you felt mad to see another man standing by her side; until you were ready to do anything, no matter how hazardous or ridiculous, for her sake, if only she said thank you and lifted her eyes to yours ; until, in fact—but there, pooh—"

Suddenly stopping himself in his crescendo monologue, he vented his emotions in a vicious kick at the red-hot gum ember that just then tumbled on to his foot. His companions, surprised at his unwonted heat upon a subject which had now for the first time been discussed among the three, sat for a while in silence, which the doctor was the first to break.

"Eh!" said he quietly, "this aged piece of marble has felt like one of us young organisms at some remote period of his life, perhaps in the Palæozoic age. Reckon it was some woman petrified him, what say?" This to a great rolling lump of crackling charcoal, which falls down from the bonfire on his side.

"Well, Coates," said Wainwright, "to tell you the truth, it happened something like that, except that I had never felt so hot about it, and the girl never said anything of the sort."

"Shure, for all this is such a quiet chap, he's scoring noo," says the doctor in a stage aside. "Well come, man, tell us hoo it really did happen. Spin a yarn, and garnish it hoo ye like so as to pass the time until we turn in."

"No," says Jack, scarcely seeming to hear the other, and keeping time to his words by a rhythmic-like beat of the pipe, with one hand in the other. "The way it was, was this. I was only twenty-one at the time, she nineteen. We had played together ever since children, had exchanged our apples and sweetmeats with each other, and whenever she came with her father to the farm on the parish duties, which ended in his taking away a pound of butter or such like, I would take her away on the sly to the dairy, and lift her up to skim her little fingers over the cream trays. So we grew up together, and when the dad proposed that I should come into the farm and share the profits, it seemed quite right that I should ask her to be the same little wife to me in reality that she had often been in fun in the olden days. Oh, I get quite hot thinking what a blamed idiot I must have looked when I asked her, for I had always spoken so naturally to her before, but somehow I couldn't find the proper words that day. I stammered and stuttered like a pig with the asthma. But she knew what I meant, for her big brown eyes got misty before I had got out a dozen words, and her face flushed and got pale by turns, and with tears she begged me not to go on, and told me it could never be. I should know one day why, if I would have her friendship. I could always count on her taking a true interest in my life, and so on. I thought perhaps she was shy, and wanted to be asked again, as the village lasses used to do when one wanted to kiss them ("What a Lothario," says the doctor)" so I kept quiet for a while, like a fox in cover, and one day I was going to ask her again, when she got almost terrified, begged me never to speak of it again, and with a huskiness in her throat, said she would rather this pain had come to anybody but her dear brother Jack. She found she must tell me she was engaged to another, that it was kept a secret from her father, as her betrothed was a young lieutenant, and her father hated all soldiers on account of his only sister having, years and years ago, married one who afterwards had so ill-used her, that she died broken-hearted soon after. She then asked me not to split about it, at which I got rather wild, though I don't know why, for how was she to know that I was not such a darned sneak as that when I had been bothering her as I had? Goodness gracious, my pipe's out!"

"I think," says the doctor, as the other seizes a small branch from the fire, applies it to his pipe, and puffs vigorously away, lying down on his back when the puffing is in full swing. "I think," he repeats, "if the truth were known, our young friend was more sorry when that lieutenant put his pipe out than noo, although he does pretend to be such a Socrates about it."

"I don't know what that may be," says Jack, still dreamily puffing away, "but I can tell you that I didn't feel as quiet about it then as I do now, and that was why I left the farm, and got knocking about in Liverpool, and so got a touch of the gold fever, as they call it."

"Well, but," says the doctor, "ye haven't finished your love-story, me lad. What became of the young lady? Did she marry the lieutenant, and live happy ever after. With the priest, her father blessing the two of them, with geese and turkeys from his parishioners' farmyards in either hand?"

"No, hardly that," says Jack. "Poor girl, her father was of the strict sort, found her writing one day to her lover, telling him not to meet her again, as she could not go on deceiving her father any longer, and the old man fell to that part of the computation service" ("commination you mean," says Coates), "where the parson and his clerk curse the congregation and seem to get cursed back again." Here Jack revived the dying flame of his pipe, and interlarded the rest of his story with puffs. "Well the upshot was that the poor girl's life got so bothered with suspicions and reproaches, that one night, without a word beforehand, she left the house, pushing a note under her old father's door saying that she was going to marry the lieutenant, and hoped for her father's forgiveness."

"Which, of course, she received by next post," says the doctor. "Why the ould man couldn't help himself, and would have to make the best of a bad bargain."

"Oh yes he could, doctor, for long before she came back again he was dead. Why a few days after he got the letter he called on my father, told him the whole story, asked him to be his executioner" ("executor," says Coates), "rode into the nearest town, and there and then got the lawyer to make a new will for him. On his way back, his stout little cob shied and threw him into the canal, which ran by the road, and the old fellow must have hit a stone, as he was found next day by a bargee with his head cut open; so he died, carrying out his vow to the last, that he would never see one of his race married to a soldier."

"Well, man, and the girl?"

"Oh, the girl never turned up again at the village, so far as I could hear; it's three years now since she left, and never a person that I know received a line from her. She couldn't have heard of his death till after he was buried, and then I suppose she hadn't the heart to go back."

"And the will? I suppose though the old fellow hadn't much to leave?"

"Yes he had, though, that was the curious part of it, for though he had been so thrifty all the time we knew him, and always collected his own tithes and so on to save expense, it turned out that he had a great store which had been piling up in a bank somewhere or other, which probably he meant to give his daughter, but which by his last will he left to a nephew; I suppose out of pure spite, as the nephew was a gay, thoughtless young fellow, and the parson had always preached at him. Why there were six or seven thousand pounds saved up. I know of that, as the lieutenant wrote to my father, and threatened to upset the will, but nothing came of it, and we heard no more of the matter, except that the nephew got gayer than ever, and a rumour came that the vicar's daughter would have been happier with her husband had she got the money."

"Well shure that's a pritty story; those women are at the bottom of everything, as the French poet says, bless his soul, and we're much beholden to you for your linguistic entertainment, Jacques, me bhoy, particularly as your pipe's out again."

Jack's only response is a nod; he thinks he has done enough talking for to-night at any rate. The glowing charcoal lights up his face for a moment, as Coates curiously scans it from under his own bushy eyebrows; but finds neither emotion nor sentiment, nor any expression, save that of physical health; then the young giant stretches out his frame prone before the fire, more exhausted by his long speeches than by a day's hard work.

CHAPTER II

CONFIDENCES

PUFF-puff go the pipes of all three, alone breaking the silence, while the music, heaven save the mark, of a concertina up at the store comes fitfully along the evening wind, enchanting alone in proportion to its distance.

"Well, Harry, me bhoy," says the irrepressible doctor, "after such a good story from our sphinx, surely ye can tell us something to keep our aural appendages warm and tingling." The surveyor starts from his abstraction and mutters, "Oh well—perhaps—why not? I don't suppose it matters to any one but myself, whether I say it or no—and I care not—at least"—he goes on, "I can't afford to care."

"Noo then, Coates, if ye go mumbling to yourself like that, I shall have to take ye seriously in hand, trephine ye, and clean out your brains, or something of that sort; it's not healthy, man, to mutter to yourself when ye have an appreciative circle or triangle of friends, including yourself, waiting to hear a yarn."

"All right, old fellow, I was just thinking aloud, you know. Well, I'm in for it I see, so here goes."

"Thrue to the core!" says the doctor.

"Too true," says Coates. "As you know, I started life in London as an architect and surveyor, with a small capital in money, and a large capital in a good education, a circle of friends, and influential acquaintances. I got on amazing quickly, too quickly to be lasting, my old-fashioned, slow-going aunt used to say, and before I was twenty-five, I was making £1500 a year, and after providing for my little orphaned sister's education, I was still able to put by a great portion of my income. All things looked well ahead. If ever a man had a rosy outlook it was mine. It had never entered into my head to be married up to that time; friends used to joke me, and I suppose mammas drew my attention to eligible daughters, as I have heard so since, but I never noticed it at the time, I hadn't in fact realized what it was to have a passion, as the French say. About this time I came in contact, through business, with an elderly gentleman of some means of the name of Clive, who seemed to take some fancy to me, and invited me on a pretext of business to his house, in a London suburb, where he introduced me to his wife and daughter. He was a cautious pupil of the old school, and as I afterwards heard, made ample inquiries about me before he took this step. His wife was a buxom matron, his daughter a lovely girl, with dark, wistful, lovable eyes and hair, clear bright complexion, an intelligent face and smile. It was a hopeless case for me from the first, though indeed at that time I thought it most hopeful. I was a frequent invited guest at their house, evidently favoured by the Clives, father and mother, and, as I thought, by their lovely daughter too. Business called me away to the North of England for a time; I returned in a few weeks, and soon received a visit from the father. Business over, he pressed me to spend the evening with them, an invitation I only too gladly accepted. While away, I had had leisure to reflect upon what I was about, and had made up my mind to propose, as I found myself harder hit than ever I had, in the hurry and scurry of business, thought. So somehow then and there in my office, I spoke out to the kind old fellow, ending up my sketch of my prospects, my love, and its object, by asking for leave to propose.

"The old man started and jerked out, 'Good God, Coates, haven't they told you my daughter's been engaged to Mr. Merrivale this fortnight. My poor boy! my poor boy!' The tears stood in his eyes as he looked at me. I seemed to be gazing on at a play, for I noticed the tears rolling down his cheek, fall drop by drop on his collar, and thought it a pity for him to spoil his linen so. This was my first thought, then the tide rushed over me, and I realized what he meant, and that it was I he was talking to. How I longed to be a little lad again at my mother's knees, sobbing away into her comforting bosom my sorrows! Then another tide, a tide of pride, surged up, and I swore to myself not to show any wound, though for that matter my face must have told the tale plainly enough. I made myself go to the house that very night to put a good face on it, but found no Merrivale there, and the daughter more charming and winning than ever. I ought to add that Merrivale was a wealthy and heavy northcountryman whom I had once or twice seen at the house, and who appeared to be very coldly treated by the daughter, though hospitably by the parents."

"Come," says the doctor, after allowing for a pause, but finding the story-teller went on no further. "Ye're as bad as Jacques, ye leave off in the most interesting part. What did it all mean?"

"Mean," says the surveyor, "I never knew, and I don't know now, and I don't suppose I ever shall know in this world."

"As ye don't believe in purgatory, ye won't in any other, for they won't have the heart to revive your misfortunes in heaven itself."

"I never knew whether the girl was a coquette, or I had been too blind a fool, for I am certain her parents didn't force her to have Merrivale; in fact, the old boy told me in the office his wife and he had fixed upon me themselves as the son-in-law they would most like, but, of course, they left it to the girl."

"Oh, they were fooling ye," says the doctor, "or thrying to flatter ye and make things smooth again."

"Not they! what did they gain by telling a lie, for so far as money-matters went, the girl would have been almost as well off as my wife; besides, I have heard the mother say that she had trained her girl to do everything that a poor man's wife had to do. So you see it's clear the parents had no particular preference for wealth."

"So you also threw up your position and came out here," said Jack.

"Not quite so fast; you see there was somebody else to think about—my sister. For five years more I worked harder than ever; but with the constant thought of getting away from it all, put by all I could, sold my business, stored all up, got a lawyer to settle the money in the proper way upon my sister, and then, with £500 in my pocket, went knocking about, now here, now there, and at last here I am. By the way, as I am telling you a true story, I ought to tell you that I've omitted a portion, but I'm really so ashamed of it that that must be my excuse. The fact is that when my hopes were thus dashed, I buried thought and feeling by a round of reckless dissipation which ended in a severe illness and kept me from my business for a month. Now you fellows know more than anybody else on the face of this globe about my one weakness, for I call it so," added the surveyor bitterly, "and I hope that if you ever need such help, you'll remember my unfortunate example, and be particularly careful to make preliminary inquiries about any girl you think you like, otherwise you may perhaps find that she is betrothed or perhaps wedded all the time she is making eyes at you."

"Come, come," says the doctor, "that's not like yourself to talk like that, Harry, so generous and kind as ye are, to speak as though life were a Dead Sea apple, all outward bliss and inward rottenness."

"Well, look here, doctor, what would you have done?" says Coates.

"I'd have sifted the matters me bhoy, looked at all the parties concerned with a microscope, and found out if the young lady really cared for me or no, sounded the Merrivale or what ye call him, and if the girl cared more for you than the other, I would have stormed the citadel and carried her off just like the young Lochinvar ye were just telling us about."

"That's all very well, doctor, but you can't go to the girl when she is already engaged and plump out a proposal. That's a mean, blackguard trick which she oughtn't to like you for."

"Well I don't see it; Shure if she'd be happier with you than the other, ye must give her the chance; ye surely don't want her to propose to ye herself."

"No; but she would first break off her engagement with the other man; surely common kindness to him should make her do that, and that would be a sign. But this young lady I speak of never showed any sign of being off with the old love in that way. Of course I made her father promise not to tell her or let her know what I had said to him, so she never knew in so many words from me how I felt; but, great heavens, she must have seen it; seen it, yes, and gloried in it, probably triumphed in it, laughed over it to Merrivale—" Coates had jumped up, and was waving his hands about in an unconsciously melodramatic style.

"Hold hard, Coates," cries out Jack, evidently much disturbed; "don't torture yourself by making believe, as the children say; take a good puff of this negro-head and a drink out of my pannikin to steady your nerves." Coates subsides with a grateful nod to his comrade, and the doctor, ever considerate of the feelings of others, turns the tide.

"Well, noo, I'll tell ye a confidence of me own, though there are more alive who know my story than ye two; what our peasant boys call the lovely craters were at the bottom of my adventure; but I was more fortunate than both of ye, as I had two to consider, and this is hoo it was when I was house-surgeon at the hospital in our grand old town of Dublin there happened to be one ward in particular which I used to consider a very good place to take exercise in. Ye can understan' that it wasn't because the ward was sunny or long or high or well aired. Not a bit of it. I am free to confess that it was because of a sunny, bright, but well-haired lass that occupied one of the beds as a convalescent. Doctors don't often look at their patients as though they were human beings like those outside walking about; they get so used to considering them as physiological structures, osseous frames covered with flesh and so on, in a normal or abnormal state, that it would puzzle many a good doctor to say whether a patient were good-looking or plain. I say this as a sort of preface, because you will see I took a great deal of notice of the pretty English girl who had come in with scarlet-fever, and who lay looking brighter every day, and, as I thought, brighter still when I came along. She seemed a born lady; but I didn't know her name, or how she came to the hospital. The nurses called her Mary, but as a doctor I went by her number and called her No. 22, never thinking of asking after her other name. Up against her bed was that of a stout middle-aged biddy who had broken her leg in a street accident, in such a way that we had to amputate. She was bonny enough for those who like a florid, large market-woman about forty-five inches round the waist, and heavy to match, which I knew myself; as when I operated upon her I had to assist the nurse with the lifting of her. Noo as Mary and Biddy got well together, I of course had to be looking after both, but scant time did Biddy receive compared with Mary. One day I heard that Mary would be going out in a couple of days, and I thought I might as well put things straight with her before that happened so as to know who she was and where she lived and all about it, for I could see she was not a common lass, and I really had quite a liking for her. So the next night, when I had made my round of the wards, I just dropped again into the ward as though I had forgotten to tell the sister in charge something or other. To put a good face on it, I waited by till the sister went away for something, then marched in, asked one of the nurses where she was, and said I would wait for her. The lamps were burning dimly, just showing the outlines of the beds and nothing more, and so I walked down to Mary's bed, No. 22, ye know, and took a seat beside it. She wasn't sleeping, for she turned over away from me, taking me, as I thought, for a nurse, and wanting to get to sleep; but with soothing tones I softly whispered to her and told her how the sky had lost its charm since her blue eyes had shone and the rippling falls of my native streams were unmusical compared with her merry laugh, and that if she went away without giving me a word of comfort, I should be desolate, and all the rest of that blarney which young gossoons manufacture for the occasion, or get out of some sentimental poetry."

Coates here interposed with a laughing gesture of dissent.

"Eh, mon, but ye never were a young man, so ye couldn't know a young man's feelings on the subject. Well, to proceed. I went on this way for some time until I was fairly out of breath, and when I stopped, I certainly expected the fair creature to speak in return, and thought I knew what her answer would be—well, what d'ye think she said? I see ye don't guess. Don't look so terribly solemn, Harry, it wasn't no again, like it was for you and Jack. The fair creature turned round with a great jerk and a heave, put her arms, and caught me by the sleeve, and in Biddy's loud voice, cried out in the broadest of Irish in a way to wake the dead, 'Shure, it's ye'self, doctor, is a darlint to take a poor one-legged creature; why av course I jump at the offer, and take ye for better or worser.' Oh bhoys, oh bhoys, it was the cruellest piece of fun ye ever saw in your life. I'd mistaken the day when Mary was leaving. She'd gone that very afternoon, and Biddy had been moved into her bed."

Coates breaks out into boisterous laughter, and even the imperturbable Jack gives vent to a series of sounds which in him take the place of a laugh, while the doctor looks on, solemnly and whimsically, surveying them the while, the very man of all others to tell a tale against himself, finally joining them with his own ringing peal, and bringing his hand down on his thigh with a hearty slap in his accustomed manner. When the little camp is comparatively quiet again, he resumes.

"Ye may just understan' that things got pretty hot for me at the hospital after that, for the sister had come up close, and had heard the last few words of my conversation, and, of course, she and all the rest of the ward heard Biddy's twelve horse-power voice; but I should have managed to live it all down, and perhaps be just through at the opposite end of this mundane sphere, plodding along respectably among my patients, if, one morning, a month after the event, an attorney's clerk hadn't poked his head in my room and served me with a slip of blue paper from her Majesty, calling upon me to show cause why I shouldn't pay a thousand pounds damages for breach of promise of marriage, made to Kathleen O'Flannagan, or something of that sort. I sold my traps, resigned my place at the hospital, gave a good dinner to about a dozen college and hospital chums, got on the steamboat, and here I am safe

from Kathleen O'Flannagan and her attorney, who may go in company
to the —— ahem!"

The doctor's yarn over, all three of our friends find themselves
suddenly rather tired, and with one accord seek their hard, but sleepful
couches in the tent, Coates, with the forethought of an old colonist, first
raking together the white ashes over the fire. The other diggers in the
distance have, by this time, done much the same. And the huge canvas
town, brimful of vice and villainy, greed and crime, sleeps without a
sound, deceptively quiet and innocent, under the twinkling of the eternal
stars, which, clear cut like the flash of diamonds in a mine, illuminate the
deep violet of the southern sky.

CHAPTER III

TWO VISITORS

NOT a sound, I said, but I was wrong, for from the tent came those unmistakable sounds which tell of heavy sleepers within—sleepers to whom the drowsy god infallibly responds at call, as a natural termination to a hard day's work; happy sleepers who know not the wearying pain of the thinker watching for, yet fearing, the early dawn, which renews his troubles without refreshing his power to withstand them.

I was certainly wrong, for there is another sound, and that an unwonted one at this time of night—foot-falls hard by, sounding plainer every minute. Is it a straggling reveller who has lost his way, and stands a fair chance of losing his life also at the bottom of one of the many disused shafts and pits which honeycomb the plain; or a police officer looking after some one who is wanted? Neither; the men, for they are two, come nearer, and in the fitful light of the stars, look neither like revellers nor police. They are no other than two of the "worthiest" of the worthies of the gold-field. One, a heavy-built man, is the doctor's old antagonist, "Bully Ben," while the other is a clever, but unscrupulous rascal, known by his comrades as "Gentleman Jim," whose presence near our friends bodes them no good. The two are mates, but what they can have in common one would at first find it hard to say, yet for the present enterprise they are well mated, as time will show.

Different as the two men were in temperament, yet more different had been their earlier histories and the circumstances which brought them together. Born five-and-thirty years before our story opens, the natural son of a Lancashire village lass, Ben, or Benjamin Griffin, had opened his eyes on to a world of bad luck. Even to those who do not believe in "good" and "bad luck" as accounting for success or failure in a way uncontrollable by the recipient, Ben's experiences must always exemplify the exception which proves the rule. The personal disadvantages attendant on a birth, not recognized by the minister of the parish, a thorough-going, strait-laced old church man, might alone have called for little comment among the class of rural labourers in which he was born, but coupled with an ugliness of visage, and heaviness of build, which amounted to deformity, Ben's life as a boy was made miserable by the jibes and jeers of his class-mates; without any predisposition to evil, being, in fact, of rather a colourless and negative mind, capable of receiving impressions for good or ill, he was yet always fixed upon as the scapegoat in any mischief, and according to the rough justice of the day, was held guilty till he had proved his innocence. The natural consequences of his continual degradation and unjust punishment manifested themselves early, and daily he became more sullen, taciturn, and revengeful—a life lost for the want of that care and love so easily, yet so rarely, given in such cases. Ten years before our story opens, he had the character of being the most drunken lout for miles around, and here, perhaps, the bad name was fairly applicable, for he could drink like any hog at "The Three Tuns" any night in the week, until prevented by pecuniary or physical limit.

Coming home one night from work, his carpenter's tools thrown over his back, sober for once, and hungry, for he had worked late some miles from his house, he chanced to be passing through a copse, when of a sudden a shrill scream rang through the night air, and in a moment a woman swept up the path and passed him, wild with fright, pursued by a man, whose crape-covered face sufficiently bespoke his vocation, but who, grasping the situation, turned at once and fled away. A few moments sufficed on this occasion for Ben to make up his mind, generally a very deliberate proceeding with him. Throwing down his tools, he gave chase to the man, but never saw him again, got lost in the mazes of the dark wood, found himself unexpectedly far out of the right way, and remembered he was supperless, so struck out again for and reached his home, telling no one of his adventure. His was but a short sleep, for within a few hours the village constable, armed with the squire's warrant, and aided by one or two villagers eager for adventure, charged him with attempting to rob the squire's only daughter, dark hints being thrown out that a much heavier charge would be brought against him. His trial at the assize town was a farce; every one believed him to have been guilty, and the lawyer who defended him, more for the purpose of form and earning a couple of guineas, than with any hope of obtaining his acquittal, would have had to have challenged the whole county had he wished to obtain one unprejudiced juryman. The tools were found and deemed conclusive evidence against him. The result was foregone—the sentence of ten years' transportation was considered by many to be erring on the score of leniency, while it brought satisfaction to most of the neighbours in and about his native village, including the parson himself, who, indeed, was not half sorry that such a *bête-noire* had been permanently removed from the midst of his parishioners. The good man's conscience had lately been pricked with inconvenient sharpness, as Ben had received little, if any, care or love from the preacher of loving-kindness to all men; so now that the man was gone, *cessante ratione cessat* conscience itself.

Ben's career in Tasmania, after he had been landed out of the floating hell called a transport-ship, had been one long series of thrashings, starvation, mutinies, heavier thrashings, severer starvation, and more desperate mutinies. The colony was then making that famous coach road from Hobart in the south to fair Launceston in the north, through the rugged forests, valleys, and gorges of the interior, which is said to have cost on the average about one human life for every yard of length. As the distance from one town to the other was about ninety miles, any person may form some idea of the death-rate in this otherwise healthy island during those fearful times. Twice Ben escaped from the gang of fellow-convicts, and twice was he brought back, his heavy frame hanging loosely from starvation in the uninhabited forests, and heavily manacled and punished; but he was more successful in a third attempt, in company with two other desperate spirits, men bedevilled by a system which even now claims its victims, preferring the well-known risks of the lone, untenanted bush to the desperate existence of the convict. He alone of the three escaped alive, met one or two of the fast-decreasing natives of the island, and by their assistance and the aid of a black dye, shipped off unobserved to the adjoining continent, which he safely reached, and when there, in the usual course of things, found his way to the gold-fields. What became of his two comrades was never known, though dark traces of their history were found by the trackers who hunted the runaways through the interminable forests, in the shape of odd bones and two skulls, which seemed to mark out some of the many camps the trio or their survivor had made. These traces pointed strongly enough to a state of things summed up in that one word "cannibalism," whose very whisper causes even the hardened convict to blanch and falter in further attempts at escape. No one of Ben's former convict comrades, of whom he had met one or two on the gold-field, had ever been able to break down the barrier of reserve that guarded this amongst other secrets in his keeping. Thus I bring the career of Bully Ben up to the date when we see him in company with Gentleman Jim.

The latter was a man of such opposite stamp and antecedents, that a short sketch of his life will doubtless interest those who follow out his career.

Born of well-to-do parents, and early educated at the best schools, he had commenced to serve his articles to a London attorney at the early age of fifteen. Sharp and clever to a degree, the inaction of an articled clerk's life suited him but ill, and the opportunities thus offered him of meeting other equally unemployed articled clerks at the gambling hells and taverns, were the first steps downwards upon a path which destroyed his own career, and brought disgrace and premature death to his parents. Good and bad luck had he at play, as have others. After one run of bad luck heavier than usual, his debts of honour (heaven save the mark) being greater than he could defray, even with the help of an indulgent though ignorant mother, he forged his employer's name for a large sum, and was found out. The attorney could not shield him from the prosecution and sentence of imprisonment which followed, as the bank insisted on this course, and young James Whitbread being a handsome youth, received much pity and notoriety from certain old women of both sexes present at his trial. When he came out of prison, his father, with some show of sternness, perhaps late in the day, accusing him of being his mother's murderer, forbade him to enter the house, and handing him £50, desired never to see his face again.

But James Whitbread was not to be daunted at such an ill stroke of fortune, and shortly after having run through all his cash, enlisted in the Militia, and by his good address and handsome, refined features, gained an entrée to the officers' mess. Stationed at Leamington, he happened to meet a country parson's gentle daughter, to whom he introduced himself as a lieutenant, and who subsequently fell in love with and married him, though against the wish of her father.

The father and daughter were no other than Jack's vicar and his old sweetheart, and as Jack had said, so it had happened that the fellow, finding that he got no advantage by his match, soon tired of the gentle-mannered, delicate girl, who was herself broken-hearted at the deceit he had practised upon her as well as at her father's death. Happily her hard, unused treatment and wretched life as the wife of a common militia-man soon came to a close, and though her last moments had been softened by the loving care of some of the officers' wives, the poor girl was only too thankful for her release. Then James turned himself to utilizing that fertile brain of his, and for some time did a roaring trade by impersonating dead pensioners until, being discovered, divers crimes were brought home to him, and at the early age of twenty-one he was transported for ten years.

The ship landed him at the Sydney Convict Depot, and his engaging appearance at once secured him an easy and pleasant occupation as clerk to a large tavern keeper in George Street, to whom he was in the language of the day "assigned." Here he had a chance to retrieve his lost position, but his instincts were all opposed to an honest course, and after exhausting the dissipation and novelties of the town, one day he disappeared. As a quantity of his master's cash likewise disappeared, the hue and cry were raised; but notwithstanding the stringent provisions intended to guard against convicts obtaining ordinary clothing or being assisted to escape, he made good his way into the interior, and for some time drove a good trade by an illicit shanty or whisky bar, which he from time to time established here and there, where police troopers were not, coupling this pecuniary adventure with the gentle recreation furnished by being his own croupier in his own gambling-hell.

A shepherd or bushman cooped up for months up country coming away for a few weeks' "spree" at Sydney with a big cheque or order on a Sydney or Melbourne firm, fell an easy prey into his snare, and was promptly "skinned and cleared out," after the manner of fisher-women with eels, then sent back to the station or run to earn a few more pounds to be spent in such jollification!

For them there was excuse enough in their quiet, humdrum life, necessarily reactive in some shape, and terribly so in the wild debauchery of a shanty; but was there excuse for him; he who, not content with thus pillaging them of their hard-earned wages under the cover of friendliness, gave them whisky heavily adulterated with tobacco, salt, and acids, to induce thirst and create burning longings for more; he who was always ready with the revolver to settle all or any of the frequent disputes caused by his cheating and chicanery at play, he who would bribe a native with a bottle of gin to spear the sheep or cattle of an enemy, or even some person "in his way," if perchance he could be found drunk or sleeping. He would say that he was doing no worse than many of the licensed hotel-keepers of the interior of that day, or with some qualification of our own times. Was there then excuse for him? Speak, poor old Tom Lamb, honest, hearty and generous to a degree, but with your one fault, your love of a "booze," as you would call it; you who at the commencement of your last bout found "the boss cheating a poor drover" out of a few shillings and insisted on restitution. How was it your massive form was never seen after that evening jogging along through the bush from the glimmer of the shanty nor anything heard of you until long after your bleached bones were found at the foot of a gum-tree, your skull pierced by the barb of a spear, and pinned to the ground with the shaft pointing up to the skies, as though appealing for vengeance. Was there excuse for him? Speak, Ned Braithwaite, going down flush with hope, youth, and money to Sydney to meet your bride, cajoled to drink "just a glass, you know, for luck" by the keeper of the shanty, and nothing loth for the heat of the day; you who awoke many days after to find your money gone, your frame racked with pains, your tongue and stomach like burnt leather, and that the seeds of an incurable disease, communicated by some passing stockman, had fastened on you while you slept on the filthy couch called "accommodation"—the death-like sleep of a hocussed man. Speak you too, sweet Maggie Scott, who waited so long at your Sydney home, anxiously expecting the arrival of your lover, or some news by the coach; you who still live a prim old maid, your features hardened and moulded by anguish, your life warped and bent away from its natural course by the news the coach eventually brought of the suicide of one Edward Braithwaite, your soul-distracted and tormented lover. Speak you scores of others who have suffered in pocket, health, and life, or life-long comfort, by the means of this one devil incarnate. Was there excuse for him? Amusing and plausible, frank-looking and handsome, what wonder that man and woman fell so easy a prey to his wiles, and that he was known in the country around as Gentleman Jim. The morals of an up-country sojourner become trained in peculiar directions and the fate of the man's victims was ascribed solely to their own folly by their friends and acquaintances. The Sydney police never tracked him down. In such a vast territory, great difficulties attend such tracking, when once the clue is lost, as he took good care it should be in his own case.

When the Ballarat gold-rush called men far and wide to the pleasurable profit of finding a fortune in an hour, Gentleman Jim came too, and finding that under the vigilance of the gold-field police a "shanty" could not be established without some risk, applied himself to relieving others of the treasure which they obtained at the sweat of their brow. This he did, not by force, for he was a coward, but by fraud, or stealth, or if force were necessary, he would apply to Bully Ben, or some other more courageous comrade, giving him a share, though a small one, of the proceeds of the theft. These two were as much feared on the gold-fields as the Tipperary boys themselves, or as a queen wasp is by a weak colony of worker-bees; but as yet, though suspicion pointed strongly to them, they had not been reached by the arm of the law, weak because of the overpowering numbers which it had to control, and because of the many disturbances connected with digger's licences about this time. The mighty law of Judge Lynch, and the Vigilance Committees of the States, had not been adopted upon the fields as a system, and in fact any symptom of such rough-and-ready justice was at once repressed by the authorities. One of the mistakes which Englishmen make, and will ever make, consists in applying forms of government, which are the outcome of centuries of experience, adaptation, and evolution from primary principles, with little if any modification to a society practically in a most primitive state, and therefore requiring a relatively primitive form of rule. However, this story was not intended to be a treatise on political economy.

Now the presence of these two worthies, at any time, so near the three diggers could bode them no good, and especially under the circumstances of the case. Gentleman Jim had, while loafing the previous day at one of the canvas hotels or drinking-booths, as was his custom, heard that the "Trinity firm," meaning our three diggers, had struck some paying gravel, and determined to see for himself if this were true, before other diggers had caught wind of it, and had established themselves in the same neighbourhood. The near presence of other diggers, would of course render his proceedings difficult and dangerous, or impossible. The costume of the two night prowlers was, to avoid attracting attention, the usual one of rough, slop-shop clothing, stained with clay and gravel. Both carried Colt's '380 revolvers in leathern pouches, strung through belts, worn round their bodies under their rough jackets, to which Gentleman Jim, with double purpose of fossicking and blood-letting, added a short knife in sheath, of the notorious pipe brand. Having carefully approached the shaft dug by the trio, Jim took from the back of the other an empty sack and a small rope, lit a dark lantern he had in his hand, and lowered this into the pit to test its depth. Satisfied that the shaft was about ten feet deep, and of almost perpendicular sides, he next caught hold of the rope, warned Ben not to let go the other end, but to stand by and give the warning of danger, and was speedily lowered to the bottom. Here for a time he carefully searched the sides of the shaft, and finally commenced at one corner, where the gravel and sand looked blacker and more porous than elsewhere, to scrape away at the ground with his knife. Failing to meet with any of the precious metal at this point, he tried another, and again a third spot. Here matters looked more satisfactory, and already two little pea-like lumps of gold had been discovered and quickly transferred to his pocket, when his knife, forced into the ground with a strong jerk, struck something evidently not of the ordinary, for there it stuck, and required a strong jerk to bring it away. The scent is getting hot now, his eyes glisten, and he wipes away the drops of perspiration which, notwithstanding the coolness of the night air, stand thickly on his forehead. He looks up for Ben, finds he is not attending, so jerks the rope. The end falls by his side; his comrade is evidently off-guard. But regardless of the consequences of his mate's neglect, he resolves to take his chance, and commences cutting away yet more rapidly than before at the ground in front of him. The gravel and sand roll out at his feet, and his lantern shows the unmistakable glint of a nugget, but this time considerably larger than a pea.

"Jim's in luck to-night. Honesty's the best policy, is it; ah, ah!" he laughs under his breath, scraping away vigorously at the surrounding soil, so as to prize out the lump. He is on the eve of triumph, when his quick ear catches a sound above, of startled exclamations and running feet.

To find the cause we must see what Ben has been doing the while. Tired after a time of lying down, with his head over the pit's edge, watching his partner's operations, he stretches himself out, and walks stealthily towards the tent, where the trio sleep, innocent of danger. Revengeful to the core, he does not think it sufficient punishment for the Irish doctor, who floored him two months ago, thus to be robbed, but hopes to have an opportunity of giving him a sound drubbing. Carefully he peers under the canvas, where a loose peg allows, but being none the wiser for his inspection, he slips round to the doorway, and parts the folds. A light breeze, passing that moment over the smouldering brushwood, fans a flame, which shows him the interior only too well, and he catches sight of his little enemy, just in time to see that he is himself observed by the awakened diggers and must run for it. He has the advantage of the diggers, while they grope about for the inevitable five-shooter, and draw on their boots, the putting off of which constitutes undressing in camp parlance. Rushing by the pit he shouts to his comrade,—

"Run fur yer life, Jim; they've got the scent on us."

"Give us a hand, then," cries the fossicker, throwing up the end of the rope as he speaks. But Ben is getting too confused to catch the rope, and the end falls back on the fossicker's head.

"You blamed fool," calls out Jim, "stand steady while I throw it round you, then catch at it like thunder or I'll riddle you with a bullet." The threat has none of its desired effect, but rather bewilders Ben the more, for though he can be well seen against the starlit sky, he cannot see his comrade, and after a moment's hesitation runs off, hotly pursued by all three diggers, who have just caught sight of him. Though a heavy man, his enormous strength and iron muscles stand him in good stead, and he makes his escape into the thick bush close by, whence a pistol-shot shows the diggers only too well that their enemy is armed, and desperate. Discretion being the better part of valour, they hide behind tree-trunks, peeping out with revolver ready, if the ear or eye should distinguish anything in the direction whence came the shot.

From the pit there comes just then, a sound of falling earth and smothered cry; Coates, remembering for the first time in the heat of the skirmish, that they had heard two voices as they ran out, hurries back to the shaft closely followed by Jack. The fossicker has been doing his best to make his way up the side of the hole, and had all but succeeded, when the fall of earth under his feet, the noise of which our diggers heard, throws him back; a heavy lump falling on his foot causes the utterance of a few of those oaths which have fortunately descended from the dining-table of our grandfathers to the camp-fire, on their path to inevitable extinction. His lantern-light falls on the lump, but he seems to gain but little comfort from his cursory examination, if we may judge from his fresh imprecations. With another strong, nimble effort he gains the top, scrambles up, and heedlessly running to the bush comes butt into the surveyor; for a moment the two lay entwined as closely as the group of the Laocoon, but the surveyor's wind had been taken, and the fossicker was fairly fresh, and had a knife to boot. Jumping up, he wrenched himself away, nimbly but easily eluded Jack, and made again for the bush, calling loudly to his comrade as he went. But Ben was out of hearing and could give no help. As the fossicker came up to the fringe of the bush, he first saw the glitter of the doctor's revolver. Then his courage failed him, and for an instant he stood like a statue, the revolver seemingly levelled at him with deadly aim, while the body of the owner was concealed by the tree; though as a matter of fact the doctor knew far more of curing than of making gun-shot wounds, the fossicker of course had no means of knowing this fact. A sharp ping through the still night-air, accompanied by a burning sensation in his right elbow, both of which seemed to *precede* the revolver report and flash, served to unloose the spell. His right arm fell to his side, and his revolver dropped from his grasp, but with desperate energy he stopped, picked up the weapon with his left hand, and with steady aim marked down the doctor who had incautiously stepped out of his concealment. Heaven save you now, bright little doctor, the man who is aiming at your head is a practised shot with either hand.

Where was Jack all this time, may well be inquired; by the side of his comrade, who still lay on the ground breathless, and gasping out as his friend came up,—

"The brute used a knife. What a ———"

"Water," cried Jack, mistaking the last words of his friend's clipped sentence for a rather natural request under the circumstances "I'll fetch you some."

So he had hurriedly fetched a pannikin of cold water, but was surprised if not shocked to find the surveyor sitting up and shouting with laughter, as he came up to him. Humorous and witty by nature, the surveyor had, by a peculiar inappropriateness which sometimes happens, noticed the involuntary pun of his comrade, and was hugely enjoying the joke, "the laughter hurting him much more," as he afterwards explained, "than his wound." The report of the doctor's revolver turned both their heads that way.

"Run, Jack; run," cried the surveyor; "shoot the thief low down."

Jack waited no longer, the blood of his yeoman ancestors was at last up; with a bound he was off, and came up with the fossicker, who, hearing the command and seeing the other running at him, aimed unsteadily, missed his victim, and sprang into the bush, Jack sending in his excitement a flying but unsuccessful shot after him.

Again the pair waited concealed behind the tree-trunks to see or hear more, but after five minutes gave up the quest and walked slowly back to the camp, their heads over their shoulders and their weapons ready. There they met their comrade stepping "painfully and slow" towards them. The doctor's practised eye soon saw that something was wrong, and with that his second nature came back to him with as much force as though he were in hospital.

"Stir up the fire, Jack; bring me a pannikin of water," cried he, running into the tent as he spoke, and bringing out a small chest and one of the old lanthorns, which were common objects on the fields, but which we have now driven off with bull's-eye and dark lantern. The fire soon sparkles up, and by its light, aided by the flickering candles, the hemorrhage from the surveyor's wound in the fleshy part of his left shoulder is soon staunched, and the wounded part skilfully dressed and bandaged, the doctor first satisfying himself that no bone is injured. When this is all finished he allows his professional severity to relax, and with a grim smile says,—

"The wound is child's-play after all, it actually borders on the humerus. I'm sure ye ought to feel heartily obliged that it wasn't a full joke, as the spalpeen sent the knife in with great force, and if it had gone a half-inch to the right ye would perhaps have had a compound fracture."

"Thanks, old fellow," replied the patient who had watched the proceedings with interest and had not flinched or uttered a sound; "I don't quite follow out your joke, but I'm sure I'm heartily thankful that the lunge didn't hit my heart, or lungs."

"Hoot, hoot, just listen to the man," said the doctor, turning to the assistant Jack, "with his jokes and jibes just after being rescued from the tomb; why I wonder ye didn't ask your friend yonder by the pit a conundrum while waiting for him to stick ye." But although the doctor grumbles, he is right glad to find his friend, after losing so much blood, in such good spirits, and smiles the while.

"Noo," says he to Jack, "we'll take it by turns to watch to-night, just to see that those murthering rascals don't come back, and if ye'll draw a twig from the fire we'll see whose is the longest, and his shall be the first watch."

The doctor's is the longest, so after packing up his medicine-chest, and depositing that and his friend within the tent, he commences his watch. Jack's loud and regular breathing soon proclaims to the watcher's amused ears the fact that *his* imperturbability has not been destroyed by the exciting events just happened. After some time a rustling in the bush close by and a muttering which trembles indistinctly on the breeze, makes his heart commence a curious thumping performance, so that for a few seconds he thinks of summoning Jack; but all is soon quiet again, and thus to the end of his watch, when he wakes up his comrade, finds the surveyor feverish and awake, so gives him a little bark, and himself turns in to court the drowsy god.

CHAPTER IV

"VITA EST SOMNIUM"

JACK in turn lies down outside by the smouldering fire, with revolver across his knees, and as he reclines the deep silence overawes him; not a sound, near or far, proclaims the presence of living being, and there creeps upon him, as he gazes up at the star-bespangled sky, that subtle appreciation of the wonders of creation, the antithesis of macrocosm and microcosm, which will at times fill the breasts of the most unsentimental of us, if circumstances be but favourable. There Orion's Belt shows over the horizon, while here the Great Southern Cross sparkles majestically above his head, out of its deep blue setting. The natural transition of his thoughts to the incident of the previous evening brings him to his friends' stories, which he had heard in detail for the first time, and lastly, to the subject of his own tale. Minutely his mind pictures the whole of his life, his innocent boyhood, his manhood, with its love-trial; and as he thinks of his Warwickshire home, with its ricks and barns, its ivy-covered homestead and tree-divided paddocks—all illuminated with the afternoon sun, as even then, perhaps, was the case,—his mother and father waving their adieux to him at the gate, as he had last seen them, never, perhaps, to see them again,—his eyes moisten unwontedly, and over his manly features comes an unaccustomed look of care. Think none the worse of him, gentle reader, that his eyelashes are wet, rough as he is, and rougher as he is bound to become, with the hard life of a digger, he will generally "be on the right side" while he can think of the old folk at home tenderly. Now he thinks curiously of the life which his old sweetheart is or may be leading—for he told his comrades the whole truth, and knows nothing of her—and, like many others, ponders how things might have been had he, perhaps, taken time by the forelock and made the girl his wife before ever a rival appeared; but then, perhaps, he muses, it was as well not—he was too rough for her—the hard life she would have led as the mother of his children, and the housewife at the homestead would never have suited her fair hands and her tenderly-nurtured spirit. Well done, Jack, thou art in very sooth as philosophical as the fox in the fable of the sour grapes. Next, he determines that from henceforth he will put her out of his mind—to which state, indeed, her memory had already more than once come perilously near—and, cunning Jack that he is, rather deems himself a hero for such strength of purpose.

A dingo's long weird howl in the bush far away here recalls his thoughts some twelve thousand miles at a leap, to find that while he has been busily planning the dawn has commenced to break. Away in the east Orion is losing his splendour, the deep blue is giving way to blue-violet, then to mauve. As the softer tones reach the zenith, the horizon far away over the hills, near the rising town of Melbourne, blushes gently as a fair young girl with pleasure; the blush deepens into a flush of rose-coloured fire, which gradually assumes the fascination of molten gold. Erebus has enfolded pale dark-haired night in his remorseless embrace, and flees away as Father Sol himself peeps above the hills, and announces the birth of another day. The dingo's howl recedes as the beast creeps away to his lair for the day; but the howl and the light together waken an Australian bear or sloth, hitherto invisible, but now, by its plaintive and infant-like cry, making its presence thoroughly *en évidence*. It repeats its wail ever and anon, until its truant mate answers from the midst of the bush.

"Ha, ha, ha, he, he, he!" screams the giant kingfisher overhead (which some unromantic person has long since dubbed the laughing jackass), thoroughly aroused for the day to its round of snake-destroying and weather-foretellling duties. Far down the plain, and right up the hill on the other side, where, at the date when this story is written, the Ballarat towns folk proudly walk along shady boulevards before pretentious plate-glass-fronted shops and offices, the blue mists hang over thousands of tents and huts, of the scores of thousands who inhabit "the diggings," while away to the north, on the slope of the White Hill, the wooden house of the chief gold commissioner and magistrate, environed by the tents and huts of the constabulary and troopers, is throwing off its misty coverlid. Distantly comes the clink of the chain and pail of some early diggers, who have probably chanced upon "paying colour," and are anxiously making hay while the sun shines. Nearer by sounds the old bugle upon which the driver of the coach between Melbourne and Ballarat blows with sportive intent, but melancholy effect, the faint echo of the coach-music at home. More and more are the sounds of awakening diggers commencing or preparing for work, and, thus reminded, the watcher turns to find the fire somewhat spent; so, with axe in hand, he walks towards the wood-pile close by, and soon obtains a good blaze. In the meantime the doctor comes to the tent door, and good-humouredly chaffs his companion for his unwonted activity, then, bringing out the materials for their simple breakfast, aids Jack to boil the tea in a bucket, to last the day out, and to lay the table. Laying the table has a familiar, homely sound with you comfortable gentle folk, but with this table it was absolutely a triumph of mind over matter, and yet not exactly a success. The dearly won victory was often worse than defeat. The table itself was of the doctor's invention and manufacture; from the first he had stipulated for some such relic of civilization, and, finding scant encouragement from his two companions, who thought it a luxury with which they could well dispense, had at last evolved the table and seats out of his inner consciousness. It was the object of remark and silent envy on the part of one or two of their digger acquaintances, who pretended to consider it very luxurious and effeminate, or, as they said, a "woman's prank." When I say that it consisted of two rough-hewn planks, which sloped with an inclination of about one in five, warped and twisted at the same time into the resemblance of the gnarled roots of an oak or gum-tree, which only served as a temporary resting-place for dry food, and even *that* suffered from the imminent risk of being deposited somewhat unexpectedly on the ground or your knees, and when I further tell that the seats were rough tree-branches nailed on to two *uprights*, called so because they had a tendency to wobble alarmingly, and to fall some twenty degrees out of the perpendicular when practically tested,—you, my readers, may guess that the doctor's invention well deserved the name of "luxury." The fact is, that as all luxury is a question of degree, and little time availed in the red-hot rush of the gold-fields even for necessaries, so the faintest echo of domestic comfort was a "woman's prank." Having with great gravity deposited the steaming bucket of black tea near one end of the table, propped a tin dish of salt meat, of an extremely tough appearance on the "table," with the aid of a couple of two-pronged forks, balancing this with a great lump of leathery "damper," or camp bread, at the far end, Jack announces, with some pretention to Jeames' style, that "the breakfast is served," this being for the edification of the surveyor, who, leaning on the doctor's arm, is making his *début*, his face somewhat pale, but his smile as ready, his eye as bright as ever.

A simple toilet preceded breakfast, each dipping his hands into a bucket of water drawn from the turbid pool banked up near their hole, and receiving a douche over his head with the rest of the contents. The surveyor's ablutions were this morning rather less complicated in virtue of his wound. For a towel they used a somewhat dilapidated shirt, and without their warranty one would have found it hard to believe that it had ever seen better and whiter days, for it would have given a mental shock to any washerwoman who had to tackle its washing. In these ablutions they were agreed to brave the comments of the diggers of their acquaintances, many of whom rejoiced in that state which our street arabs consider a sure preventive of catarrh, that is, a total abstinence from cold water applied externally, and considered washing another "woman's prank." For the rest, until their clothes became worn-out and beyond patching, they served equally as day and night habiliments, to remove which was of course an unnecessary waste of time. Such were the amenities of the gold-fields!

Jack laid aside his pipe and ladled out the tea, while the doctor cut up as deftly as a woman the bread and meat for the surveyor. Let not a medical reader start incredulous at such a diet for a wounded man. Refined distinctions of diet were then unknown on the fields, and all had pretty well to fare alike. The meat and bread did not belie their appearance, and gave the doctor plenty of work. Whilst thus engaged, with pardonable pride, he draws his friends' attention to the indispensability of the table and seat, now that one of them is an invalid; and as he slyly points to a broken branch jutting out at right angles to the seat, and digging the unwary surveyor viciously in the back, "See," says he, "how Nature herself architects for us, and adapts her ways to the grand achievements of civilization."

The breakfast passes, and while Jack lights up for a short "smoke," the surveyor, with his thoughts intent on their quest and the events of the previous evening, asks Jack just to step over to the hole and see if their visitors left anything behind last night to identify them.

His friend strides away a dozen yards, stoops down over the shaft, and suddenly commences cutting such capers, throwing his cap up into the air, shouting, and generally behaving with such unusual emotion, that his comrades think him beside himself, and the doctor starts in pursuit, but no sooner reaches the edge of the hole than the infection seizes him. The surveyor puzzled though convulsed with laughter at their pantomimic gestures, shouts for information, the request being apparently unsuccessful in its object, for both men at once commence lowering themselves over the side of the hole and disappear from his view. The next minute comes a cry of "Yo, heave ho!" and as from Tongariro comes the hot coal, and as from a New Zealand geyser the gush of living water, up jerks a great nugget, and with its acquired momentum rolls a yard or two towards Coates; in a second another lesser nugget follows to the same accompaniment, and then the doctor's head appears above the level of the edge, helped up by his comrade from below, to whom upon reaching the top the doctor in turn stretches a helping hand.

The surveyor now at once comprehends both the reason of his friends' antics and the imprecations of the night fossicker, and is only prevented by his maimed state from imitating his friend's boyish glee, so sudden is the revulsion of feeling caused by fortune after toil and anxiety. Jack regaining his pipe and his coolness is the first to raise a doubt as to the genuine character of the nuggets.

"What," says the surveyor, with a trace of contempt in his voice, "do you think that I, an old digger, am to be taken in. Why, man, I know the very smell of gold. But just to prove to this unbeliever that the glitter is golden, we'll give it a touch of acid." With that he fetches his acid bottle from the tent, and successfully scrapes and tests the two nuggets. Then balancing them in one hand he roughly guesses their weight at twenty pounds troy, which he soon figures out at about 800*l.* sterling value, assuming that they are the pure metal throughout. This he soon settles by determining the specific gravity of the lumps.

"Now, Jack," says he, "the safest place for these is the bank, so I guess you'd better go there first thing, have the lumps weighed and cash them, pay all but 20*l.* into a joint account for us three, and start down to the store to settle up our score and get us some fresh tucker; I'll superintend cooking to-day if one of you'll just act the scullion. We must celebrate the occasion with such a banquet as the Honourable Corporation of the City of London loves, but after a humbler scale. Now, doctor, what's your particular weakness?"

"Oatmeal porridge and Killarney cream," smilingly replied his friend.

"That's modest! And yours, Jack?"

"Don't ask Jack, man; why of course he'll reply negrohead. His tastes are tobacconalian to a degree."

"Oh, all right," says Jack, "I'll treat myself to something, but I'll have to think it out, for I don't know what I especially care about, so that I don't starve. What's your order, Harry?"

"Beef-steak and fried potatoes," cried the surveyor. "The doctor and I are giving you a good morning's work, my boy. You won't find oatmeal or potatoes very easily, and as for cream, you may as well make up your mind for a journey to Sydney or Wollongong for such a delicacy."

"Oh, I'll manage somehow," says Jack, who has the while been engaged in packing up his treasures in brown paper, and now sets off across the plain to the bank.

"I'll bet you a pound to a penny he gets them, too," cries the surveyor, when their friend is out of hearing. "When Jack and I were first chums, and my money hadn't run out, I had an attack of dysentery, and the camp doctor, you know him, young Jones, fresh from England, told me I ought to have stout and oysters. 'My colonial,' I said, 'if you had ordered pearls and diamonds it would have been about as wise.' My friend the doctor got huffed and left, but Jack followed him, as I afterwards found out, and as he still found him leaning to stout and oysters, Jack determined to have them. He left me in the care of a neighbouring digger, paying him, I think, a pound a day, set off to Melbourne, and came back in three days, having coached the whole way and back for two dozen stout and a few dozen Sydney-cove oysters. So you see there's hope for your Killarney cream yet."

"Noo," says the doctor, who has been clearing away the few table impedimenta which have not already deposited themselves on the ground, "ye'll just take it aisy for a time while I see if there's any more of the dross where those lumps came from."

"Well," says the surveyor, "I'll just turn to and see if I can't sketch out this new water-race we want so badly, and if you'll help me about midday to take the levels, I think we'll manage to have it up in a few days, and so manage to work much quicker and surer."

"All right," says the doctor, "ye can go after I see to your arm."

This being satisfactorily arranged, and the arm dressed, the doctor shoulders pick and shovel, and commences vigorously throwing up the soil and gravel out of the pit, while the surveyor silently plans the construction of the water the first of its kind on the fields. Leaving them thus engaged, let us follow the steps of Jack.

Stopping here and there to interchange a "How d'ye do" with an acquaintance, he reaches the bank, an inconspicuous weather-board building, whose only title to distinction is the word "BANK" in capital letters of about a foot high over the low doorway. As this bank is destined to play a somewhat important part in this story, I had better describe it somewhat fully. First then, it stood in the main street of the canvas town down which the coach ran, and was about half a mile from the troopers' camp.

It consisted of a main building about twenty feet square, surrounded by a deep verandah, with two additions, like small bulblets on a tulip bulb, the one on the western side the other at the rear of the building. These two rooms were respectively the manager's bedroom and kitchen. The main building, with shingled roof, was unequally divided into two parts by a partition partly glazed which ran the whole length of the building, the front one for the clerks with a long counter all across, the after one for the manager, a shallow room about six feet deep. There stood the huge safes and strong boxes which held the precious metal and coin, and out of this room opened the entrances to the two additions aforesaid.

The kitchen was the only room with a fireplace, its chimneys being of the usual colonial type of wide wooden inverted cone-shape, puddled round with clay for about five feet from the ground, to form a fire-proof fireplace.

When Jack entered, as it was yet early, there was but little business doing, a half-drunken digger was endeavouring to prove, to the clerk's amusement, that he had a banking account, and wished to write on "one of those derned little pink pieces of paper," so as to provide himself with funds, while a respectably dressed man was seated in the window-sill, the only available seat, waiting to see the manager.

Jack was recognized by one of the clerks who had previously cashed one or two of the little piles of gold-dust which he had brought, and accordingly, before his astonished eyes, Jack unloosed the nuggets from their brown paper envelope, turning them out on the counter with a heavy jerk. The exclamation of the clerk brought the others around, and even the tipsy digger came gravely over; but the man in the window-sill looked quietly out of the window, apparently unconcerned. The tipsy digger offered to purchase the nuggets then and there, for a fine new pick, cradle, and two dozen paper collars, his sole property beyond the clothes he stood in. Of this offer Jack took no heed, calmly asking the clerk to weigh the nuggets, and let him know their price. The nuggets received a scrape or two to test their purity, then wiped clean, they are placed in the scales, which register twenty pounds, this being equivalent, at 3*l.* 12*s.* 6*d.* per ounce, to 870*l.* in value, at bank price, subject to the nuggets being found to be pure throughout.

The quiet man at the window is still looking out, and, apparently in an idle mood, tips his slouch hat over his left eye, screwing up his face in a curious and by no means prepossessing manner. Another digger walks in, and without noticing the man at the window, approaches the group, and deposits a small bag of gold-dust on the counter. While one of the clerks is weighing this out, he, of course, notices the nuggets which lie on the scales, while the clerk seeks a cheque-book to hand to Jack, who is for the first time to rejoice in the full honours of a banking account. Of course the new-comer asks many questions about the nuggets, where they came from, who belonged to this party, and so forth, many of which Jack answers with the candour of innocence, though, as is his wont, curtly. The quiet man, tired of waiting, soon goes out, and is followed, at short intervals, by the fresh-comer and Jack, who, obeying his partner's injunctions, has obtained about twenty pounds in gold, and deposited the balance of the purchase-money in the bank for safe keeping. The drunken digger staggers out after them, alternately vituperating Jack for not accepting his offer, and entreating him to come and have just one glass at the bar, so as to settle the matter in a friendly way.

Jack takes his way to the store where he is to purchase the one or two provisions they require, and to see if he can find the luxuries laughingly ordered by his friends, whose requests he views seriously. As he passes along various "hotels," booths, and other stores, he meets an acquaintance, who asks him if he has heard of the stroke of luck of some diggers at Poker Flat; he (the acquaintance) is just hurrying to find his mates, strike camp and away down to the Flat.

"By the way," he says, without giving him a chance to reply, "there's a letter for your mate Coates up at the post-office. I saw it there just now; came in by last night's coach."

So Jack takes her Majesty's post-office on his way, wondering who besides his companions could have struck the luck, and receives from the hands of so august a personage as her Majesty's postmaster himself a letter for Coates, and another for the doctor, both from the old country. Pocketing these, he resumes his course, and enters the store, a nondescript building of weather-boarding, canvas, and odds and ends of case tops, eked out and patched with pieces of rusty sheet iron and tin. Its interior is less obviously rough, for every spare inch of space seems to be occupied. Here the straw of a partially opened case of champagne half hides a few dozen pairs of digger's boots; there a tub of salt fish and very salt butter stands amid a perfect forest of diggers' tools, baskets, shovels, and the like, while overhead swing slop-shop coats, shirts, and trousers, smoked sausages, herrings, women's bonnets, pipes, and a thousand other luxuries and necessities of the "field." The store boasts no counter, space is at a premium, the proprietor walks about, and for convenience discards effete civilization in the shape of a coat and waistcoat; his bushy bearded face is the picture of health and vigour, to which the pale face of an assistant, pock-marked and short-cropped, serves as a foil. Here, as at the bank, business is quiet. All sober diggers are at work, and all diggers "on the spree" have scarcely got over their previous night's debauchery. So Mr. Williams, the store-keeper, who is punctilious as to the use of the word "Mr.," treats Jack to personal attention, a distinction which Jack appreciates, as hitherto the trio have not by a long way proved the storekeeper's most profitable customers. These attentions become still more pointed when Jack mentions his message; but having discharged his debts, and obtained a fresh supply of goods, he poses "Mr." Williams with his friends' special requirements.

The surveyor's commission is after some delay executed, though the beef-steak is wiry, and the potatoes sweet; but the storekeeper and his assistants are searching high and low to find the doctor's oatmeal. While they are thus engaged, a girl's merry voice breaks upon the silence of the store,—

"I say, dad, I want some sugar and plums for the pudding to-day."

Jack turns at the sound, and sees, framed in the doorway leading to the back of the store, so pretty a picture that he is content to gaze, unmindful of polite usages. A girl of seventeen or eighteen Australian summers— equivalent to about twenty-two or twenty-three of the English seasons—

her eyes dark and shaded by lashes, which rival her long glossy hair in jet
tones, her cheeks ruddy with the glow of youth and life, her lips full and
sensuous, her chin dimpled and roundly moulded, stands upright in the
doorway, smilingly showing her white row of teeth, and, well aware of
the fact, flushing slightly at the sight of the unexpected but good-looking
stranger. Her dress is varied, verging decidedly on the florid. Those were
the days of the crinoline monstrosity, but fashions on a gold-field are at
a discount, and the little lady had with considerable ingenuity adapted a
bright print dress to hang in unconsciously artistic folds from her waist.

"Jest see, now, mister!" cries Williams; "did yer ever see a more bootiful
sight than that in yer life? Fit for a lady in the Queen's own castle, that
she is, both for booty and fine dress."

Jack certainly agrees in thought with her proud parent, but not being
a born gallant, finds no nimble words on his tongue-tip, so maintains an
awkward silence. However, he so evidently appreciates the high colouring
of the picture that the storekeeper smiles approvingly.

"What are you doing, dad?" says the girl.

"Why, Mister Jack, here, wants some oatmeal for a friend of his, and
some Kill-early cream, so he says, and though we know we can't raise the
cream, we fancy we can muster the groats."

"But why trouble, dad, to look so long, when you have all these oats"
(pointing to the bags) "and the coffee grinder?"

"Bless her!" says her father; "what a clever creature she is. It isn't the
first time, I say it, but, gentlemen"—this to Jack and the assistant, who both
feel highly flattered at the unusual address—"I'm proud of that girl."

"I'll grind the meal if you'll get me the grinder," says Jack; then,
attempting a compliment, he adds, "and if the young lady will look on."

"Young leddy she is, though she's my darter, and young leddy I always
meant her to be, though for that matter I've seen that she won't make
one of them useless young leddies as don't know batter from butter, or a
suvrain from a guinea. So ye'll stop a bit and just light up the store with
yer eyes, won't yer, my dear?"

Jack looks up so winningly, that after much pretended diffidence,
and a good deal of blushing and giggling, Edith promises to stay "just a
minute." The first stiffness wears off quickly, and the two young people
soon become quite friendly, and chatter away briskly. Jack's mill grinds but
slowly, but exceeding small, like some other mills we wot of; in fact, he

pays so little attention to what he is doing, being able but indifferently to do two things at one time, that I fear he is quite sorry when he finds that he has ground up more than enough meal for his wants.

"Didn't I hear you say that you wanted cream?" says the bewitching maiden, turning her eyes full upon Jack. "Well, then, why not use some of dad's butter: put it into a saucepan, with some flour, sugar, and a little water, and there you'll have melted butter, quite as good, you'll find, as any Killarney cream." Jack takes the hint, and purchases a pound of very salt butter for the modest sum of 10s., and now that his other purchases are packed up, seeks some pretext for stopping a few minutes longer with Edith. A bright thought strikes him—he has bought nothing for himself. He takes the girl into his confidence, and soon has all the unlikeliest of her father's merchandise laughingly thrust upon him. At last, in hunting about, Edith lights upon a card of cheap fancy jewellery, now so common, then more rarely seen, which had somehow found its way into the storekeeper's miscellaneous repertoire. Her delight at the discovery is so great that Jack purchases the set at once, and insists on her accepting it, the which, after much pressing, she does, her ultimate decision precipitated by Jack's misunderstanding her coquetry for feeling, and ceasing to proffer the gew-gaws. Her thanks, expressed by rosy lips and bright eyes, quite daze poor Jack, who feels himself becoming ever more and more entangled in the enchantingly delusive web she thus spins for him. Had he been acquainted with the natural history of the vampire, the parallel might have suggested a caution, but then perhaps this story had never been written.

Having no longer any pretext for delay, Jack sets off for his camp, having first promised himself the pleasure of soon looking in again, and, wily dog that he is, tells Mr. Williams out loud that he will possibly call on the morrow for some of the goods which he now leaves behind. Worthy Mr. Williams almost disconcerts the plan by attempting to convince him that he can "carry the lot," the weight in fact being less than he has often "tackled before." Incontinently Jack has to rush away to prevent such a catastrophe as the failure of his little plan, leaving the storekeeper to add, "Good fellow, that, but a coorious critter in his ways; he ain't got yer eddication, Edie. Lor', what a blessed thing that eddication be! See, now, how ye've improved out of all knowledge sin' ye've been in Sydney!"

Mrs. Williams had died when Edith was of tender years, and Williams had managed to keep his daughter at a middle-class Sydney school until a week or two before our story opens, when she had been reported "finished" by her schoolmistress.

The girls' school was no worse than were girls' schools, or young ladies' seminaries, of the usual run at that time, and while the pupils were as strictly guarded as the inhabitants of the harem, at the same time they acquired little knowledge, scientific, literary, social, or otherwise, but a good deal of coquetry and frivolity, which, while it would not be called positively, was yet negatively, hurtful to their intellects and morals. Edith was accustomed to her father's loving though injudicious remarks on the few occasions he had visited her, and naturally considered them her due, while she held a sway over the man which he would not have acknowledged but yet tacitly admitted. He had been somewhat perplexed what to do with the girl, for he was coining money, as the saying goes, at Ballarat, and did not care to leave, but the "young leddy" settled the matter for herself by coming "for the fun of the thing," as she said, and keeping house for him, replacing the Chinaman who had hitherto superintended the storekeeper's *ménage*.

Poor Edith! had you but known how little fun "the thing" possessed, you would have stopped in Sydney, content to marry some respectable squatter, or even shopkeeper; but there, the tale must run its course, uninterrupted, to its natural end.

As Jack neared Poker Flat he noticed an unusual stir and bustle in the vicinity of his partners' camp, instead of one tent there were many already pitched, and others being set up, men were staking out holes and throwing up the "dirt" on all sides, and the whole aspect of the place had changed.

To explain this we must try back a couple of hours, following the steps of the half-drunken digger. Having deceived innocent Jack, and learnt all he wished, suddenly he became sober after a fashion much to be envied by the votaries of Bacchus who drink deep and long, and forthwith called upon one or two of his intimates to whom he told the news of the nuggets at Poker Flat, advising them to follow his suit, and "hump their belongings down to the Flat, peg out claims, and await the run of luck." Very soon a little procession in the direction of the Flat moved across the diggings, and the news communicating like wild-fire, a small army of the curious and speculative gathering strength like an avalanche, arrived at the Flat.

The surveyor was busily sketching his plans, but happening to look up saw the procession, and took in the situation at a glance. Calling to the doctor he bade him take a few of the pieces of brushwood that lay about, cut them into twigs and directed his friend, while he pegged out as far as he legally could, a claim where the tent stood, and another in the close vicinity of their hole, first similarly "claiming" the ground on which the shaft and the upturned heaps of gravel or "mullock" were situated. This, by dint of hard work, the doctor had just finished when the first of the adventurous diggers arrived; these having thus to be satisfied with claiming and pegging out as near to the "lucky hole" as possible. This done, their secondary operation was the erection of tents and huts, which, of course, were placed as near the respective claims as possible, and it was at this point that Jack came upon the scene with his load of provisions. The surveyor at once constituted himself cook, the others occasionally lending him a hand, thus varying for a space the fresh work which each of them was doing in digging out his cubic yard from the fresh claims pegged out that morning, so as to constitute *bonâ fide* possession. The new-comers were busily engaged in the same way, many of them being satisfied after they had thus "dug their yard," to sit idly by, waiting to see "which way the luck would turn." By midday our three friends were regaling themselves with a meal which was, by comparison with their recent diet, almost luxurious, but they spent little time in chewing the cud.

The surveyor, assisted by his friend the doctor took the levels for his water-race, and Jack fell to splitting up into planks the trunks of one or two gums, which they had felled for the purpose of building themselves a log-hut some time since. This work was laborious, and so slow and tedious, notwithstanding the great muscular strength and energy he displayed, that the surveyor saw that he must devise some other method of building his race if it were to be at all serviceable. And now was a most fitting time for it, as the fresh camp of diggers at the spot would contribute their quota by way of rent, so that it might become quite a profitable undertaking. He bethought him of the native method of making canoes, bark huts, and the like, and forthwith set Jack and the doctor to work sawing a ring round the bark of the neighbouring gum-trees, about two feet from the ground, and again some eight feet higher, Then splitting the bark perpendicularly on opposite sides, and prizing it off from the trunk, they found themselves supplied with two huge pieces of thick guttering, about eight feet long and two to three feet wide, which they strengthened by nailing cross-struts from one edge to the other. This work was comparatively simple, and by nightfall they had about eight trees thus disbarked, giving them some 120 feet of guttering. This they carried, or rather Jack did, for the doctor had to assist the surveyor's cooking again, close to their tent, the surveyor as pleased as punch with their afternoon's work, and inviting them cheerily to come to supper.

CHAPTER V

"MR. EH-EH-DIGGER"

NIGHTFALL was closing in, and the fire burnt briskly, its welcome warmth never so welcome as after such a day's work as they had one and all performed. The surveyor's arm gave him a few twinges as he would move about, but was reported to be progressing extremely well, so well that the Doctor expressed his surpise at such a deep wound healing by "first intention," and declared that he had never come across such a curious patient.

"It must be the cynicism and misogynism, me boy, that's in your blood that drives out the germs of disease before it, and gives ye such a healthy tone and colour. Shure, I think I'd better be after trying the same specific myself. I scarcely shall take any credit for curing you, why ye mind me of a case which I had at home."

"Tell us it, old fellow," replied the surveyor.

"A stonecutter was driving a blasting-hole in a quarry close by, and having got to the end and located the powther, he commenced, somewhat foolhardily, ye will agree, ramming it home with the iron crowbar or drill he had used before, when, as bad luck would have it, the bar struck a spark, the powther ignited and shot up the bar like a cannon-ball; it hit my patient, Heaven bless the rascal, under the chin, came through the roof of his tongue, broke away through his skull with a piece of bone on the top of it, and went careering away to the sky. Ye would have thought the rascal wouldn't have wanted to have shuffled off this mortal coil then, but would have been clean whisked out. Not a bit of it, he stands bolt upright, rather surprised, and mumbles as well as he can, 'May the Holy Virgin give ye a long dose of purgatory, ye spalpeen, for being so quick! if ye had but just given a kick before ye went off; I wad have taken the hint and sat upon ye.' This was what he was heard to mutter, and while his mate was sick with the sight, the rascal went first and found the bar, and then came on to me for a piece of plaster, as he said, to keep the wind and rain out. Bedad, I gave him some plaster first and a good talking to afterwards, but the rascal was labouring again in a couple of months little the worse for it, except his temper, which afterwards acquired an evil reputation."

"That's a good yarn, doctor," says Coates.

"I assure ye it's as true as Gospel, every word of it."

"It might be that, and yet not be, as you would have said, veracious," returned the other.

"What do ye mean, man; ye surely don't disbelieve the Gospel?"

"Never mind, doctor," says the surveyor, seeing how suddenly the good Catholic had become serious; "just you have a turn at your oatmeal before it gets frozen, and tell us what you think of it."

The doctor helps himself from a large billy to the stodgy food, and is liberally supplied by Jack with the melted butter from a pannikin in amongst the hot ashes, and the sugar out of a canvas bag, which generally hangs with the rest of their larder from the tent pole. Though the doctor was an Ulster man, and a Connoisseur of the article, whose name alone the dish possessed, yet such was the sharpening effect of the air on the appetite that Spartan history repeated itself in this little camp, and he pronounced the half-burnt, wholly smoked, and lumpy mess of porridge, smothered in a sea of paste,—being the flour and water of Edith's receipt, the butter having incontinently refused to mix, and floated on the top like very salt and yellow oil,—he pronounced this dish quite a *pièce de résistance*, and indeed fit for an Irish king, far surpassing the menu of the dinner-hour.

The surveyor, perhaps from being rather less hungry, by reason of his comparative inaction, or from being himself the cook, and therefore not compelled to bestow praise, smilingly tasted the mess, but making no farther adventure, addressed himself to Wainwright, with,—

"Well, Jack, what was your choice?"

Now, Jack, are you on the very horns of a dilemma. The forenoon's experiences in the store came back again to remembrance, lost for a time in hard work, and the poor fellow falters between facing the chaff of his mates by telling the truth, or, and this is foreign to his nature, cleverly fencing the question.

"Ah," says the doctor, "Jack's got a surprise for us to-morrow morning, I'll be bound. I'm shure with such an appetite as he's got he'll have chosen some thing bulky and gross, so that there'll be no stinting at his feast."

"No," says Jack, bound at last to protest or confirm the statement by silence; "I didn't buy anything to eat, I left that to you two; I bought a—in fact something which you won't care to hear about."

Jack's blushes are too obvious now to be mistaken for the shadows cast by the fire, and the surveyor, fearing some entanglement with either the men or the women of the canvas town, whose reputation, especially that of the latter, is not lofty, resolves to bring broadsides of chaff to bear upon his friend, and thus discover the cause of his embarrassment. Consequently, after some badgering, blushing hotly, and awkwardly glancing at the two, Jack is forced to tell the story of the morning, of course proving a better limner than nature in describing Edith. As the narrative nears its end the two friends, who have been assuming preternaturally grave airs for some time, burst out into shouts of laughter, the doctor first disclosing the cause.

"Oh, boys! oh, boys! My poor sides! What a Lothario and Lochinvar rolled into one! Oh ye Don Juan! What, haven't ye had enough ixperience of the little god without risking his wiles and caprices again? Did ye glance up, noo, very tender like? Did ye look very romantic with your torn shirt and clay-stained breeks? Oh! oh! oh! oh!" and again the little doctor rolls off in shouts of laughter at the notion of Jack making love to the girl at the store.

Jack looks highly offended, and is walking off in high dudgeon when the doctor, grieved to give his friend pain, steps round and pats him on the shoulder with a "There, me boy, ye must forgive me; I was, perhaps, careless of your feelings, and I'm sorry for it; but it seems such short notice for ye to tell us one night of one 'vourneen, and next of a new one."

Peace being restored the conversation proceeds the surveyor remarking on the curious fact of the other diggers having so to speak, smelt out their luck, and thus like bees to honey, congregated about the spot.

"I suppose you didn't tell any of your friends," says the surveyor to Jack, "that we had got such luck, or was there anybody up at the bank besides the clerks?"

Then Jack tells the story of his experience at the bank, whereat the surveyor becomes somewhat thoughtful, and questions his friend closely as to the appearance of the half-drunken digger, then of the digger who questioned him, and lastly of the man at the window-sill. When Jack tells that this last man had his one arm in the fold of his coat, as though injured, the doctor cries out,—

"Why, perhaps that was the murthering hound I shot last night coming to see if we stored the nuggets or kept them here."

"That's what I think," said the surveyor; "but I can't make out whether either of the other diggers was in league with him or not; for if they were, who was it spread about the report, for some one must have done so, and it couldn't have been the fossickers, who, now that all these tents and fires are around us, would stand little chance of doing any more business either with our hole or our store in the tent?" Then, turning to Jack, he says,—

"Should you know any of them again?"

"Well, the two diggers I should," said Jack, "but not the man on the window-sill, he never turned his face once. I don't think he cared a bit about the matter, for when all the others came up to see the weighing and talk it over, I noticed by the reflection in the glass partition that he kept looking out of the window, and only once moved to tilt his hat on one side."

"Was that before or after the digger walked in?" asked the surveyor.

"Before," answered Jack.

"H'm," said the surveyor, rubbing his week's stubble thoughtfully, "and what was the drunken digger doing all the while? Do you think he was getting sober?"

"Well, now you talk about it," said the other, "I did notice that he walked away quite briskly after he got outside."

"Well then, my friend," said Coates, "I think I can explain the little drama you took a prominent part in. The man in the window was doubtless the man whom the doctor pinked last night, the digger he called in was a mate who had been waiting outside, and had planned to knock you down and run away with the nuggets, just when they were in the scale, and I think the two were checkmated by the unexpected presence of your friend, the drunken digger, who was no more drunk than I, but up to some game himself and they saw it; but what the game was I can't yet tell, unless it was to hear of any stroke of luck, and hurry to the source. You just look round amongst these new-comers to-morrow, to see if any one of them is the drunken digger, only don't raise suspicion."

"Why, shure we've got a Bow Street runner in our midst," cried out the doctor, "a very Townsend in disguise. We'll put up a sign over our tents as the grand folks used to at the routs, 'Townsend will attend,' and perhaps by that means prevent the light-fingered gentry of the neighbourhood from purloining our Lares and Penates."

"Well, Jack, you've had a run of adventure to-day; any more yarns?" smilingly asks Coates.

"I don't think so. Well, yes, I've got this cheque book, and—ah! here's another book which the clerk told me you'd know what to do with," said Jack, putting them out as he spoke, while there fluttered to the ground the two letters he had received that morning. "And, bless my soul, there's the two letters I got from the post-office; one for you and the other for the doctor."

"Two letthers! why, ye omadhaun," cried the doctor excitedly, "ye say it as cool as a cucumber. Are letthers, ye spalpeen, so common here that ye can afford to treat them so superciliously? Two letthers, bedad, who are they for? hand them over."

"Dinna fash yerself, doctor, darlint," said Coates, who used an inimitative gibberish of Scotch, Irish, and English when he wished to tease the doctor; "there's sorry a one from your ain lassie, the sweet Biddy, or her attorney."

The doctor answered not, he was already busily reading his missive by the light of the fire, which he had stirred into a blaze, so the surveyor followed suit, but, before he had finished the page, gave vent to such expressions of surprise that the others insisted on knowing their reason. So, glancing through first to see if there was anything of a private nature, Coates read as follows:—

> "Burbidge's Hotel, Melbourne,
> "July 1st, 1854.
>
> "MY DEAR HARRY,—As I did not hear from you in reply to my last two letters, I have come over, just as I promised you I would, to take care of you. We sailed from home on the 6th of April, and, after rather a boisterous passage, we arrived safely on Wednesday last. I feel quite well now, I'm glad to say, and am staying here for a day or two until I hear where you really are, as they tell me in Melbourne that I shall never find you among so many thousands on the gold-fields, and that you may, perhaps have moved away.
>
> > "Your affectionate sister,
> > "MARY E. COATES."

When the reading had finished, the three looked at one another ruefully, and particularly at each other's garments, when the humour of the situation struck the doctor, whose merry peal infected the others. When gravity had reasserted herself, Coates thought out the position, and said,—

"Well, I must start at once and persuade her not to join us here, for that wouldn't do at all."

"No, my patient, ye're not going to do that," said the doctor. "The jolting of the coach would be murther to your shoulder, so ye'll have to commission Jack or meself upon this delicate mission."

"I'd rather not have the job," cries Jack, getting rather nervous. "I'm not a good hand at talking, and would rather face a rowdy with a five-shooter than try to persuade a lady against her will."

"Well, then, you're the only one we can send, doctor," says Coates.

"I'll go," says the doctor, "but hoo about ways and means?"

"Well, I should think you'd better start off to Melbourne by to-morrow's coach, go to some decent tailor's, and get fitted with some clothes; but no, perhaps your digger's clothes will prove the most forcible dissuasion she can have."

"What, man, am I to approach the young lady just as I am, with bowie-knife and revolver? Perhaps ye'd like me to rap out a half-dozen oaths, and go down three parts drunk. I didn't reckon on this when I accipted. I shall have to consider the position afresh," smilingly says the doctor.

"I vote for the digger's clothes," says Jack.

"Well, well, if you're both against me, shure I must surrender, but I'll be after giving them a good brushing and furbishing before I call upon the lady."

"That's forbidden, too, old fellow," says Coates with a sly twinkle. The doctor's even temper becomes ruffled for the first time in his friend's experience, through the good fellow's one and perhaps pardonable weakness, that of vanity; so Coates surrenders the point, and gives him the benefit of the brushing. The question of shaving next comes up for discussion, when the two others are unanimous against such a *barbarous* practice; the surveyor emphasizing the pun, and diverting the doctor's attention thereby, secures this point. Next they discuss the methods to be pursued to gain their purpose, which are duly settled; and lastly, the surveyor remarks on his sister's curious references to previous correspondence, which must have gone astray, as he has not heard from her for twelve months, when she was living near Dublin.

Jack brings out of his pocket a copy of a recent *Argus* (the *Times* of Melbourne), announcing the expected resignation of the Governor, Mr. Latrobe, and the probable appointment of Sir J. W. Denison or Sir Charles Hotham, with comments on the likelihood of either being able to cope with the increasing difficulties of the gold-field question.

"Shure, noo, what's all this throuble about the gold-fields? Can't they let us alone, and drop the licence fees altogether?" asks the doctor.

"Oh, the trouble can be summed up in a word or two," answers Coates. "From the first the diggers have had to pay for a licence, but ever since Latrobe tried to double the fees of 30s. a month in 1852, and failed through the determined front of the diggers, there has been constant agitation, got up to induce the Government to drop all fees whatever. The governor admitted quite lately that the tax costs some thousands more to collect than it brings in, and you may rightly ask why he continues it in its present shape. The fact is that he, Foster, and Childers make a series of experiments, for which he bears the blame, and the crown lawyers advise Government not to give up the licence altogether, as mining is a Crown right."

"Why, in the name of fortune, don't they put an export fee on it, then, as it all has to go out of the colony to be coined?" resumed the doctor, "that wouldn't cost much to collect."

"It has been proposed and recommended by Gold Commissioners, but the Government haven't been able to pass the necessary laws," answers the surveyor.

"Why not?"

"Oh, there's a large class of adventurers on the diggings, many from the old country, chiefly Irish, and others forming the scum of Europe, who live by agitation and the confusion it occasions, so can't afford to let the matter be settled."

"We can't be much worse off than we are at present," replied the doctor. "I saw half-a-dozen men chained together like felons being taken up to the Commissioner's camp, and all because they hadn't got their licences. Why, it might happen to any of us if we forgot to take it out, or we got so low again as we were the night before last."

"That's quite true. There are two men here I know, called Huxter and Jackson, commonly known as Jake; only last week they were haled up just like convicts, simply because they had forgotten to take out their licences for the month. I happened to see them, and at once bailed them out; but Huxter, who's the brain of the two, is very bitter against the authorities, though as honest and quiet a man before as you would wish to see."

"Here I see it says that very probably the new governor, whoever it is, will come to have a look round the fields," continued the doctor.

"Well, heaven send him a clearer brain and firmer hand than we've been accustomed to," replied Coates; "but we've had enough of politics to-night, so let's turn in."

First, the doctor drills Jack to be his substitute in dressing his friend's arm during his absence, and then the three retire to their tent, remarking as they go, the difference between their surroundings of the night and those of the night before; *then* a death-like silence pervaded the place; *now* the hum of diggers chatting over future hopes or past hits forms the running accompaniment to the crackling of their brushwood fires, which glow around like the camp of a beleaguering enemy. The earliest streaks of dawn find the doctor and Jack astir. The doctor makes a more elaborate toilet than usual, the babbling brook serving the double purpose of cheval glass and hand-basin, the blue vault the ceiling of his dressing-room, the horizon its walls. In the meanwhile Jack prepares his friend's breakfast, and makes valiant though futile efforts to dust the long-stained clothes back to their original purity.

After a hasty meal the doctor makes the best of his way to the coach-hotel, where, even though the morning is thus early and chilly, a small crowd of inevitable loafers stand around, their costume as well as language sufficiently showing the cosmopolitanism of the gold-fields. "All aboard," states, rather than queries, the driver, who is a big man in his way, and waits for none, being in fact her Majesty's mail-man; and the coach is off its human freight consisting of twelve or thirteen lucky or unlucky diggers and others having business in Melbourne.

The track close into town is in fairly good condition, with the lower-lying parts corduroyed with felled trees, but a few miles further on the absence of road-making of all sorts becomes conspicuous by the frequent cries of the driver to "hold hard inside." The winter rains have softened the ground, and the drays and coaches with their dead and live freights have cut up the roadway terribly, so that the coach is often at an angle of thirty degrees from the perpendicular, one side running on the top of the road, the other in such ruts that the hubs of the wheels themselves slide rather than run over the ground. Altogether the driver's appeals, though directed to the fortunate occupiers of the inside seats, are capable of application to all without reserve, for the motion of an up-country coach on a rough track is near akin to the working of a cockle-boat on a lee-shore with a choppy sea, and is followed often by as disastrous results upon one's internal organs. Often the driver leaves the track and finds an easier path through the bush which closes in on either hand, or across the plains which here and there stretch out their grassy surfaces invitingly. The kangaroos sit on their haunches, staring at the rumbling coach with its noisy freight; for the passengers, bless their hearts, are enjoying fun in their own peculiar way with whisky, champagne, and revolver-shots. The sheep, which here and there dot the plains, are more shy, and scuffle away at a distance; while parrots, parroquets, and a thousand other birds screech and scream their annoyance at the disturbance of their solitude. The day, though in mid-winter, is warm, and nature is looking at her best; verdure and freshness after the recent rains gladden and refresh the on-looker, while countless flowers are unfolding gay blossoms, and spreading out their dainty carpet, where so recently the black hard soil seemed relentlessly and everlastingly sterile. The doctor's spirits rise with the occasion, and he pours forth many an old college and hospital song, sung erstwhile at the "wines" of his associates, thereby earning the clamorous praise of the other passengers, who now are approaching that jovial turn which too soon ends in the lachrymose or pugilistic phase of intoxication. They are thus amusing themselves when a distant report falls upon the ear to the right, answered by a couple of shots to the left. The diggers have sense enough left to look to their revolvers and pistols, which most carry, for these are troublesome times, and "Black Jack" and his gang are becoming rather too close in their attentions to the occupants of outgoing coaches, freighted with gold-dust, who have not availed themselves of the military escort. The driver takes over the organization of the party, bidding them fire in rapid succession a barrel apiece, thus apprising the enemy, if it be one, that the numbers they have to cope with are not insignificant. As there are fifteen in all piled up within and without the vehicle, the discharge of the single barrels becomes a somewhat unsteady, but unmistakable fusillade, which apparently convinces the enemy, if again it be one, how useless an attack would be; and they roll on undisturbed, except with the conviction that there's many a slip between the cup and the lip; and those who carry the most gold make a resolution to drink no more fire-water, in which resolution they determinedly proceed, until the lapse of an hour or so reminds them at once of their thirst and conveniently defrauds their memory of adventure and resolution.

Late in the afternoon the track somewhat improving, but passing among high hills, they make a stage where they sight the up-going coach in front of the half-way house. The coach rattles down the hill, its leathern springs swaying the body from left to right, and in keeping with the sway the passengers are in full chorus, echoing the doctor's good-tempered Irish song with as many different imitations of the brogue as there are throats, all save one or two "insiders," who are sleeping the sleep of the just, if we may judge by its soundness. So they pull up abreast of the other coach, itself standing opposite one of two weather-beaten huts, which bears the dignity of calling itself "hotel," while the other is called "stables," though a disinterested observer might find it hard to discover which is the cleaner within or without.

Not until they have pulled up are they aware that the up-going coach is unusually dignified by the presence of a lady passenger, whose head is curiously and somewhat timidly thrust from the coach window, scanning the on-coming noisy coach-load. The doctor first espies the fact, and signals the others to be quiet; but the fun is too brisk to be stopped, and soon the eloquent blood tinges the doctor's cheeks as some fellow strikes up a ribald song. Jumping down, he walks away to the hotel, desiring not even by a strange lady to be recognized as a willing consort of such men, and in passing the coach peeps rather sheepishly at the face of the fair passenger, who, he finds, is eyeing him somewhat amusedly.

The merry eyes, the brown air, the mischievous but demure mouth, are surely known to him, though the tanned healthy face is not. Then with a sudden rush of recollection he finds himself within two yards of the fair heroine of the hospital, of whom he had unbosomed himself to his friends two nights back. His first impulse to spring forward and take her hand in his is somewhat rudely checked by a hearty but unsteady slap on the back which one of his quondam associates gives him.

"Come alon', ole man, an' have a booze, don't waste time—hic—ah! ah! I sees what ye're after—hic— fine gal, ain't she—oh lor!—hic."

Here the speaker expressed his satisfaction by giving his nose two or three taps and winking violently. The doctor, who might have enjoyed the humour of this very unpleasant situation on another occasion, was bewildered and confused; moreover, he could see that the girl shrank back into the coach, looking somewhat disgusted, but still half amused. Shaking, himself free of his hanger-on, who was fain to content himself with bemoaning the "flash ways of sum cusses," he hurried into the hotel, found out the driver of the up-going coach, and after some trouble elicited from the way-bill the name of the traveller. What was his surprise to see the name of Coates booked a week ago for the very inside seat occupied by the lady passenger! Was she Miss Coates or a substitute? Was she going through to Ballarat? Who had booked the scat? Was she going to meet any one? and a hundred other questions the excited little doctor plied the driver with, but to all was the same answer, "Didn't recollec'," until after much imbibing of "plugs" and "three fingers," as the various potions of fire-water were then called, the driver did recollect "that the leddy had been seen off by the missus of Burbidge's Hotel, who hoped she'd find her brother all right."

This, then, must be the very lady he was going to Melbourne to prevent coming up, thought the doctor, and this was the way, after all, that he had first met her, he who would have arranged all so differently; and yet she looked so amazingly like the Mary of the hospital, and it was so utterly impossible that the two could be identical, that he "faltered where he firmly stood," and hesitated to adopt the most sure course of asking the fair object of his doubts to solve them.

However, mail-drivers cannot wait for ever, and very shortly each driver was calling "all aboard," so the doctor tried a ruse. Calling up to the driver of the up-going coach, loud enough to be heard inside, he wished him to tell his friend Coates, if he inquired at the coach-office, that he, O'Donoghue, had got half way all right. The plan succeeded admirably, for the lady, putting her head out of the coach, asked the doctor in the pleasantest of tones, mixed with some anxiety,—

"Pray excuse me, Mr. Eh-Eh-Digger, but do you happen to know a gentleman of the name of Mr. Coates?"

The doctor was amused, but answered "Yes," and asked if the lady wished to meet Mr. Coates (the mister came very near sticking altogether in the doctor's throat, and as it was, caused a smile on the bystander's faces).

"Well, yes, I do. I'm a particular friend of his—in fact, I'm his sister."

"By the Holy Virgin," ejaculated the doctor, "but you're the same young lady that I'm commissioned to find and turn back."

"Now, then, all aboard, all aboard," cries the down-coach driver.

"All aboard, all aboard," echoes the other driver, both anxious to move on.

"Here, Tom," cries the doctor to his former driver, "catch it—something for yourself. I shall be after going back again."

The man catches the coin, whips up the fresh quartet, who plunge to the collar, and soon bustle the vehicle out of sight, while the doctor tumbles into the other coach, and finds scant room, except by sitting on boxes and parcels, with which, except place for the lady passenger, the inside is crowded.

However, once firmly ensconced, he commences to unfold his tale, which is at first received with some suspicion by his listener, who has not been in the world for some few years without having gained some caution. Then, too, his voice is somehow familiar to her, which perplexes her the more, as she does not ever remember to have met, this sturdy, bearded, handsome, but roughly-clad Irishman.

Again, his appearance on the other coach was not the best introduction he could have wished, and he has an uphill fight at first. She has not realized, and cannot now believe, that her enterprising, well-educated brother is simply a rough digger, like the good doctor appears to be, so she hears all that he has to say, but does not commit herself. As to turning back, which he earnestly pleads, or rather stopping at the next stage until the following morning, and then returning by the down coach, she will not hear of it, she has not come all this way to be fearful of a little more bumping and jolting. But when the doctor talks of the rough life of the gold-field, and tells her the tale of the other night's experiences to emphasize his point, her English courage rises to the occasion, and though she pales, she decisively expresses her intention to proceed at once and nurse her wounded brother. Finding her thus determined, and as the night is drawing on, and the road becoming rougher, the good fellow makes the best of what he feels to be a very bad job, padding the coach in her vicinity with sundry wraps and cloaks, and wrapping up her feet in his thick pea-jacket. For this, the slice of bread and meat, and the cup of tea which he brings her at the next stage, strong and murky though the latter be, dry the bread, and stale the meat, she expresses her thanks so prettily that the doctor is amply repaid for all his anxiety, and congratulates himself on the providential chance that made him espy her just at the nick of time.

"Well, you know, Mr. Eh-Eh-Digger," replies Mary Coates with a smile, "I don't quite see yet where Providence has been so generous;" then, seeing the doctor's face fall, she adds—"to you."

"Shure, I think I have the advantage of yeself in more than one point, and particularly in the point of company," gallantly replies the doctor. "Somehow it seems to me that I have had the pleasure before, but I cannot quite say where."

"Well, I too thought I had heard you before, sir," replies Mary, "but I don't remember ever to have seen you. I was cudgelling my brains just now to find out when and where, if at all, we had met, but the person whose voice resembles yours was a gentleman whom I knew many miles from here years ago."

"Was that same gentleman a doctor, Miss Coates?" inquires our friend.

"Yes; how curious you should guess that! Did you know him?"

"Perhaps so. Was his name Michael O'Donoghue, of Dublin Hospital?"

"That was his name. How strange that we should both know him!"

"Yes," says the doctor drily, "that it is; but I never courted his acquaintance much. I never liked his squint, ye know, and I can't say he was very generous or amiable to me; folks used to call him my worst enemy."

"Oh, I'm sorry to hear you speak so," indignantly replies Mary; "he was as handsome a man as God has made, as generous as he was handsome, and as amiable as generous. If he was anybody's enemy, I can't help thinking— you must forgive me—that it was that person's own fault."

"There I think ye are right," says the doctor, whose tell-tale flush is fortunately lost in the night air. "May I ask where ye met this happy man, who has so won your praise?"

"At the hospital you mention. At that time I was a governess in a family, and, having caught a fever, was shipped off at once, like a servant, to the hospital."

This conversation had been carried on under what may be mildly termed disadvantageous circumstances. The lady was, thanks to the doctor, warm and as comfortable as possible; the jerks and bumps of the vehicle being effectually neutralized by the padding around her; but her voice had to be raised or lowered to suit the exigencies of the case, while he himself, perched upon boxes and packages, with his head inconveniently near the roof, with which it spasmodically came into violent contact—his knees almost drawn up to his chin—his hands employed the while in hanging on to the various lumber of the coach to prevent their toppling over to Mary's side—found so little natural romance in his position that he had to evoke his most brilliant spirits to the rescue in order to produce even a most ordinary conversational effect.

A great snag at this juncture, which almost tore the front wheels out, and tested the strength of the leather springs to their utmost, prevented our doctor from explaining his own relationship to Michael O'Donoghue, and they had scarcely settled down after the heaving and bumping they had then suffered before they heard the sharp sound of many horse-hoofs on the frosty track behind them.

CHAPTER VI

A WOMAN'S WIT

THE doctor had just arranged himself to explain, and had got as far as "I must apologize, Miss Coates," when a sharp order without of the passing horsemen sent a cold-water rill down his back. The words were simple, but too significant in those troublous times "Bail up! Bail up!" came the stern order of the foremost horseman, joined in by a chorus of "Bail up!" from his followers. The affrighted driver let his horses plunge forward, a police inspector on the roof sent a bullet down amongst the horsemen, and an oath and thud told that the bullet had crippled some one or his horse. The coach plunged forward, but not for long. What chance had a cumbrous laden tumbril on such a track against light mounted horsemen, valuing life but as a toss of the dice? One or two of the roof passengers, who have heard terrible tales of wholesale butchery by bushrangers on attempts at resistance, fall, some upon the constable, others upon the driver. The coach stops, and the leader of the gang, mounted on his panting mare, draws up alongside, and with a sneer asks the driver "whether he could crawl away with that old caravan from Black Jack and his good men. The first man that stirs has a bullet in him," says the rascal. "I've a good mind to give you all a good supper of cold lead for knocking down poor Ben's horse. Who shot him? Get down, all of you, and stand in a row. Who shot him, I say?"

The driver and passengers are all getting down as fast as they can, and as he steps down the inspector steps forward courageously, and cries,—

"It was I, Black Jack, or whoever you are, and I wish it had been you I had shot instead!"

"Brave words, my boy!" laughed the rascal satirically, "and if I hadn't got my arm just touched a bit" (pointing to a bandaged arm) "they would be your last. Now, who are you that talks so big, I want to know?"

Mary all this time is pale but courageous, hiding in her corner, while the doctor is peeping out of the window, and notices in the pale moonlight, as it were in the flash of a second, the broad grassy plain upon which the coach has debouched, the row of eight pale-faced passengers with hands up in air, the mounted horsemen, six in number, their faces blackened and their revolvers levelled at the passengers, and the single dismounted horseman, with his face also blackened, one wounded arm, and the other wound through his horse's reins, who is holding the cheering conversation with the inspector just chronicled.

The constable's answer comes short and quick—he knows his minutes are few, and so he is reckless:—

"My name is Inspector James Cochrane, and it's yourself I'm after, Black Jack, and its yourself shall come to your end through me."

"Oh! oh! Oh! oh!" laughs the other. "Here, Dozer, you can shoot pretty straight, close up as well as I can, though I can shoot with my left arm, and should like to have the killing of this buck myself; still I'll be generous, and he's your quarry to-night. This is the inspector, boys," cries he to the others, "who made Tom Blake and Three-Fingered Williamson swing. Now, then, Mr. Inspector, you shan't say you hadn't a chance, for you shall run to the scrub yonder, and the Dozer shall have practice in shooting at moving targets. If you get away, let the Dozer answer for it."

"I run for no one," says the inspector. "There's never a man can say that James Cochrane ever turned his back to his enemy, and never a man shall."

"All right, my joker," calls out the Dozer; "then you just stand aside from your mates, or you'll get some of them hit through your precious pluck."

The brave fellow complies in order to save his comrades; but within the coach the doctor's blood is up—his eyes are glistening unwontedly, and his revolver, the barrel hardly four paces from the braggart "Dozer," is vibrating with the excitement of the moment.

"Black Jack," as the leader is called, gives the word. "One—two" comes distinctly the death-knell of the constable, but the "three" was never heard, for a report which buzzed in the ears of all drowned the word, and, to their astonishment, was followed by the fall of the braggart, not his intended victim.

"The beaks are upon us!" cried the leader, and, springing to his horse, was hastily riding away, the others following, when a peremptory voice of one of the others called out,—

"It's some skulker inside the coach; I saw the flash from the coach window."

They all remember they noticed the same, and as their courage revives the doctor slides boldly through the window head first, falling heavily to the ground, in his attempts at imitating the harlequin at the pantomime. Mary nervously thinks, even in the excitement of the moment, of the curious figure he cuts. He is pounced upon in a moment, his smoking weapon wrenched from him, and himself placed side by side with the inspector, who grips him by the hand, as a token of his thanks for respite.

Black Jack gets down one of the five great lamps that burn over the coach, and turns it within, hunting, as he says, for other skulkers. There, of course, he sees Mary, now thoroughly frightened, and pale as a sheet. He laughs noiselessly, and, with a bow worthy of the notorious Claude Duval, he opens the coach-door on the other side, and insists on Mary alighting; then, apologizing in sarcastic tone for his enforced rudeness, he leads her to the end of the long line of passengers, and surveys the throng.

"Now," said he, "who's the man with the nugget? Come, out with it, or we kill all the lot of you, barring the lady,"—this with a fresh bow to poor Mary, whose throbbing heart, fearing a moment ago lest she might be killed, now dreads lest she may be reserved for a worse fate.

"Come, come," says the other impatiently, as none answer, not knowing, in fact, to what the rascal refers; "I'm not going to be humbugged like this. Who was the digger who changed coaches at the halfway house?"

"I!" said our doctor laconically.

"Well, what did you do with your nuggets, you fool!" threateningly asks the other, holding his weapon so that the cold iron scratches the doctor's nose,

"Banked it yesterday morning," answers the doctor.

"That's a lie!" answers Black Jack, "You took it out again, and are taking it down to Melbourne."

"Michael O'Donnoghue tells no lies," replied the other.

"Oh! oh! so you're a good little boy, are you? but come, come, we can't waste time with you. Hallo! let's look at you again. Why, cussed if you aren't the chap that shot me the night before last. So, so, my joker, you don't escape me this time. My arm's going to be revenged. Two of you search the coach for the nuggets, while the others keep guard. This fellow wants us to believe that he went down to the half-way and came back again for the pleasure of the thing."

"No, I don't; I went down to meet this lady," hotly answered the doctor, "and, bedad, if you're so clever, ye ought to know that too."

One of the others has approached the two.

"I say, Jim, don't waste words like this; what are you going to do? Why, blamed if it ain't the little doctor chap who knocked Bully Ben down at the store a couple of months since."

Bully Ben himself strides up as he hears his name mentioned, and looks so threateningly at his lighter-made and disarmed foe, that Gentleman Jim—for it is he, Black Jack being his cognomen when in the free-booting saddle—intervenes.

"Doctor is he? well, then, he shall doctor me, and shall be well paid; in fact, his fee shall be in lead, and last him his lifetime."

The grim meaning of the rascal is too obvious to be unintelligible to the other passengers, and the doctor is just repenting his precipitancy in rescuing the inspector, when Mary Coates steps forward, fearless of the weapons aimed at her. Standing erect in the moonlight, one hand raised to the skies, the other pointing to the dead man by her side, she impressively addresses the leader,—

"Stop, man! Stop in your crimes. I exhort you all, by the dead body of your comrade, cut off thus without hope of salvation or repentance, pass on your way, take all we have, but spare our lives; if you don't, as sure as there is a God in heaven, our spirits shall haunt you to the very gates of hell."

Some excuse must be made for Mary, that her address was thus melodramatic, but it was intended to be partly so, and for the rest I must leave my readers to place themselves in her position before they criticize her too closely. The words certainly had considerable effect on most of the lawless crew, who were unaccustomed to the ways of the drama, particularly when enacted with "properties" so real as dead men and real actresses, but Gentleman Jim merely laughed and chid his comrades for being afraid of the threats of a woman.

"Hell, where is that?" said he. "I don't know it; besides, what do we care, a short life and a merry one, isn't that our motto, boys? and the devil take care of the future."

"That's it. A short life and a merry one," chorussed his fellows, relieved to follow suit, and to be released from their fascination.

"Madame, we are extremely indebted to you for your dramatic performance," said the rascal, turning to Mary, with his slouch hat in hand, "but to tell you the truth, we can't protract the scene, so we'll have to ask you to postpone the rest of it, and we assure you that you shan't want for an audience, for at our leisure we will hear the rest of it, as we purpose asking for the honour of your company."

"Never," cried poor Mary, at her wits' end thus balked of success just as she hoped she had achieved it. "I'll die first."

"Oh! dying's easy enough, my dear, in some cases; but bless your pretty face, you won't die just yet."

The doctor is beside himself with rage, and is trembling from head to foot, to whom turning, Gentleman Jim cries,—

"Now then, Mr. Doctor, here's my arm, but honour bright, you know, no tricks with it, or there are other ways of dying, and more like surgical operations than being shot, such as being tied to the tail of a kicking horse, or pulled at the end of a coach by your feet, and so on."

"Honour, ye murthering ruffian," cries the doctor, "take the word out of your mouth, why ye soil it by the mention. Do ye talk of honour? Well noo, I'll make a bargain with ye, though I'm sore to have to with such a rascal. I'll bandage ye up efficiently and surgeon-like on one condition alone, that this lady is allowed to go on to Ballarat with the coach, and is at once handed safe and sound to her brother."

"Done with you," cries the other, whose exertions have told on a badly-set bone, and whose promises never weighed very heavily on his conscience. The doctor hesitates awhile, divining the rascal's faithlessness, but finally calling the others to witness the promise, proceeds to bind up the arm, setting it with splints improvised from broken branches.

The two searchers have ransacked the coach, tossed open all the trunks and packages, but of course found no nuggets belonging to the doctor, and report the result.

Disappointed at their non-success, they are for riding off at once, but Gentleman Jim has other plans in view.

"Look sharp with them, then," cries one of his fellows; "it's about the time of night that the military escort pass along, and if they come to-night, we shall have our work cut out to get away with whole skins."

"Oh! never fear," says Jim; "I heard up at the bank one of the clerks asking the manager when the escort was going down, as the safes were getting full, and the manager said that the regular escort was going to be kept up at the fields for some time longer as the police wanted reinforcing for licensing business. But come along, who's got a bit of rope?"

Another search in the boot of the coach reveals a piece some yards in length, which the thoughtful driver provides against accidents, and a joyful shout proclaims another discovery.

A small box, a foot square, very heavy, is pulled out by the united efforts of two bushrangers, one of whom has already broken through the cover and tosses out a small golden nugget. The box is reversed, when out fall the contents, a heap of bright golden nuggets of all sizes, from a pea to a chestnut, to the apparent amazement of all the party, including the passengers. The keen eye of Gentleman Jim looks down the row and notices one who looks more annoyed than surprised, a dark-haired young man, one of the two who had seized and disarmed the inspector; he steps up to him, takes him aside, and after a few words seems to come to a thorough understanding with him.

"Put them in your pockets, boys, and load up the saddle bags," says Jim, "we're in luck tonight."

This order is promptly complied with, and two of the bushrangers with Jim proceed to the nearest tree, over a limb of which the rope is flung, coming down nearly to the ground on either side.

The poor doctor feels that for him there is no longer any hope. The inspector, however, whispers that he will not die the disgraceful death of hanging, as this is not the custom of the rascals; they are going to be tied up and shot at as they swing. The good fellow feels little consolation in this, and envies the inspector his iron nerve in the face of such a death; but the recollection of his heroine's presence braces him up, and he forces his nerves into subjection and resolves to die game.

Poor Mary is distraught; she, too, has guessed the meaning of the rope, and, placing little trust in the promise of the chief rascal, feels the awfulness of her position acutely; but what can she, a weak woman, do amongst so many men? Her fellow passengers are terrorized by the revolvers which command them, yet fearlessly and tearlessly she chides these terrified men; but without effect. In the meanwhile the doctor and inspector are being tied under their arms to the opposite ends of the rope, and are set swinging some four feet from the ground in opposite directions. The brutality of the proceeding is increased by the fact that they occasionally swing against and bruise one another. Two of the bushrangers are left to guard the helpless, cowed, trembling passengers, while the other three and Gentleman Jim take up a position about thirty paces distant, and in regular order fire at the dangling feet of the two hapless men, Gentleman Jim having precedence. The second shot takes effect in the inspector's knee; but no cry escapes his throat, nor anything tells of the wound save the helpless hang of the leg and the agonized sweat on the man's pale brow. The third ruffian takes, his stand and aims, but his shot goes wide of the mark; a double report sounds through the night air, the aiming miscreant falls shot through the spine, while one, two, three succeeding flashes and reports from the bush behind the ruffians announce a flank movement, and strike terror home to their hearts, who naturally think themselves surrounded by a large force.

"To horse," comes the harsh cry of the leader, running back to the coach, and soon the gang is in saddle and full flight, not without a hasty but unsuccessful search by Gentleman Jim for the girl, whose absence is unaccountable by his comrades. With an oath he is off and the silence of the bush soon buries the tramp, tramp of the crew, who have thus left two of their number on the field.

The frightened passengers stand as though paralyzed, but one, two, three minutes, elapse before aught stirs in the bush to disclose their mysterious but well-timed preservers. In the meanwhile the doctor and the inspector have released themselves from their perilous position, the doctor first in order, then gently letting down his partner in danger to the ground, and supporting him, as his practised eye notices the broken limb.

The driver next realizes the position, and at the doctor's call, helps the inspector back to the coach, where by dint of great care in piling up boxes and packages, the poor fellow is provided with the best litter available, the doctor attending to him in the meanwhile with his usual womanly tenderness and manly skill. The man who is shot through the back has ceased by this time to groan, and turns out on examination to be as dead as a door-nail. The doctor's thoughts then turn to Mary Coates, whose absence he for the first time notices. Cooe-ing aloud soon brings her back to them, pale-faced and trembling all over, while the passengers recovering their senses, proceed to impart to one another the obvious reasons why they did not rush upon and overpower the bushrangers. They can boast between them three revolvers and one pistol of the old horse

type, and with a little pluck might have done wonders, so the doctor is
disgusted, and looks for his own weapon, assisted by Mary, who comes
across it, as though by accident, flung under the coach. The doctor holds
out his hand and receives the weapon by the barrel, but is fain to let it go
suddenly as his hand is burnt, and the barrel still smokes.

"This is curious," thinks he, as he has not fired it off for many minutes
(the seconds had seemed to him like ages as he hung on the tree), and on
examining the charges sees that they are all fired, though he had taken
the usual precaution on starting from the half-way house of looking to its
loading. Then as he looks at the alternately pale and red face of Mary, it
flashes upon him that this gentle girl's courage has saved his life, and her
disappearance and reappearance from the bush are now accounted for.
He says nothing, but steps up to her and raises her hand reverently to his
lips. Then he hastily reloads his weapon, the other passengers see to their
own firearms, and the inspector receives back his revolver, the trunks and
packages are repacked, and the coach rumbles along again on its way, the
horses trotting forward as unconcernedly as though they had merely spent
a few minutes' breathing time, while the driver and his human freight re
silent, each revolving the adventures of the night in his or her mind.

Miss Mary is seated on the box-seat, for the inspector monopolizes
the interior, while the gallant doctor wedges her firmly in, encouraging
her spirit, exhausted and half-fainting now that the excitement is over, by
telling her of her brother's anticipated joy at her safe arrival, and reminding
her of her brave deeds. She faintly smiles, and wishes she had not come
from Melbourne against the advice of her hostess, in which wish the
doctor, be it said, heartily concurs; then she also wishes him not to talk of
her part of the matter, being deeply impressed by the death of the second
ruffian, whom she assures the doctor she had not meant to kill.

Without further adventure they reach the next station, where Ned
Manning, the station-keeper, greets them with, "What in the tarnation
kep' ye so long on the way, Bob? Why ye're two hours behind time." This
comment, of course, causes the first version of the story to get abroad. The
station-keeper has heard nobody pass, in fact seen none since the coach
went through that morning, except half a dozen tramps on their way up
to the fields. He is at first "struck all of a heap," as he says; but the next
moment, being an old soldier, fetches out his rifle and shot gun, and laying
his hand affectionately on the weapons as they gleam in the lamplight,

promises the "'rangers a warm reception when he does come across them." Poor old plucky Ned, what a meaning had your words in days to come! The old fellow's daughter makes some hot coffee, which stirs the whole party into life, "warming the cockles of their hearts," as the driver promises them it would, and filling them, especially those who dilute the liquid with the contents of their flasks, with that courage whose source is generally traced in Holland. The doctor surreptitiously introduces "a little of the high-priced article," which he has asked for and obtained, in Mary's cup, ordering her quite professionally to drink it as medicine, when she at first hesitates. The inspector is not forgotten; his wound is dressed with cold water, the doctor cursorily satisfying himself that there is no bullet there, and making the poor fellow as comfortable as possible, while a judicious dose of the high-priced article aforesaid stimulates him to perform the rest of a journey which is of such an extremely painful character to him. If you want a good idea of pain, reader, just break a bone—to sprain an ankle is sufficient to give you a "notion"—and then ride on a rough road in a lumbering vehicle. Every horse's tread is registered on the wound, almost as painfully as though it were in fact trodden there, every sway, swerve, jerk or bump makes itself felt, not only in the wound, but apparently upon the whole of the nervous system, and the limb, though well set, is given to starting on a spasmodically compensating species of movement, which only adds to the sufferer's agony.

At last the dawn appears, the moon pales, and the Australian sun rises in all its vivid colouring, looking so brightly and freshly at the anxious, worn travellers that the doctor upbraids it with being an imposter or a bad ruler, either ignoring or not knowing the deeds of violence which went on within its realms when its back is turned.

CHAPTER VII

A ROYAL RECEPTION

AND so they drive into Ballarat, which is just awakening to the rush and turmoil of another day. The doctor at once secures a room for Mary at the hotel, accompanies the inspector to the barracks, where he hands him over to the divisional surgeon, explaining the accident and its treatment. Then shaking his *confrère's* hands, he hurries back to the hotel towards the camp, where he expects to find his friends just waking up. But the news of the night's adventure is spreading like wildfire; the doctor is waylaid, and made to tell the matter in detail, which he does by omitting any mention of Mary. Interrogated as to the strange rescuing party, he maintains a steady silence, but finds from his hearers that the driver has heard part and guessed the rest of the truth, and the "lady on the coach" has become a heroine. A crowd collects opposite the hotel, and the proprietor is sent in to call Mary to the door, so that the assembled multitude may do her homage; but the old German host is frightened, and consults his wife, who, coming forward to an upper window, explains that the lady is almost dead with fatigue, and gone off into a sweet sleep. The doctor also gets up, and tells how dangerous to her health and more excitement would be. But the mob is not thus to be balked of its cheers. "Fetch her to the window!" resounds like the war-cry of an army, and, fearing consequences of refusal, upon the doctor's advice, the hostess proceeds to wake up poor Mary, and leads her, half-bewildered, to the upper window, where the presence of her kindly friend the doctor reassures her. At sight of her the diggers madly shout and cheer, surging this way and that, and throwing up hats, coats, and any thing else handy, much to the personal danger and detriment of their unheeding fellows, thus doing homage, in their rough way, to the pluck of the young girl before them. A digger named Jackson, of great, massive, broad shoulders and sturdy frame, stands prominently forward in the veranda, while his friend Huxter, an energetic backwoods' orator, of slight build, but with long-bearded face,

climbs on his shoulders, facing the mob, and waves them to be silent; but
this he long seeks, in vain. At last a few moments of comparative quiet allow
his voice to be heard, and, ever ready for a speech, the mob stand at ease.

"Feller countrymen and—others," says Huxter—including in the last
comprehensive word rather more than half his audience—"this here is a
sight fit for the nobs, and as there are many of us who'd like to express
our satisfaction in better and more substantial ways than cheering and
mayhaps the leddy wouldn't care to drink with each and all of us" (Mary
nods her head to this doubt smilingly), "I don't think we could do better'n
make up a leetle pile, and hand it up to the leddy, to encourage other
wimmen to do likewise. As I ain't just now much in luck myself I can't
start the pile with more'n a couple of yellow boys; so here goes."

Taking off a greasy slouch hat, he solemnly dropped into it two
sovereigns, during which operation his efforts to get at his pocket
endangered the stability of his seat, and almost brought him on his nose;
however, after some staggering about, his human platform recovered his
equilibrium, amidst the laughter of the good-natured crowd, who caught
the idea at once. In went all sorts of treasures—here a gold pin, there coin,
again gold-dust, again little nuggets, until the improvised bag was running
over with wealth, and yet generous would-be givers were yelling for a
chance to get at and fill it. They fought one another in their attempts to
bestow donations, so that the leader had to send round another "bag."
This time Jackson's hat performed that function. Meanwhile, Mary was
earnestly speaking to the doctor, who finally motioned to the crowd to
give him ear awhile.

"Me friends," said he, smilingly, when the shouts had subsided to
murmurs, "I've had a rare tussle on your account to get your handsome
present accepted, as the queen of our hearts—God bless her!"—(here the
interruptions by the crowd took the form of vociferous and prolonged
hurrahs; when they had toned down, he continued) "refused to take
anything for what she considers to have been her duty; but I've just been
telling her how angry—I mean, how grieved"—

("Angry's the word," says one of the crowd).

"Ye'd all be if she didn't accept this offering, and so she's made up
her mind to do so, and to thank ye heartily for it, and to start with it a
hospital close by, where those of ye who are sick or hurt may get well
under careful nurses and doctors."

This speech is greeted with another burst of cheers, the crowd swelling every minute, and the "bags" having now come back to Huxter, he and Jackson form a "deppytashun" to the upper floor, where, in the sight of the whole crowd, they present the two "bags" into Mary's hands, an act greeted with further thunder from the throats of the crowd. The "deppytashun" steps down, and Huxter again mounts his obliging friend; silence of a sort is enforced, and the "deppytashun" pronounces a benediction in this wise:—

"Boys, the lady took the rhino and asked me to thank ye all amazingly; but she said that by the living Jingo (Mary dissents smilingly) she only did her duty, and that as England expects every man to do his duty, so it expects every Englishwoman to do likewise, which is good argyment for a woman, and—well, she said a lot more which I disremember, and ended up by wishing us a long life and a happy one; and she looks right down pale and sadly; so, boys, I think as we've done all as we ken do for the present, we'll dissolve the meeting."

"I second that, Huxter," says the platform.

"Hold yer tongue, Jake," cries the other. "So, boys, here's three cheers more for the leddy, and one for the Irish doctor, who's been hung until he's good mate, as he'd say."

The cheers were given, and the crowd separated; the doctor leaving strict injunctions with the hotel people to keep Mary quiet, and, fearing no further disturbance, set out at last for the camp, where he arrived, after dodging many a digger, and getting a hand-shake from nearly every other, because of the fame that had gone before him. Even Poker Flat had heard the news, though rather distortedly, the facts having been represented as a wholesale successional massacre of twenty bushrangers by a single girl, firing from the roof of a running coach, and the story was served up with various strange exaggerations, themselves increased by the loud cheering up at the hotel, faintly heard across the plain. The two were somewhat anxious about their friend, but doubtless he would long before the fray have been nearing Melbourne, and they would hear news of him and the object of his quest in a day or two.

Judge then their surprise when the doctor interrupted them at their frugal breakfast—the beef steak had long disappeared, and the porridge with cream had been reserved for banquets when the appreciative doctor presided. Taking his seat and discussing a tough piece of bread, he was soon in the thick of his story, telling his tale to ears that drank in every detail.

When he had finished, the surveyor thanked him for the care he had shown to his sister, and was for setting off at once to meet her at the hotel, a course which the doctor dissuaded. Then Coates asked if he had recognized the head ruffian, to which the doctor replied, "As well as a black corked face would permit." Yes, he thought he could swear to him in a court of law, though he had seen him both times at night.

"I think, doctor, you'd better see the superintendent and have the neighbourhood scoured," says the surveyor.

"That's being done noo, me boy. The police with the black trackers have by this time set off for the scene of last night's drama."

"I don't believe they'll find the *dramatis personæ*," said Coates. "These people make it worth everybody's while to hush up the matter. They threaten the people and bribe the police."

"Ye forget that they've shot down one of the police themselves this time, and why ye should doubt the virtues of the Victorian police, I cannot understand. D'ye know there's the flower of the Irish people among them, turned out of their native counthry by the Saxon's misrule. The inspector himself is the son of a great county (Mayo) family. Noo, me boy, I'll wager ye they don't get off by bribery."

"Well, we shall see," says the surveyor; "but now what's to be done about my sister? She can't come here, you know."

"Why not?" says the doctor, who has become amazingly loth to second Coates in his wishes to keep his sister at Melbourne.

"Why, my dear fellow, you know well enough. What would the world say if she were to come here to the gold-field unescorted by any one and without a roof to her head?"

"As for the roof; I'll provide that," says the doctor, "and it's her own house she'll have to keep; besides, man, ye don't know how they all count her their *mavourneen* now, and sorry a hair of her head would anybody harm unless he wanted to be lynched off hand."

"Well, well, we must see what the little body says herself," replied the other.

"Little body is it ye're saying. Oh it's yourself is a little body, me boy. Do ye know, she's as tall as yourself and as slim as a gazelle? Oh, those eyes of yours will have to be opened a good few, I see."

Then the doctor had to go into an elaborate description of her; but he took care not to hint at having seen her before. There was, in fact, growing up within him, with the speed of Jonah's gourd, a very different feeling to that which had prompted him to pay "attention" to Mary as she lay in the hospital, and he was half ashamed of having spoken as he had about the girl to his friends.

Then the doctor had to inspect the surveyor's water-chute, which had progressed considerably, as he had hired the services of one or two of the lazy diggers, who were "shepherding" their holes around still awaiting the run of luck. The bed of the stream had been boarded and pegged, thus narrowing it at a point where the chute would join it. Here was a hinged board which would, so to speak, shunt the water down its natural or its new bed as required.

In the afternoon the three had a call from a detective, dressed as a digger, who was getting up the case against the bushrangers. This man had a long conversation with the doctor and the surveyor, the last of whom gave him the benefit of his suspicions. Jack was also called upon to describe the clothes and general appearance of the diggers who had so interested themselves in the nuggets when he called at the bank. He had not yet adopted the surveyor's advice to search amongst the neighbouring diggers for the drunken man, a piece of advice the detective echoed, and thereupon departed, promising to call when he had any news to impart useful to the three.

The doctor then walked to the hotel, accompanied by Coates, who was obstinate upon the point, and there they had an audience of Mary.

After the first greetings of brother and sister were over, the doctor, who had delicately remained without, was called in and shyly greeted by Mary, who had, in the turmoil of last night's encounter, obtained the information of her unknown friend which she had so much wished for, but which, now in the possession, filled her with confusion for the glowing terms in which she had praised him to himself. For his part in this little comedy she had not forgiven him, though it is but justice to him to add that he had not for a moment anticipated the effect upon Mary of his sly abuse of himself.

The consultation, which followed dispelled the awkwardness of the situation, and, after much amusing argument, the surveyor, who did not see his way yet to return to Melbourne, having a good excuse in the refusal of his "medical man," consented to his sister remaining to nurse him, overborne in fact, against his better judgment by the other two, who were unanimous whenever the lady took the initiative, the doctor agreeing to the most unreasonable remarks that Mary made, and which she intended mischievously to see if he would follow her lead through thick and thin.

But Mary was to stop at the hotel until a frame-house was built for her, which would soon, the doctor assured his hearers, be erected, and in the meantime she could, as she wished to be doing something useful, apply at the police barracks for hospital nursing for a few days.

The treasure collected in the two hats had to be stored away, and the bank was settled upon for the purpose, though the money was as safe in her own possession as in any strong room. Of this she was made fully aware by the sentry-go of two or three diggers around the hotel, relieved from time to time by willing comrades. Such was the enthusiasm instilled into the hearts of these rough diamonds by the pluck and daring of a single woman!

The bank was closed for the day, so it was settled to deposit the money and valuables on the morrow, and leaving the surveyor at the hotel, the doctor trudged back to the tent, right glad to find so much luxury in his hard couch—luxury by contrast to the many fatigues and anxieties he had lately endured.

On the morrow the three settled down to their respective duties.

Towards evening the detective again called on the party, requesting Jack and the doctor to walk up with him to the police barracks, where their presence was required. They both complied, leaving a friendly digger to look to Coates, and on the way Jack caught the officer by the arm, pointing out a man whom he recognized as the drunken digger at the bank, standing by the side of a bark, but near our friend's claim, and engaged in close conversation with a dark, well-dressed young man, who, in fact, was no other than the young passenger of the coach who had attracted the bushranger's attention. The detective carefully observed the two without being himself observed, and made mental notes to shadow them at no distant date. Proceeding, they reached the barracks, and being ushered within the enclosure found themselves in a long room, dimly lit, with two beds at the upper end, on which there appeared to be men sleeping. The detective approached the beds, followed by Jack alone, and drawing off the sheets disclosed the dead bodies of two men, at the sight of one of whom Jack started. In answer to the detective's question whether he recognized either, Jack replied that one of the men was undoubtedly the sober digger at the bank, who had exclaimed so loudly as to the nuggets; the other he did not know, and had never seen before.

"These are the two highwaymen, bushrangers, or what you like, who were killed in the attack on the coach yesterday," replied the detective, "and as I thought, the digger at the bank was doubtless the mate of the man with the wounded arm, who is no other than Black Jack, Gentleman Jim, bushranger, fossicker, robber, and lately attempted murderer. The mystery of the drunken digger is not yet solved, and why they didn't all attack you and rob you of your nuggets I don't know yet, but I'll get to the bottom of it some day, I dare say."

The doctor had now approached, and identified as well as he was able, the man whom Jack had recognized as the bushranger whom he had himself killed, while the other was the one who had been killed by the shot from the scrub. Having made a deposition to this effect before the police magistrate, who was then sitting, it was arranged for Mary's sake that the inquest which would take place the next day would be formal, and not require her presence. Accordingly on the morrow the coroner holds his court, and the jury, much to Mary's and the doctor's satisfaction, find both men "killed in self-protection, by or on behalf of the passengers of the coach." The bodies are taken to the bush, where a hole has been dug for their reception, and there to this day they lie, two men formed in the image of their Creator, and once perhaps the pride of mother, father, or friends, yet dead and buried like dogs,

"Unwept, uncared by all."

The same day the Melbourne papers brought by the coach, gave a detailed account of the attack on the down coach, some six or seven miles beyond the half-way house. The story, from the lips of the driver, said that just as he was fording the "Found-drowned Creek" in the twilight, he heard the patter of horses' hoofs on the road behind, and before he could climb the steep bank on the other side, the bushrangers "stuck the coach up, turned out all the half-asleep or half-drunk passengers, ransacked their pockets; and learning that one of the party had turned back at the half-way house, and was returning in the up-coach, had finally ridden away cursing their luck at not finding a large nugget. This accounted for the knowledge the ruffians displayed of the doctor's movements, and the exhausted state of their horses on attacking the up-coach some three hours later, as they had then ridden some twenty-four miles since the first attack on the coach.

The doctor was as good as his word as to Mary's house, for finding out the good-tempered Goliath, "Jake," and the spokesman of the other day who had started the collection, he explained the situation they were in, and at the end of the third day had the pleasure of seeing a frame house transported on two trollies, carefully threading the honeycomb of holes and pitfalls over the field. The "house" was not pretentious, but was a nucleus, consisting of one living-room and a small cupboard, called by courtesy a bedroom, at one end, both of which rooms possessed glazed windows, then at a premium on the fields. It was neatly and strongly put together, facts, indeed, tested by its journey, while over the low doorway was an inscription, in extremely unsteady letters, which had a tendency to illustrate rather the curve of beauty than the straight line of duty, whereby it was manifest to all men that this was another of the offerings of the diggers of Ballarat to the "Queen of our hearts." The doctor's gallant words had become a stock-phrase with them, and the brown-haired, gentle-mannered girl had indeed become, so far as absolute sway was concerned, "the queen of their hearts," a phrase which became shortened, without any discourtesy to her Gracious Majesty at the other end of the globe, into "The Queen."

We must pass over the installation of "The Queen" in her palace, with the arrangements of which she was mightily pleased and amused; her subjects soon withdrew and left her with her brother and friends, showing that delicacy of thought which manifests itself often in the roughest of the rough. We must also pass over many weeks which ensued, weeks of heavy hard labour on the part of the doctor and Jack, the surveyor supervising the work all the while, completing the water chute and making great progress with their gold-digging, which had proved extremely lucky. Mary presented them with such hitherto unknown delicacies that Coates gravely questioned her more than once whether she was keeping within their means or trenching on her own. As the delicacies were simply the result of good cooking, instead of the miserable makeshifts they had been before accustomed to, it may be rightly guessed that their expenses did not materially increase. She also nursed Coates back to complete forgetfulness of his wound, and then her motherly tenderness sought wider fields, so that Miss Mary soon became known to many a sick digger, his wife or child, as "a ministering angel" of the most practical sort. The hospital grew into definite shape, the proceeds of the diggers' collection having amounted to more than 300*l*. Easy come, easy go was their motto, but Mary hoped that the easiness of going would only be manifested in her scheme, which she wanted to be an example of thrift to them. The diggers erected the frame-house for the hospital themselves, movable as for Mary's house, but larger and less highly finished (save the mark!) except that it was ornamented by very similarly jovial letters, all at sixes and sevens, which chronicled the *raison d'être* of the building, and gave its founder's name.

CHAPTER VIII

WORK FOR THE DOCTOR

ONE warm afternoon in the early part of August, Mary pronounced the fittings of the hospital complete, and, *nolens volens*, received her first patient, a digger, whose curiosity had prompted him to feel "summat in the wind catchy-like," and who came to be relieved. Yet another and another came, although she explained that the doctor was not yet at hand, each with some fancied or small ache or pain, until she fairly broke out into a cheery laugh at her dilemma. Patiently they waited outside in a row, winking to one another solemnly, and admiring the general aspect of the hospital, "for all the world," as Mary told her brother, to whom she hurried, "like a parcel of schoolboys looking at an apple orchard through iron railings."

She had engaged two women, the best she could get, to act as nurses, and had intended for some weeks past to ask the doctor to throw down the pick and shovel and take up the probe and lancet, though she feared the exchange would not prove of pecuniary advantage to him. But whenever she had intended to speak, her timidity had proved the victor, and enforced silence. This afternoon matters were at a crisis, so she had to speak out. Her brother, to whom she applied for advice, fraternally told her not to make such a bother about so small a matter and smilingly kissed her; so she sauntered to the bush where the resounding axe-strokes told her the doctor was hard at work, and as she went she reasoned herself out of her timidity, and resolved to go straight to the point. Jack was working in the shaft at the time, and it was in fact for the supports for a tunnel of this very shaft that the doctor was so hard at work. Jack's presence, she admitted, would not have materially assisted the matter, as Mary looked upon him in the light of a big, overgrown boy, and made great fun of and with him; but what had she to fear; was the doctor a woman-eater? At the self-questioning she laughed aloud, and the doctor hearing the laugh, stopped in his toil over a fallen log and smiled a ready welcome.

Now I regret to say the doctor had lately been engaged in a species of infanticide, the infants being the creation of his brain, or adopted out-and-out from his "college and hospital bachelor" friends. Such early literary creations of his as "The Delights of Freedom" and "Celibacy—the Perfect State," "When a Man's Single," &c., had been steadily and surely throttled, until a sort of tolerating recollection of thoughts and opinions which had formed the subject of his college songs and arguments alone remained. He had left negative and adopted active resistance to that former self of his. He had let the little divine *retuarius* cast his fatal net over him, and, gladiator-like, plunge the trident to his very heart. No thumb had he held up for mercy. No, he would not have stirred his little finger to soothe the pleasurable anxiety and pain he felt or to dispel this sense of exaltation, fool's paradise, as he more than once told himself, though it was. Since we last saw him, toil and heat had alike reduced his waist measurement to normal tally, and vastly improved his physique, so that he looked very manly and strong as he rested on his axe, his kindly smiling eyes lighting up his bright comely face until, as Mary had perhaps somewhat flatteringly said, he looked as handsome a man as God made. The recollection of this remark, as he stood there smiling in the afternoon sun, flushed her face crimson, the approximate cause of which the doctor intuitively divined, and himself flushed hotly.

"Miss Mary," said he, "I'm going to take the liberty of asking your very humble pardon for a bit of boyish prank, I oughtn't ever to have played, and wouldn't speak of it noo, were we conventional folk in a conventional place, but" (glancing laughingly at his own costume) "we aren't. I don't think ye'll misjudge me for making a clean breast, as the boys say."

The girl recovers her composure at the evident embarrassment of her friend, and asks him to speak frankly, like he would to her brother.

"Well noo, that's not quite possible, letting alone that I should say ould fellow and the like, I don't compare ye any more with Harry than I should a mackerel with a sprat."

"Who's the sprat, doctor?" asked the girl mischievously.

"Why, Harry, of course," replies the other, with a smile.

"Well, well, now I did expect to have a compliment from an Irishman, not to be told I'm so big and clumsy," says the merry girl, assuming an offended air.

The doctor is metaphorically on his knees in a second begging pardon, which is laughingly granted, while she has skilfully drawn him away from the awkward confession he was going to make. The cause she has long forgiven; as she knows more and more of his self-denying, loving, lovable, and humorous character, she sees how little of the thoughtless butterfly there is in him, and how much true merit, so she has long since ascribed his mischievousness in the coach to its real source.

"Now, doctor, as you've said all that you want to say, I'll just put you through a catechism which you may answer or not, as pleases your majesty."

"It ill becomes the queen of all our hearts to call a poor digger your majesty," cries out the doctor gaily.

"Come, come, I never called you a *poor* digger, that's too bad of you," replies Mary, "but that's what I'm coming to, you must not be a digger at all. For Mr. Wainwright it's all very well, his mind is more suited to it."

The doctor bows his acknowledgments.

"But for you and my brother, it's just like using one of your fine-pointed lancets to sculpture away a piece of marble; your lancet may make some impression, but it suffers more than the stone in the long run."

"So ho," says the doctor, "Jack is the chisel, I suppose, and where is the gavel, I mean the mallet, to knock him against the stone, I should like to know."

"Well, he doesn't possess any ambition, which I assume you mean by the gavel, but borrows that from both of you. Now, doctor, don't put me off the track, and then turn round and call women hard names for not following up a point, but just tell me, don't you feel yourself that this is not the life for you, this wood-cutting, pick-axing, money or gravel-grubbing existence; don't you feel that you would like to be back at your professional work again?"

"Well, I don't know," returned the doctor gravely. "Ye see, though ambition is at a discount, as one may say, here, yet the ills and cares of life are few and the responsibilities are *nil*."

"No, no, doctor, that won't do," replied Mary, pushing home her point. "Your responsibilities may not be so evident as they were with actual patients under your care, but they exist just the same. I'm not going to preach to you" (she sees a humorous expression on his face), "but a clever professional man's duty and responsibility are not of his own making; his talents are the world's and he must use them for the world, not to please himself."

"Me dear young lady, I never intend to spare meself where I have work to do, but then ye know that the cleverness which ye are good enough to accuse me of is a good deal imagined by your kindly heart, and I doubt whether I should do more harm than good by going back to practice me profession. Here, at any rate, I could do no harm, and me services are sometimes useful, especially to such men as 'Black Jack,'" says the doctor smilingly.

"Well, supposing somebody were to tell you to commence at once with more active professional work among this army of diggers, this immense canvas town, what would you say?"

"That there are plenty without me, Miss Mary."

"Yes, there's old Doctor Martin who's always drinking with the diggers, and unable even to pour out a cup of tea steadily, and then that poor little fair-haired mother's boy, McGregor, just out from Aberdeen, but are these your expected rivals? The fact is, doctor, I've set my heart on one thing, that is that you should be the doctor at my hospital, and as you can't possibly be digger and doctor in one, it's come to this pass, that I want you to choose one path or the other."

The doctor had smiled over "the mother's boy," but now looked very earnest.

"Miss Mary, say not another word; if ye had told me of this before, I would never have argued the matter with ye. Provided ye got your brother's and Jack's consent to my leaving the firm, I'll become the doctor of the hospital and whatever else ye order."

"I'd rather you had consented to do it for the patients' sakes," replied perverse Mary, though she had gained her point, and would not have the doctor's answer different.

"All right then, let it be for the patients' sakes, bless their hard skins and soft hearts, over which you rule, gracious queen," replied the doctor.

"The next thing is the salary, doctor," said Mary ingenuously blushing. "I'm afraid I shall appear rather selfish to you on this point, for the remuneration is very small and the committee can only see its way at present to give the doctor 50*l*. a year, unless contributions come in more generously than we anticipate."

"I shall not think my remuneration small; in fact, I shall be very much honoured if ye' accipt my services without any salary at all," said the doctor.

This Mary refused point blank to do, as the committee have made up their minds to a paid doctor, and the few substantial members have promised to assist annually, and they will value a paid doctor so much more than a volunteer.

Of course Mary won her point. Who could resist her pleading as she sat there on the end of the felled tree, her face all flushed with life and spirit, her blue eyes looking up appealingly to the sturdy, sun-browned man at her side, her dimpled cheeks quick as electricity to respond to the other's smile, her merry eyes ever ready for a laugh, yet full of feeling?

At the evening meal it was settled that the doctor should become a sleeping partner in the claim, which had, since the opening of the story, netted more than a thousand pounds for each of the three diggers, and that he should take up his abode as he pleased, either at the diggers' tent or the hospital. The doctor would not listen at first to the sleeping partnership, but when the other two appealed to Mary, whose assistance experience told them was always fruitful, to second their efforts in convincing him, they gained their point, and the surveyor drew up the articles, much to the amusement of the others, with such legal phraseology as his memory supplied, writing on the doctor's knobbed table which stood opposite the frame house, a monument to ingenuity and ignorance combined.

But notwithstanding the entreaties and arguments of all, the doctor would have nothing to do with the surveyor's chute, the water revenue of which, paid by adjacent diggers, was in itself a moderate income. This, he maintained, was the surveyor's own invention and Jack's handiwork, and was fairly the property of his two friends, and no others, and so obstinate was he that this point was at last conceded to him.

So the doctor was duly installed as medical adviser at the hospital, the committee being in fact entirely in Mary's hands, and accepting her nominee without discussion or comment. At first his position seemed to be a sinecure, for, after the diggers had learnt, as they soon did, that their wounds, pains, and ailments would not be treated by their "queen" in person, their enthusiastic desire to share the practical benefits of the institution decreased in fervour, and, perhaps fortunately so, as the beds of the hospital soon afterwards became filled with genuine patients, while the applicants for out-relief regularly increased in numbers, and the fame of the institution and the skill of the doctor spread over the fields. O'Donnoghue had of course sent for the rest of his instruments and professional appliances, which he had left at Adelaide, and, pending the arrival of further supplies from the old country, had made large demands on a firm of Melbourne wholesale druggists, so that the hospital was in a few days duly furnished to meet all reasonable requirements.

While these events were passing, Jack had more than once gravitated towards Mr. Williams's store, expressing such willingness to procure provisions that Mary's suspicions became aroused, and her curiosity did not rest satisfied until Jack had confided to her the tale of Edith's charms, and she had, of course, as any true woman must, sympathized with him, and herself accompanied him to the store to see the girl. She had assumed towards Jack the motherly air of an elder sister, being greatly interested in the phlegmatic and stalwart young giant. So she was somewhat disappointed when she discovered, as soon was the case, that the girl was coquettish, and vain and selfish to a degree.

Coquettishness she could have forgiven, for had she not herself inherited this womanly attribute, but vanity became her not, as she construed it as synonymous with selfishness, and this was her abhorrence. However, though she did not care for handsome, brightly-dressed Edith for her own sake (in which Edith did not think herself much the loser), she took an especial interest in her in Jack's behalf, and by womanly example strove, without incurring the odium of posing as a preacher, to instil in the younger girl's mind worthier thoughts than those of dress and flirtation. In this she received little encouragement or assistance from Jack, or even the store-keeper himself, who was quite satisfied with his imperious daughter, and denied himself many of those comforts and liberties sweet to male minds in order to dance attendance on her caprices.

The custom of the store had considerably increased in consequence of the chance which many a digger hoped for of a chat with "Williams's pretty darter," and, although the old man never admitted that such a state of things was desirable from a paternal point of view, yet, because eminently gratifying in a commercial sense, he comforted his conscience, or its substitute, by considering that she could take good care of herself, and that "he was proud of that girl."

Her handsome face and quick tongue attracted a wide circle of admirers, so that often of an evening one would peep into the store, where a flickering lamp, hanging from the roof, shed its uncertain light over the motley heaps in the interior, to find every point of vantage occupied by open-mouthed diggers, laughing, perhaps, over the discomfiture of one of their members who had pitted his wit against hers.

Jack did not attend these "receptions," preferring to pay his court alone, a course which the girl herself instinctively encouraged. I think, if Master Jack had plucked up courage at this juncture to avow the love which he actually felt, he would have met with success and saved himself many hours of anxiety and her much irremediable injury and loss of refinement.

The girl felt flattered by the feelings which she could plainly see she had stirred in the breast of the young Hercules, and appreciated the modesty and diffidence of his manners in contrast with the brusque familiarity of the general run of the men who frequented the store. Her young butterfly nature was then incapable of loving, as women delight to love, with self-denial and self-forgetfulness, often wasted on a being purely animal, on four or two legs immaterially; but she certainly regarded this stalwart, half-bashful lover more warmly than any one else, including her father.

Even the shop assistant was not too small a fry for her wide-spread net, being enslaved at the very commencement of her appearance at the store, and there after kept a jealous, almost unwilling slave of her every behest. His was the curious, anomalous position which some men appear willing to occupy, sacrificing their ease and comfort, denying themselves luxuries and almost necessities to obey the commands and caprices of a woman who despises their very obedience, and openly notifies them of her contempt. His name, Jeremiah Wilkins, for the sake rather of brevity than euphony shortened to "Miah," and pronounced "Mire," had been doubtless conferred upon him by a pious mother, with a view to his future welfare; and insomuch as he continually carried with him a pocket edition of the Old Testament, from which, in and out of occasion, he liberally quoted, he for his part doubtless thought he was carrying out the intention indicated in his nomenclature. But nature to him had not been altogether kind, or shall we go back to first causes and blame his father and mother, for he was capable almost of any meanness which is ascribable to unconditioned, ill-educated men, and carried his obtrusive religion only in his mouth and pocket. His sanctimonious nature, added to a long, pale, hairless face, surmounted by hair of the colour mis-called "red," though not then recognized as aesthetic, procured him the sobriquet of

"Saint," which term, though used in ridicule, he, with strange blindness, appropriated to himself as seriously befitting his character. Thereafter he allowed his jealousy, passions, and meanness full play, deeming his outward saintliness a cloak for all.

It may be surmised that he looked blackly upon the coquetries of his handsome mistress with the other swains who came to the store, and still less approved of the solitary *tête-à-têtes* which were accorded to Jack; he had, in fact, often to be brought back to allegiance by a smile or look from the glancing eyes of Miss Edith: these never failed in their purpose. The girl was doubtless much to blame for the air of proprietorship that "Miah" sometimes assumed, and which she, in the presence of others, haughtily repudiated, for her capricious coaxing had on many an occasion turned the poor fellow's head, a feat, on account of his conceited vacuity, by no means difficult.

Amongst others who about this time caused this humble moth some amount of perturbation, and even gave modest Jack a feeling akin to jealousy, was a gaily-clad butterfly, otherwise a slim young fellow, of shaven, handsome face, winning eyes, and ingenuous mouth, who sought the store from time to time ostensibly in search of provisions, being, according to his own account, a "new chum," just out from the old country. His real motive was cleverly concealed from all but the keen self-consciousness of Miss Edith. At times he came accompanied by Griffin, *alias* "Bully Ben," at others by Jacob Saltner, the young clerk whom we have before seen riding on the coach when it was attacked; more often, indeed, with Jacob than Ben, who roughly classified women as "playthings for beardless boys." The handsome new chum was, as my readers have doubtless guessed, no other than Gentleman Jim, whose career since last we saw him posing as a bushranger, had been somewhat chequered. "Bully Ben," though one of the lawless crew who attacked the coach, had not come under suspicion, having, long before the trackers set out, returned to his tent. His horsemanship was notoriously of so dubious a character that his absence was not noticed, and his part in the fray unsuspected, so he had been enabled to work quietly upon the fields, amassing a little heap of gold-dust, notwithstanding his frequent drinking bouts, and awaiting the inevitable return of his mate. Jim could not trust for escape to such fearlessness, and had, indeed, returned very much the worse for wear, after six weeks' absence, ragged, footsore, haggard, and sick, after having been hunted up and down country by the police and trackers, escaping imminent capture from time to time only through the friendliness and assistance of shepherds on outlying stations, who, being many of them old convicts themselves, sympathized with a fellow-sinner. The rest of his gang had been dispersed, one caught, and, on the evidence of the down coach driver and others, convicted and sentenced to death, while the other three had for a time become lost, for all he knew and cared; they were totally forgotten, as he had taken care that they should all "plant" or "*cache*" the nuggets they had turned out of the boot of the up coach. These nuggets were, as he had suspected, in the possession of our friend Jacob Saltner, and were, in fact, imported by that enterprising rascal straight from Birmingham, for the purpose of "salting claims," being merely masses of worthless metal, lead and brass of skilfully adjusted weight, neatly moulded and gilded.

The method of salting claims is almost too well known to be here explained; suffice it that it consisted of scooping out a little of the earth of an unsuccessful claim, hiding therein one of these nuggets, and then selling the claim to some digger new to the custom, showing him a few little pea-like nuggets and dust, "just dug out," and allowing him to test the claim before buying. Of course, if the bird was ensnared to this point, his complete plucking was easy: the pick tumbled out the loose earth and spurious nugget, the claim was at once purchased for five or ten pounds or so, and the victim successfully fleeced. A more virtuous "salter" has been known to use a real instead of a counterfeit nugget; but the deceit and consequent loss of the victim was generally only one of degree.

Now Gentleman Jim had taken Jacob Saltner into a partnership with "Bully Ben" and himself, prevailing over the scruples of the "honest man," partly by scruples and partly by plausibility; the nuggets formed their chief capital, and their partnership had thriven wonderfully, although only of a few weeks' duration, fattening on the frauds thus practised. How the three remained unpunished would have been a mystery anywhere else; but their prey was the solitary digger, whose appeal to violence on discovery of his loss would be useless under the circumstances, by reason of the superior opposing numbers, and whose appeal to law would have been equally useless in such turbulent times, when every one was a suspect until proved otherwise. Finally, the victim's appeal to the help of fellow-diggers generally would have evoked laughter and contempt for his innocence.

It is true that Inspector Cochrane, who had noticed the episode of the nuggets, had at the time determined to watch Jacob, but the healing of his wounded knee had been much more tedious than he anticipated, and, together with the pursuit of the bushrangers by his subordinates and the licence disturbances on the fields, had driven all thoughts of the circumstance out of his recollection for the time.

It was curious that none of the passengers or the drivers of the coaches had run against and recognized Gentleman Jim; but this may be accounted for partly by the fact that at the attacks his face had been blackened and bearded, and now was white and shaven, and that it was the easiest matter possible for one man to be altogether lost amongst a crowd of sixty thousand or eighty thousand diggers without any disguise whatever. Hence the immunity which the rascal enjoyed, and as often happens in such cases, just when all who had met Black Jack, including our friends, were congratulating themselves that he and his gang had been exterminated by the law or the surer famine in the bush, the chief rascal was hatching fresh plots in his fertile brain, and collecting around him a fresh gang from the ever plentiful crop of rowdies who abounded on the fields. Amongst these were some of the Tipperary boys, Irish miscreants, and convicts, whose notions of law and order—never very constrained even under the benign influence of a complete system of civilized government—procured to themselves such powerful wings on the fields, under the less perfected and necessarily less vigilant system which there prevailed, that they flew away altogether, a state of matters which the "boys"—in which they differed from their victims—accounted decidedly advantageous.

Shortly after the hospital was instituted, the new governor, Sir Charles Hotham, arrived at the fields on his tour of inspection, and was most enthusiastically greeted by the fickle mob, who a few months later were howling and railing at his policy. As he was inspecting the various parts of the canvas city it was of course to be expected that the new hospital should be brought before his notice, and the circumstances of its endowment explained. Miss Mary and the doctor were also, of course, introduced, the former receiving a gallant laughing compliment on her accession to the throne from the brave officer, which tinged her fair face with crimson blushes. Neither she nor the doctor were forgotten by the governor in after-times, as matters proved. Altogether, the effect of the governor's visit was very reassuring, and at last matters seemed likely to settle down comfortably on the field.

Time went on, and the inspector got about again; the doctor's hands were full; Coates turned his busy brain to account by surveying a roadway through to Streatham, a neighbouring township, and got the contract for erecting a new bank, while Jack worked away steadier than ever at the three claims, which still yielded a steady show of colour and gold-dust, with occasional small nuggets. The "Trinity" firm had purchased the claims of one or two neighbouring diggers, and seemed to be the object of especial favour on the part of that capricious quean Fortune, prospering where others had failed, turning up "dust" out of the most hopeless places, and banking their proceeds successfully. Coates often took a spell at the claim, and the doctor, who to his dismay, was adding fat instead of muscle to his frame, occasionally came down to keep himself in "trim," as he said, and spent a few hours with pickaxe and shovel, but, to his friends' amusement, reaped such blistered hands and aching back after these constitutionals as he had never had as "Mr. Eh-Eh-Digger." His professional practice on the fields was increasing rapidly, and becoming very profitable, for the successful diggers would never hear of receiving gratuitously the professional attendance so often necessary after their bouts of success and dissipation, while they often assisted their poorer brethren to find the doctor's expenses, never asked for and often refused in such cases by the kind-hearted fellow. Mary and he often met at the hospital and elsewhere; at committee meetings his opinion was always consulted, and generally ruled the day, while Mary's was invariably law, her popularity having lost little beyond its initial enthusiasm. All seemed prosperous and happy around the three friends and their circle, when trials came which shook and tested their mutual help and affection to the very foundations.

CHAPTER IX

VOLCANIC RUMBLINGS

IT was in the early part of October, and a baking hot afternoon, that Gentleman Jim, alias James Paterson, as he now called himself when in broadcloth, approached Williams's store, and after a little mild flirtation with fair Edith, proposed a walk in the cool of the scrub which ran up close behind the house. Edith, who was *ennuyée*, and had not seen Jack or "any one interesting" for some days, with characteristic neglect of conventionalities, jumped at the proposal, and without more ado accepted the other's arm, telling poor jealous "Miah" to inform her father that she would be back in time to get his tea. Her bright fresh colour had considerably paled, what with late hours, a little anxiety, and, above all, the heat of the weather, and her plump cheeks had thinned down to more angular shape since we first saw her helping Jack to grind oatmeal; but she was still handsome, and her large brown eyes as keen and bright as ever, though a trifle bolder than before.

The versatility of Gentleman Jim allowed him at this time to be maturing a desperate plan for robbing the chief bank at Ballarat, and yet to be playing the soft-cheeked suitor with pretended love for Edith Williams. Had her vanity allowed her more *clairvoyance* and discrimination, she must have seen through his pretence, for his was a purely selfish animal passion, which sought all, and would give nothing in return. She herself was debating,—or I should say wondering, for debating required too much concentration—whether she preferred the Herculean but "slow" Jack, or this vivacious new chum, as he still called himself, and in her heart would, I think, have been right glad if the manlier lover had come forward, and, heedless of her coquetry and caprice, claimed her arbitrarily. Now, as ever, she gave herself up to the pleasure of the moment, and chatted away briskly to the man at her side, beguiling the time with repartee and fencing his amatory speeches.

"Come, come, Miss Williams, or Edith, if you will let me call you so," cried he, proceeding, as he noticed she did not dissent, "don't let your humble adorer remain in such doubt about your feelings towards him."

"But what would Saint Miah say to you talking thus?" queried the girl mischievously.

"There you are again, trying to turn me off the track; why, you know you don't care a brass farthing what 'Miah' thinks of your actions, now do you?"

"Well, you're rather hard on him, but it's true I don't pay much attention to his preachings; you see, a man like that is no good off his one subject, and I can buy a bible without marrying it."

"Now you must answer me 'yes' or 'no'; may I call myself your husband or not, Edith?"

"You may call yourself whatever you like. Some call you good-looking, some don't; but as to calling yourself husband, you'll have to go through rather a long operation before you do that, for you'll have to show me that you love me, and my father that you can support me. I don't mean," added she hastily, as he moved nearer towards her on the rock on which they were then sitting, overhung by gum trees, and near a very attenuated brook, "I don't mean carry me, but keep me in dress, a good house, and all that sort of thing."

"Oh! bless your soul, I can do that; why, don't you know, I've got about five thousand pounds in the bank to draw from," answered Gentleman Jim. The remark was not true in fact, but only in spirit, inasmuch as the standing balance in specie in the bank safes, which he was plotting to obtain, amounted to about five thousand pounds, as he well knew.

"Well, that's a good beginning," replied the girl "now how about the other point?"

"That's certainly rather harder," said he, "for if you can't see how deeply I feel your coldness and indifference, how my sleep is disturbed, my health suffers, my very occupation is neglected, for thinking of and calling upon you, how shall I make my love plain?"

In these statements the lover drew largely upon his fertile imagination, but who was there to tell the belle of the store that he was not in earnest; at any rate, she looked touched, the balance was going against Jack, and Jim saw it.

"Your face, my love, is always in my eyes, and is fairer than the moon. Your eyes dazzle me more than the sun, and your figure is like a young kangaroo's."

Having exhausted his mental *repertoire* of metaphors for the nonce, Jim was silent, but approached near enough to place his arm round the girl's waist. Edith was half convinced, and especially by his appeal to her good looks, but thought this action rather premature, so quietly moved out of reach, and archly said,—

"Well, that's very pretty, but I think you ought to ask Mr. Wainwright's opinion."

Had she looked up, she would doubtless have been fully convinced, but not in his favour, for the demon rose in his eyes and mouth when he saw the ripe fruit so close to hand, yet eluding his grasp like an apple on All Hallow E'en; but, curbing his impatience, he replied,—

"Wainwright. Why, what is Wainwright, the lumping piece of clod, to you, the fairy of the fields, the queen of all our hearts?"

"Not so," answered the girl rather snappishly. "You forget that the queen of the fields is quite a different woman. Miss Coates, so good and prim, and such a favourite with you diggers."

"Oh no," laughed Jim; "so very good—yes, at shooting, so very prim in acting. Do they call that slip of a girl with the pug nose, Miss Coates then, their queen. Pooh! pooh! you little jealous muff; why, she can't hold a candle to you."

"Well, about Mr. Wainwright?" queries Edith, evidently pleased at the broad compliment.

"Why, I say that Wainwright,—Mr. Wainwright, if you wish—is a great lumping booby of a fellow, unable to laugh or joke; and, as for mating with you, it would be like a princess marrying a rhinoceros."

"Well, I want a strong man to take care of me," says Edith smilingly, "and you can't say he is not that."

"Oh, I've heard he's strong enough; but if you want strength, there's my mate Ben, stronger than any two men I know, and can live in the same house as ourselves, if you like."

"No, I don't like Ben, he's so rude to me, and I certainly shouldn't like a husband to have to depend on a friend for protecting his wife."

"Oh, I'll do all the protecting you want, Edith" says the other boastfully.

"Would you?" says Edith. "Why, folks say that the other day, when you had just left the store, and commenced saying something which the others didn't like, little Phil Morris challenged you to fight, and you wouldn't do it."

The man flushed scarlet; it was indeed true, but how annoying that she should know it. He had used her name slightingly, boasting of her affection for him, and one of the more modest of her admirers, a younger, smaller-made man, had contemptuously challenged him to mortal combat, or to swallow his words; so, to save his crown, the boaster had performed the last-mentioned undignified but simple operation. How much she knew he was unaware, but with his usual *aplomb*, which was never long a deserter, he casually remarked,—

"So Mr. Jack has been telling tales out of school, has he; now that's what I call a real manly thing to do, nothing of the coward or sneak about it, all's fair in love and war is his motto, ain't it?"

The honest fellow, overcome with virtuous indignation at such base offences, sprang up and commenced viciously knocking the rock with a stick.

"Mr. Wainwright," said the girl, with some approach to dignity, "is a man who would tell no tales behind folks' backs; he has, indeed, no cause to, such tales are generally told by others. If you wish to know very much who it was, I'll tell you. It was my father who had himself been—oh!—"

The abrupt silence of the girl, and her long-drawn exclamation, caused Gentleman Jim to look round and ascertain the cause: his startled glance took in a face of ashen hue, with parted lips and affrighted, dilated eyes, whose gaze was fixed helplessly, and as it were by a species of fascination, on a brown snake which, disturbed by the rhythmic blows of her companion's stick, had crawled out of its hiding-place, and was now swaying its malicious head to and fro within two feet of Edith's.

I wonder if any of my readers, otherwise brave and ready to face a mad bull or do other daring deeds, has ever been startled in a moment from apparent heedless security to deadly danger by the appearance within striking distance of the venomous head of a poisonous snake, whose four diminutive tooth marks are as fatal as the rending jaws of lion or tiger, and almost as quick in deadly effect as lightning, so insidious the poison, so small the hurt. If so, he or she can remember the strange loathing fascination and tremor felt, and can fully appreciate the paralysis that seized both the girl and her companion as they remained petrified out of flesh and blood into rigid rock. While the stick had beat time the snake had, after the manner of his kind, kept up a corresponding regular motion of its head and neck, which were raised from the rock as though fascinated itself; and had Gentleman Jim but continued the regular blows of his stick all might have gone well, and by a dexterous stroke he could have broken the viper's spine. But the man's hand was paralyzed, and the sway of the reptile's head confused the girl's brain, exercising such a horrid fascination over her, that she had herself to sway her own head in imitation; the snake's eyes seemed to her now thoroughly excited imagination to grow of monstrous size, as when one suffers from congestion of the brain, they swayed her breath, her circulation, her life, and without shriek or cry of any sort, she fell prone forward at the same time that the snake, loosened from its own fascination, darted at her face. The two met in that hideous embrace, though but for a moment, but the coward turned and fled from the spot beside himself with terror, and released from his spell by the sudden movement of the snake. A loose stone in the bed of the rock tripped him up, and he measured his length, grasping with his hands to save his fall what appeared in the hurry of the moment to be a dead branch; as he scrambled up he felt a prick in his own hands, and to his terror, found that he had caught hold of the consort of the brown snake, and was himself bitten. To leap to his feet, regardless of the girl, and to tear through the scrub towards the fields and the hospital, was the work of a moment. As he ran he cried out to two passers-by that Williams's girl and he were viper-bitten. Now the two passers-by happened fortunately—or perhaps as subsequent events proved unfortunately—for Edith, to be Jack and Mary, who had together visited the store, and were returning by the scrub, whither "Miah" had informed them his young mistress had walked. He had not told of her companion, for he took a gentle saintly delight in picturing the mutual recriminations and blows which he fancied must take place between the girl's two rival lovers when they met, in which dispute he cherished a hope that he might act the lawyer, and gain the kernel of the nut. When the two saw a man thus running at full speed from the bush, and heard his words, they were for a moment staggered, but Mary's quick wit instantly grasped the situation, and suggested, "Stop the coward, and ask him where he has left Edith?"

To hear was to obey, for more reasons than one, and before the other had made good a dozen yards further, Jack's hand was on his collar, jerking him back, and demanding, in a stern voice through set teeth, where the girl was.

The valiant boaster of a few minutes since cringed and craved leave to hurry on to the hospital before the poison spread, but Jack was inexorable, and in half the time it takes me to write this, was running back towards the fatal rock, dashing through the tangled scrub, through wattles, ferns and bushes, and crashing down the tangled undergrowth like a rogue elephant through a paddy field. Mary followed as closely as she could, but was soon met by Jack bearing hurriedly along his unconscious but lovely burden, and deftly steering his way through the forest with the skill of an old stock-horse.

Again Mary supplied the orders. "Take her to the store, bring her out of her swoon by cold water over her face, smack her hands, loosen her dress, and give her as much spirit as she can take: I'll run on and fetch the doctor."

With this he complies with such speed that for a second she admiringly notices how gallantly he bears his sweetheart like a feather in his arms.

With her usual pluck she sets out intending to run right across the fields to the hospital, where she knows the doctor will be engaged, as typhoid fever is rife on the fields, but though the spirit is willing the flesh is weak, and she is not sorry, after five minutes, to attract the notice of a passing digger who bears up alongside and takes orders from her to fetch the doctor at once to Williams's daughter at the store. With a sigh of relief; she sees her messenger cast off his coat and waistcoat, and slip his arms out of his braces, thus to gird himself for his race, for is he not specially honoured by being made the queen's messenger? Fearing he may have some trouble with the doctor, he hails another digger, who stands open-mouthed at the unusual sight of a man running on such a hot afternoon, and the onlooker, hearing the nature of the errand, joins as enthusiastically in the race. Gentleman Jim has by some way the start, and has arrived at the hospital gasping out to the doctor that he has been bitten by a black snake on the hand and is just being treated, when the two diggers, breathless and red hot, pull up short, and demand the doctor's immediate attendance, according to the queen's orders, at Williams's store.

"All right," says O'Donnoghue, "in a minute, as soon as I've seen to this man, who is also bitten."

But the orders are peremptory, and respectfully but firmly they insist on his coming back with them at once, they remember nothing in the queen's orders about "minutes," only the words "at once."

The doctor, half-amused, attempts to remonstrate while his patient reviles the diggers and alternately prays them to allow his wants first to receive attention. Seeing that they will waste precious time in words, one seizes the doctor by the feet, the other by the shoulders, and they are thus about to transport him incontinently across the fields, to his personal inconvenience if not injury, when his unconditional surrender and reasonable prayer to be allowed to carry along the necessary drugs and appliances relieves them of this unpleasant and tiring duty. Leaving a few hasty words with one of the nurses as to the treatment of Jim, and placing in his pockets articles most likely to be wanted, he sets off at such a jog-trot across the fields that he soon distances his companions.

Arrived at the store, he is awaited by Mary, who explains as well as she can the accident and the treatment she has adopted, in which the doctor concurs. He is at once ushered into the little room used by the storekeeper and his daughter as their dining-room, where on the floor, stretched on a mattress and pillowed in Jack's stalwart arms, the patient lies. Without any fussiness the doctor examines the girl's neck where the four little punctures with livid blue marks round them tell so forcible a tale, finds her drowsy under the combined effects of the poison and copious doses of whisky, and whispering Jack to leave unless he has nerve to watch the cautery, proceeds first to excise and then to cauterize the wound. The storekeeper happens to be in the room, is beside himself with grief, and is accordingly taken out by Mary, who to her disgust, finds awaiting them the ubiquitous "Miah," with his mouth full of appropriate texts, exhorting repentance, and affecting to give consolation. The storekeeper's patience with this religious verbiage, hitherto tolerated, is exhausted, and his overwrought feelings find vent in a kick which assists the unfortunate "Miah" some feet nearer the store-door, where he tumbles over an incoming customer with whom he rolls and grapples in the dust.

The storekeeper laughs nervously, and assists to dust down the customer, whose language does not bear repetition, and Mary returns to the chamber of sickness and perhaps death, with a curious recollection of the natural sequence of pathos and bathos.

Jack bears the operation on his sweetheart manfully, though feeling somewhat sick, particularly when the poor girl's moans and semi-conscious movements proclaim her sufferings, but by strong effort he masters his weakness, and remains the imperturbable Jack of yore, so that when the doctor has applied these immediate remedies and given the patient a cupful of whisky, with a strong dash of ammonia, he curiously scans the face of his friend and turns toward Mary nonplussed and puzzled at the other's coolness.

All through that night the three watched by the side of the girl's bed the fierce battle which youth and strength fought against shock and death. The father had, I grieve to say (but as this purports to be a veracious story cannot deny) dosed himself to sleep with a bottle of the same fine stock whisky which was feeding the little spark of his daughter's life. This event had at first very much shocked Mary, who was the only one who knew of it, but she soon felt consoled in the absence of the poor querulous fellow from the sick room and the consequent stilly silence so much wanted. Besides, she knew him in general to be an abstemious man, whose mental equilibrium had evidently been upset by the shock.

Towards morning the girl's youth won the victory; slowly, but surely, she regained consciousness, and was pronounced by the doctor to be out of imminent danger, but still in need of careful nursing. Mary, of course, promised to take personal charge, while Jack with characteristic delicacy left the room, aroused Williams from his stupor, and assisted "Miah" to put the store to rights before setting out for the camp. He reached home in the early morning to find Coates terribly disturbed by the absence of his sister and friend, and much relieved though sympathetic over the cursory account given by Jack. When Jack mentioned that on reaching the girl he found both snakes trying to make off into the undergrowth, the one actually wriggling out from under the girl's weight, and that he had in his frenzy broken its back with a branch, Coates suggested keeping the skin and presenting it to the doctor as a curiosity, for which purpose he accompanied Jack to the top of Canadian Gully, where they found the reptile so terribly smashed by the mighty blow which Jack had dealt, that Coates abandoned his intention. The young man seemed indeed to have been gifted with the strength of two men for the occasion, as he was utterly unable on this second visit to lift the massive gum branch which had literally flattened the snake out like cardboard.

While this catastrophe had disturbed the even flow of the placid life which our friends had been enjoying, disturbances on the goldfields had re-commenced. The landlord of the Eureka Hotel, one of the many licensed houses which catered for the vitiated tastes of dissipated *nouveaux riches*, had in a brawl shot a digger, and the matter had created extraordinary excitement because of the peculiar circumstances of the case. The interchange of shots and the death of a digger was by no means an uncommon event, but in this case the brawl had been provoked by the landlord himself, and the wretched man had been butchered in the sight of all. Yet on the examination of the landlord before the bench of magistrates the case against him had been dismissed, and the murderer had the impudence and hardihood to boast of the means he had employed to gain his acquittal, which were no other than bribery and corruption of one of the bench, a venal creature who had obtained his commission as Justice of the Peace, heaven only knows how. This episode, unimportant as it was in itself, was pregnant with disaster and led to fierce and bloody struggles. The diggers were infuriated, and all the land-sharks rising out of the sea of discontent always seething among such a motley crew, posed as the champions of miners' rights and liberties. Certain periodicals, for pecuniary and other purposes, stirred the mud; up rose the diggers' advocate; up rose Melbourne papers with frothy articles, the purport of which was that the authorities were evidently leagued against the diggers. It was the old grievance of one law for the rich and another for the poor; let the diggers take the matter into their own hands; did they not remember that in California Judge Lynch and the Vigilance Committees were all-powerful?

Huxter was in his element, he preached and harangued, he frothed and spluttered over the wrongs of diggers, working himself and his audience to such a pitch that they were ready, with few exceptions, to pledge themselves to the most extravagant courses. While his friend was thus engaged, Jackson, a head and shoulders taller than most of the crowd, scrutinized them closely to watch any signs of dissent with his learned friend. If any appeared he would shoulder his way through the mob and would emphasize his friend's arguments in a way which gave opposition no chance. Jackson believed implicitly in Huxter, who, unlike many others who were then agitating the mob, believed in his words and himself.

The consequence of all this spouting was that a couple of weeks later the mob took the law into their own hands and attacked the Eureka Hotel. It was at night that they approached the building; ominously quiet were its precincts, sadly had the receipts fallen off since the fatal bullet had struck one of the convivialists, only the roughest of the rough now consorted there, and hatched plans and plots worthy in their complications of political or revolutionary movements. The landlord was standing in his door as the mob came up, and seeing their determined march and hearing their clamour, thought it best to make himself scarce; so that when the forerunners angrily inquired of the topers at the tavern for the landlord, he had removed his family to the scrub behind, and was himself in hiding to see which way events would go. Events went rather adversely for him, for finding they were balked of their victim, the more orderly part, among them Huxter, returned, while the rest of the mob commenced pillaging the stores at the hotel, gladly aided by the topers, and finally, reckless of their own danger, some set fire to the hotel over their heads. The wooden building, flaring up like a tar-barrel, was soon gutted, while the proprietor, pale with anger and fear, watched from the scrub close by, muttering anathemas on the diggers' heads. After all was over and the place hopelessly destroyed, the troopers appeared and took prisoners the few stragglers who seemed to gloat over the landlord's ruin, the rest having become satiated and dispersed to their homes.

The outcome of this episode proved that the broom at Government House was making clean sweeps, for the landlord was put upon his trial, and upon the same day that he received his just sentence the corrupt magistrate was struck off the commission and disgraced. But the diggers were not satisfied with this act of stern justice, for from what they considered an excess of zeal the authorities prosecuted the leaders of the movement, amongst others, Huxter and Jackson. These two were fortunate enough in being able to show that they were not at the spot when the hotel was burnt, and had counselled the more headstrong to take no such course; but others, not so fortunate, were convicted and sentenced. The diggers, who had been praising the Governor for the prosecution of their enemies, now reviled him as forcibly for the imprisonment of their friends; and a Ballarat Reform League was started, with a secretary and other officers, to agitate, amongst other matters, for an immediate release of the imprisoned diggers.

Thanks to Mary's assiduous attention and the doctor's skill, Edith quickly rallied from her shock, became convalescent, and able to thank the stalwart, blushing Jack for his doughty deeds, the valour of which Mary had taken good care should not suffer in her telling. Once only she asked after her companion, and then with a shudder, as she learnt that he was lying delirious at the hospital, having frightened himself into a fever over his wound, the poison of which had been distributed through his veins by his violent exertions more rapidly than in Edith's case. Upon this an attack of typhoid had supervened, itself ushered in by violent hemorrhage. Released from his duties at the store, the doctor worked night and day for the miscreant, as the nurses had their hands full, and cases were daily requiring attention.

The good fellow had a high sense of his professional duty, and though at first he had not the faintest conception that he was fighting for the life of a man who had compassed his own death a few months back, after a few days he made a pretty shrewd guess who his patient was, and fought with the fever rather the harder from a combination of sense of duty, pertinacity of spirit, and superabundant kindliness. He would fain, out of this kindliness, have assumed that the patient's ravings were not his uncontrolled, and therefore natural, instincts and recollections, but rather the outcome purely of his fevered state; however, he found it hard thus to deceive himself when he considered his own experience and treatment at the rascal's hands, and made up his mind, much as such a course was contrary to his nature, that as soon as the patient was well enough he must, for the good of the public, inform the police of his suspicion. Procrastination, ever the thief of time, proved fatal to the doctor's schemes, which had otherwise brought this simple history to an abrupt close, for at this juncture an unlooked-for complication caused him first to hesitate and then to abandon his intentions.

The fact is, that Mary had become interested in this case on account of the man's friendship for her late patient Edith, and had more than once relieved the nurse of her care, until she found herself taking more and more interest in the delicate-looking, attenuated man, who, for all his fever, had not lost the handsome contour of his face, and was, with convalescence, quickly recovering the arch, winning expression of his eyes.

Do not, fair reader, believe that a man's face is always an index to his character, or you will, on occasion, go astray in your reckoning, as indeed Mary, a confirmed physiognomist, actually did; for the frequent conversations she had with the man impressed her more and more, until she experienced a feeling of fascination which she continually struggled to overcome, but which seemed in its intangible and incomprehensible entity to defy her.

He adopted, but not to exaggeration, a quasi-polished style, which astonished and at the same time attracted her. That she had not guessed his identity with Black Jack is, I think now, at this distance of time, quite clear; and the reason may not be far to seek, as on the only occasion when she had seen him the excitement of the moment had not allowed her time to notice the similarity of his then harsh and bullying voice with the mellow and softened tones of her patient. She realized in all its despicability the man's cowardice in abandoning Edith to her fate when himself hurt; but as the virtues of the lady in *Comus* become all chained up in alabaster at the sorcerer's enchantment, so her contempt for his failing, which indeed was notorious, as she found on inquiry, seemed paralyzed and ineffective when the man was himself present. When away from his bedside she became hugely vexed with herself, and in her womanly way vexed with the doctor, whose quiet eyes she felt were looking through her.

The doctor was, after the awkward fashion of men, daily pluming himself on his power of repressing feeling and putting on a cheerful face in this miserable chaos. It may be supposed that his Mark-Tapley nature underwent some strain, for he had daily and hourly to sacrifice his own feelings and his own sense of right to the girl's infatuation, which he thought, without any prejudice, was not elevating to the nobility of character and purpose with which, in his own mind, he had, as with a divine halo, girded her round about. So he forbore to tell his suspicions to his friend and compatriot, Inspector Cochrane, who occasionally came round to the hospital for a chat and smoke. Nay, he carried his sense of chivalry to the woman of his love so far that he deemed it dishonourable to acquaint her brother with the dreary comedy which was being enacted under his very eyes.

Once, indeed, maddened by seeing the rascal's ascendancy over Mary's mind and heart, which he had hoped might some day surrender to his own siege, he determined that the torture should cease, and the bushranger—for so he then thought him to be—should get his deserts; and for this purpose he asked Cochrane to accompany him into the hospital to identify a patient; but on entering the long, low room into which the building had by this time of necessity developed, Mary, seeing them, and ignorant of their mission or the character of her patient, yet construing the forlorn and stern expression so unusual on the doctor's features into some menace to the man, had pressed the doctor's hand, and with flushing cheeks and downcast eyes, eloquently yet in silence begged for a respite; which the doctor, who was fast regretting his disclosure to the inspector, willingly but sadly granted.

The inspector noticed the scene, but of course misinterpreted the cause, subsequently offering his congratulations to his friend on his good fortune, congratulations which would have seemed to the poor fellow ridiculous in the extreme had they not been so pathetically wide of the mark. At the time he had diverted the attention of the inspector from the patient with whom he had intended to confront him to a quiet, orderly young digger, fresh to the fields, whom starvation and fever at the outset had well-nigh crushed, and who of course was utterly unknown to the police.

Cochrane laughed at the doctor's suspicions of such an unsuspicious character, and often afterwards smilingly asked him how the terrible Black Jack progressed. Mary soon hastened away from the place utterly ashamed and half-regretful of her momentary impulse and her continuing weakness, reached her frame-house, and to the consternation of Coates, fairly and for the first time in her life to his knowledge, broke down in an hysterical fit of weeping. Even then matters might have been set right had Coates but exhibited the appearance of that sympathy which he felt; but as he did not, the precious opportunity apostrophized by Shakespeare passed and the wheel of Fate rolled on.

After this the doctor attempted to obtain an interview with Mary so as to discuss the position with herself; but she, guessing his object and thoroughly alarmed at herself, frustrated all his attempts, worked harder than ever, and the old friendly companionship between them faded away into the background until it appeared to both but a sadly-pleasant recollection, to be classed in the mighty catalogue of might have-beens.

CHAPTER X

"IN THE SPRING A YOUNG MAN'S FANCY," ETC.

A FEW days after the events which I have just related, Mary happened to be sitting in the little surgery which had been attached to the hospital, where the doctor's drugs and instruments, neatly arranged on shelves around, looked down on the window-flap table at which she was writing and the (comparatively) easy-chair which was consecrated to her use alone.

The hot, heavy November afternoon disinclined her for the exercise the need of which told in her pale cheeks, and, had not her letters been business circulars, she would doubtless have been engaged, with the rest of mankind, in taking a siesta. A young pet kangaroo, or joey, as it was called, the gift of the broad-shouldered Jake, reclined by her side, stretched out in a sleep undisturbed but by an adventurous ant or two which would mistake the great mass of red wool for some luscious article of food, and attempt by ridiculously inadequate efforts to remove it. The chirrup of the grasshopper without and the click-clack of an insect or two alone disturbed the reverie into which she had fallen, not an unusual event for her now, disturbed and worried as her mind was by various conflicting thoughts. A sharp knock at the door brought her and her pet from dreamland, the latter timidly crouching under the table, while she bade the knocker "come in," and turned about her chair to receive the visitor.

She was not quite prepared for the appearance round the corner of the pale gaunt face of Miah, for it was he on a message from Williams; and remembering her last encounter with him, she could not repress a smile at the recollection. The man was quick to notice the smile, but misinterpreting the cause, was emboldened to introduce the rest of his body into the surgery, where he stood staring now at the fair occupant, now at the rows of bottles and cases which impressed him with child-like wonder.

Having in silence delivered the rare present of some fresh fruit, which the girl graciously received and acknowledged in a short note to Williams, he continued staring at the bottles and Mary in such a ludicrous way that she broke out into one of her old-time musical laughs, communicating by infection a ghost-like resemblance of a smile or vertical crease on each side of the man's lean, long-chopped visage.

At a mischievous suggestion by Mary that he should try the contents of one of the bottles to bring the colour back to his face, he turned tail and fled, heedlessly bumping into another visitor. This one, who was no other than Gentleman Jim, was so taken aback that he rapped out a hard oath at the "clumsy fool," receiving in return a rebuke from Miah with the usual scriptural text against swearing. The other, forcing his equanimity, turned with a smiling face to Mary, who was somewhat shocked at having heard such an expression from his lips for the first time, and apologized, humbly praying for her forgiveness, begged Miah's pardon, much to that worthy's astonishment, and passed in, closing the door behind him. Miah, recovering his astonishment, winked to himself, and, stealthily creeping to the side of the house, crouched down in pretended sleep under the open window, remarking that his was a good cause, in that he might gather some news to convey to Edith from the lips of her absent admirer.

The new-comer, gravely patting the head of the kangaroo, which, innocent of all guile, approached him expecting such a caress, hoped he was not disturbing Miss Coates at all, and noted with some satisfaction the embarrassment which Mary evidently felt in his presence. Whether he had guessed its cause is neither here nor there; it is probable he had, but as he certainly believed it was caused by affection for himself, the result was the same so far as his conduct was concerned.

Now he was naturally born to *finesse* in all matters, and took good care that she should not read his thoughts. So he discoursed on many subjects, enlisting her sympathy, now with one tale, now with another, and finally telling a cleverly pathetic, though mendacious history of himself. It is true that he impugned himself constantly, but the faults for which he blamed himself so openly were such minor sins that, as he expected, he soon found Mary defending him against himself, and, though he knew not that she was even then mentally accusing herself of wrongful suspicions, and blaming the doctor for instilling them, he could see that she did not look unfavourably upon him.

Then he touched on his approaching departure from the hospital, where he had received so much care, and of course won the girl by his frank thanks and compliments. Miah, listening the while, could hardly realize that this was the same man whom he had often heard profanely handling the names of Edith and other women. His motive in all this incipient flirtation, for such it had become, was purely and simply of an indolent sensual nature, combined with a ready tact *pour passer le temps.* It is possible, but hardly probable, that he thought seriously of Mary as his wife, though the mind shudders to think of such an ill-assorted match. How much longer he would have continued the self-conscious chit-chat which suited him so well, Miah could not have said, for at this juncture the doctor, who had some business in the surgery, came in, and as Gentleman Jim always had a rooted aversion to meeting at close quarters the little fellow whom he had so nearly killed, and, who he could see read him aright, and but for Mary's sake would long before this have given him up to justice, the interview came to an abrupt end, the rascal walking straight away from the hospital to Ben's tent, where he was certain of a shake-down.

Miah followed, and overtaking him soon let him know that he had overheard his conversation, being, in fact, overjoyed to find that he had a chance of ridding Edith of one of his dangerous rivals.

But to let Edith slip from his net did not suit Jim's book, for he flattered himself he could still win back her troth, so concealing with marvellous energy the anger he felt for the eavesdropper, he pressed him to visit his tent, and escorted him thither. There they were fortunate in finding that Ben, having made a few pounds, had laid in a plentiful supply of whisky, besides other liquors less innocent but possessing finer names. The fact that he lay fast asleep, a votary to the divine Bacchus, was of itself a small disadvantage to the new-comers, who indeed felt that the cup would pass all the freer and the contents go all the further with only two to participate in the feast.

Miah, of course, found some appropriate quotations to apply in contempt of Ben's wretched condition, and in exaltation of his own moderation.

"What," says Jim turning round, "have you never been the worse for drink?

"Never," solemnly assures the other.

"Well, I'll bet you ten pounds you'll be very much the worse before an hour is over; you simply can't refuse such whisky as we've got here."

"I never bet," replied the other, "but I'll make a wager for your mate, and if he wins I'll go shares." He then drained a tin cup of the liquid with such composure as would make Jim tremble for his bet and the success of a further plan he was just then maturing, were it not that his fertile brain hit on a method of quieting his companion for a time. Miah's refusal to keep silence on the other's double-dealing had made it incumbent on Jim to impair the Saint's activity for a time. As the pure liquor appeared powerless, he had to resort to other and more questionable means. It was a case of cunning against cunning now, and in such contests Jim smilingly congratulated himself that the result was generally a foregone conclusion. Fumbling beneath a heap of odds and ends which lay in scattered confusion at the end of the tent, he secretly pulled forth a bottle of paregoric cough mixture, which he happened to have amongst many other oddments, a legacy from an unfortunate consumptive deceased digger, and former occupant of the tent. He had little difficulty in introducing it into the tin cup of liquor from which he had been himself drinking, and, apparently unobserved, exchanging the cup with Miah's comparatively empty pannikin, for Miah was holding forth with the enthusiasm of a fanatic on his favourite topic, his own saintliness, and the vice of all around. Even the weaknesses of his master and Edith were not spared, until almost spent of breath, he took a good pull at the contents of his tin, apparently drinking a strong dose before he ascertained that the after-taste was somewhat medicinal. The effects of the opiate, combined with the weakness of his frame and his rather copious libations, appeared soon evident in the sleepy tone, glassy eye, and lethargic movements he displayed. Stupidly, incoherently, and with difficult utterance, he spoke a few words, his head nodding slowly forward, until he fell over, log-like, to the eminent satisfaction of Jim, who, after waiting a few minutes, pronounced him properly hocussed.

The approach of footsteps, and the intrusion of a man's head, interrupted Jim in his meditations upon his success, and upon the details of that other and more important enterprise he had in hand. The intruder looked at the occupants of the tent, smiled grimly, and laconically said, "All dead-heads."

Jim started, turned round, and warmly welcomed the new-comer as one of the happy band which delighted to call him Gentleman Jim,

Captain, or Black Jack indifferently; the man acknowledged by a laconic "Here's luck" the acceptance of a tin cupful of spirit which the captain handed to him.

"Where's the others?" asked Jim.

"Comin', I b'lieve, very soon."

"Why did you let this fool get drunk like that?" inquired Jim, pointing to Ben.

"Couldn't help it, none of us; got on the rampage last Tuesday se'ennight, and been like that ever since. His first lush was a good'un for the rest of us, but this time he stuck so close to hisself that we ain't had a chance to 'elp him out."

The approach of three others, Jacob Saltner, an Italian, and a German Socialist, brought this desultory conversation to a close. They had evidently been summoned to a council, and after they had one and all tossed off a cup apiece, and drank luck to the Captain's return among them, Jim called out,—

"Take Ben out and duck his head, so as to get him to a bit, one of you."

This order having been complied with, the two reappear, Ben, semi-conscious and very much the worse for wear, having, in fact, got into an incipient state of *delirium tremens*. He grins in ghastly wise as he sees his friend, and, remarking on the pallor of his face, wishes, with sundry oaths, to know why they've brought down that plague of a ghost to torment him. "I didn't cook him," says he, "it was the others, not him, I swear it!"

So mumbling he soon falls off into a sleep, from which there is at present little chance of awaking him.

"Bedad, who's this, Captain?" says one, kicking the recumbent form of Miah, thereby almost causing that worthy, who is malingering, to disclose his fraud.

Jim's action with the paregoric bottle had not been, as he expected, unobserved by Miah, who had, in fact, swallowed very little of the liquid, and had, in a very creditable style, whereby the astute Jim had been deceived, simulated drunkenness, and was now anxiously debating within himself whether to run the risk of listening or disclose his sobriety at once. In the end his curiosity overcame his timidity.

"Oh, he's all right; he's drunk as a lord, or a couple of 'em; he's been drinking the paregoric out of this bottle; leave him alone."

The others laugh, while the supposed victim smiles grimly to himself. The purpose for which they are met is soon disclosed, the quickly recovered captain had again brought forward his plan for robbing the bank, a feat which was then as hazardous as it was novel, for was not every digger who had banked dust or nuggets a special constable, who would defend the building and the contents with his life. But if the project was ever feasible it was so then,—the licensing laws were still the burning question of the fields, and even the honest diggers were fast crossing the line which separated legitimate from unlawful agitation. Of the assembled company, though all were dressed and worked as diggers, few had paid for licences, and many were their fellows in a like defiance of the law. It was no easy matter for many of the diggers to find the heavy tax of thirty shillings per month with which they were one and all saddled, whether rich or poor, successful or failing, well or ill. Taking all this into his consideration Jim hoped that by judiciously inflaming the minds of the more temperate amongst the diggers into the state of suppressed mutiny which the more turbulent felt, he might secure his object of diverting the attention of the authorities and the diggers generally, so that when matters were ripe a raid on the bank must be successful. As for the question of licence or no licence he cared not a rush, in which many of the agitators of these momentous times agreed with him.

His four followers applauded his ideas, but asked for details. Then Jim showed a plan which he had prepared of the bank, and divulged the method he had devised for gaining access to the safes without explosives, which might prove tell-tale and uncertain servants.

A bank clerk was wanted then, so Saltner was to offer himself for the post, and, by hook or by crook obtain impressions of the keys. Saltner, after some demur, consented to accept the risky post thus assigned him on the assurance of the others that his fresh arrival at the fields, and his clerk-like appearance, suited him pre-eminently for the task. So, after a good pull together at the rest of the whisky, which was—fortunately for Ben's chances of regaining sobriety—fast disappearing, the rascals arranged to meet the ensuing week, and took their leave. In going out, one of the conspirators by chance stumbled on Miah's pet corn, which so exasperated that individual, that, without thinking of his *rôle* he rapped out a sharp epithet at the astonished miscreant, much to the surprise and dismay of the other occupants of the tent. Jim was the first to realize their position and its consequences. Doubtful how much the wretched man had heard, yet fearing the worst, he was for at once despatching him, and deputed one of the others to take the eavesdropper away, and to see to it, with as much *sang froid* as though he had ordered the drowning of a rat. The terror-stricken man prayed for life, and swore so vehemently that he would not betray them, that some of the party, among them Saltner, were for enrolling him a member of the band. Jim, however, who knew his man better, and placed little reliance on his word, at last compromised the order by sending him away, gagged and bound, to an old disused pit, some thirty feet deep, at the edge of the fields, where few, if any, people passed, thus satisfying the more squeamish of the crew; while carrying out his intention to silence the poor wretch for ever.

With a dirty rag over his mouth, which was stuffed full of corks, his hands bound behind his back, and his feet hobbled together, more dead than alive, the poor apprentice was huddled by two of the crew across the dark plain, lowered down the shaft, which fortunately happened to be dry, and by an ingenious arrangement of the ropes, was left at the bottom, the ropes being pulled up hand over hand. Every inch that they receded against the star-lit sky seemed to the terror-stricken man one more league towards a certain death. The pair alone did not relish their job, as it was essentially cold-blooded, and there was nothing to fire them with the necessary cruelty, but they carried out their orders to the letter, and as their steps and voices receded into the distance, poor Jeremiah broke into a profuse perspiration and swooned away. The loneliness of the night, the discomfort of the corks, the tightness of the man's ligatures, and the horrors of his coming death, all helped the aims and objects of Gentleman Jim, and there we must leave him to speed away to the other events which were taking place.

The next day, Saltner, having transformed himself into a dapper clerk, applied for and obtained the position at the bank. His credentials, which were cleverly forged by Jim, were beyond doubt, besides, the astute manager could not possibly be mistaken in the evident business-like look and cut of the man, and therefore engaged him for a week on trial.

In less than two days the impressions of the keys were obtained and the moulds prepared and keys cast, the pseudo-clerk finding out in the meantime the arrangements of the staff and building.

Upon the licence question, the expected crisis seemed so much nearer than Gentleman Jim had anticipated, that he found he would have to antedate by some few days his attack, to be successful, and before the arrival of reinforcements for the constabulary which were daily expected.

So on the 28th day of November it was settled that the night of the 1st of December should be the time at which they should all meet at the rendezvous and make the attack. Horses on the fields were at a premium, but the conspirators had their eyes on five, which meant that they intended to steal them, and before the date fixed for the attack they could probably "eye" enough to horse the whole mob.

The manifestations of disaffection on the fields were as follows:— The Ballarat Reform League had sent a deputation to Melbourne to "demand" the release of the prisoners who were still suffering punishment for the attack on the Eureka Hotel, and although they had not yet returned with the Governor's answer, which might turn out satisfactory after all, the more disaffected had that very day insulted and hooted a detachment of the 12th Foot on its march into quarters at Ballarat, where the Governor was concentrating as many men as possible. The time was evidently not far distant when force on one or both sides would be resorted to, and it was obviously to the advantage of Jim's scheme that he should not postpone it until order had been, as it must inevitably be, restored. In this, as in other points connected with his plan, he showed great foresight. The morrow saw fresh complications, the return of the Governor's answer, a firm, but sorrowful refusal—a mass meeting of twelve thousand diggers at Baker's Hill—various inflammatory speeches by the diggers' advocates, in which, I regret to say, Huxter and Jackson distinguished themselves, and, as it were, an impress of popularity given to the Ballarat Reform League, of which tickets of membership were issued. Greatest of all acts of insubordination, a German Socialist advocated the burning of licences, counsel promptly followed by a regular holocaust, the flames of which roared and crackled a burning insult to the powers that were. The next day serious rioting took place, shots were fired, prisoners were taken, and finally the diggers elected a commander who was lucky enough to escape the collapse of the rebellion, and eventually, as a respected and respectable member of legislature, made—not broke—the laws of the land.

The same evening Coates and Jack were seated outside their hut, their present substitute for the old bell-tent, discussing the passing events and their future plans. Passing to personal topics, Coates said,—

"Do you know, Jack, I can't help thinking that that confounded hospital work is running away with both the doctor's and Mary's health, if not their good looks. I wish I could persuade the doctor to give it up and have a spell here for a while, so as to gain his former strength; and as to Mary, I think I shall send her to Melbourne at once for change of air."

Jack replies laconically, "Guess she won't go."

"Well, well," says the other, with a smile, "of course I shouldn't order her to go, I should look decidedly foolish if she refused, but I mean I should find some excuse for going myself, and getting her to accompany me."

"Give you a good excuse," says Jack, cutting up his sentence with puffs of smoke into regular periods. "Edith wants to go to Melbourne for some reason; let Miss Coates know that she still wants some one to look after her."

"Ah," says the surveyor, "that's a good notion but how about Edith, why not Miss Williams, as of old?"

Jack flushes up under a skin many shades swarthier than when we first saw him six months ago. "She said yes, you know."

"Dear me," says Coates, "I congratulate you, my boy, pass the tea, and we'll drink a right good willie waught. Here's luck, and plenty of it. But I say," this rather mischievously, "how did you get the courage to do it?"

"Miss Mary told me what to say," replied Jack, which was literally true, as Jack had, the day before, requested Mary for a few words in private, and then begged her help, which she, of course, promised to give to the best of her power, but equally, of course, would not accept the responsible position of advocate, with which Jack wished to entrust her. He had accordingly repeated Mary's tender suggestions almost word for word; and as Gentleman Jim was out of the way, and in Edith's bad books, while Jack was her hero for the time being, and looked at by all around with favour, she being still rather weak and sentimental, had readily given her assent to the suit of the stammering Hercules, and was at that very moment, in true consistency, crying herself silly that she had done so.

However, we must not leave Jack, whose pipe is actually going out with suppressed excitement. Coates was bent on teasing, and asked,—

"How did you manage to dispose of the handsome new chum you told me of?"

"Disposed of himself, by running away," replied Jack.

"Oh, ho!" laughed the surveyor, "so you were the gallant cavalier that won the day by bravery. "Well, come," he continues, as Jack, not understanding the joke, looked annoyed, "I'll be present at the wed ding and give you away, and that's a thing I wouldn't do for anybody else."

"What, not your sister and the doctor?" asks Jack.

"I say," replied Coates, answering one question in the Socratian style by another, "what do you make of these two? They puzzle me. Why, O'Donnoghue seemed so struck with Mary, and Mary seemed to feel equally friendly to him, while it appears that Mary is the doctor's old flame of hospital renown; but now they're terribly stiff and stilted with one another, though they think others don't notice it, and the doctor hasn't ever proposed, though I'm sure he has often been on the point of committing that indiscretion. I don't believe in marriage myself, but I don't want to see two people who do, made miserable by not understanding one another."

"I think," says Jack, deliberately, "she's in love with some one else."

"Oh, that's too comical," laughed the other; "why, who is there on the fields fit to look at her, and she never sees anybody from the barracks?"

"Well, I still think it," says Jack, drawing conclusions from his own rather recent experience with Edith Williams. "I saw that fellow who sat in the window at the bank talking to her the other day at the hospital. I'd swear to him in a thousand, for I noticed the reflection of his face in the glass when I first saw him, and what's more, he's Edith's old flame, and no more a new chum than you or I. He's grown a beard."

"My gracious, you a detective, too! But I say, if that's true, the performance is getting interesting, but devilish close home, my boy. Talking to Mary, how? when? and where?"

"He was sitting up in a chair, just getting about, for he's been sick. Looks love-sick now, and as saintly as a siren."

"A seraph, you mean," says Coates, correcting his friend abstractedly. "I must talk to Mary about this to-night, when she comes home. But now, how about the Melbourne trip? Will you come too, or will you go to take care of the two girls? Perhaps you'll be wanting to tie the knot in Melbourne at the same time, eh? how's that?"

"I'll go if you like, but she won't be married yet. Old Williams says that she must wait a year at the least," replied Jack.

"Oh! if you don't want to go, I won't trouble you," returned the other. "I'm wanting to see the Minister of Lands about these roads, and the waste bits of land up yonder, so I'll kill two birds with one stone. The fact is, I'm becoming somewhat alarmed about these licence riots, and want Mary to be safe away and out of the reach of danger. Inspector Cochrane, the doctor's friend, is wearing a grave face, and told me last week that the authorities had sent to the Governor, asking for a reinforcement."

"I can't blame the poor devils who can't scrape even a living together, for refusing to pay such a heavy licence," said Jack.

"Perhaps not on moral grounds, but the law must be complied with at all costs, whether it be good or bad," asserted the surveyor.

And as Jack was not a political economist or a student of ethics, the subject dropped, the puff-puff of their pipes alone breaking the stillness of the camp.

CHAPTER XI

THE VOLCANO SMOKES

HURRYING footsteps caused the two to look round and simultaneously feel for the revolvers which in these troublous times invariably hung from their belts. Inspector Cochrane and two constables in long cloaks were the new-comers, the men standing a short distance off, while the inspector exchanged hurriedly a few words with the two.

"Did ye hear of the licence riots down the field to-day?" asked the inspector. "Some of our fellows badly hurt. I myself got a stone on the head—no respect for authority, you see."

"So soon!" cried the surveyor. "We heard shooting, but didn't pay any especial notice. There's always a good deal of that going on, you know, what with quarrels and drunken sprees."

"Well, it's an accomplished fact now, the first blood was let to-day. We pounced on a nest of Tipperary boys, who were working claims down at the gravel pits. They replied to our requests by levelling their five-shooters and heaving stones at us. That was too much for us, you know. We have had threats and murmurs, but not open mutiny; so we went for them, and tried to wipe them out, but they were too strong for us at first, so I ordered a retreat while I sent for reinforcements. Then the gold commissioner came up with a posse, read the Riot Act, and we charged them, and this time gave them something to remember us by. You see the boys have been so insulted lately by the diggers that it's hard work to draw them in when they do get the chance to retaliate. I know some of them had a taste of lead which will give them a fright for weeks to come. One of those we've taken, called Bully Ben, we have long been after, and another, a young new chum, who has, I learn, been bank clerk, and was one of my fellow-passengers when the bushrangers swung the doctor and me, was also a good catch. [This was true. Saltner had indeed been captured, having taken French leave at the bank.] Ben gave three of our boys fits before we could get him up to the barracks, and I think the clerk is going to turn Queen's evidence against the lot. The poor fool thinks it'll pay him, and doesn't see that he'll have to reckon up with his mates. Well, I've not come to yarn, but to ask you from our commandant to lend us your help if there's another riot. We have promises from about five hundred diggers and others already, and there are plenty more who are hesitating only to see us well supported before coming over to our side. The two detachments of infantry came up, as you are aware, three days ago, and others are on their way up now, but we don't want to use them unless we are forced."

Well," says Coates, "to tell you the truth, I don't expect to be here after to-morrow myself; and I'm most likely going to take my sister down by coach to Melbourne, but for what it's worth you have my promise, and Jack here will doubtless help you."

"No, I don't think he will," says Jack. "The fact is, I'm not one to take up arms against the Government myself; but I don't see why I should help if the Governor don't act fairly by the diggers. Latrobe didn't know his own mind, what's more; and Hotham's a new broom."

The inspector now has his work to show the fairness of the tax, in which he fails, for his heart is not in the wretched work, digger-hunting and capturing being by no means to the taste of himself and many other members of the force. So he sets himself next to exhort Jack to be a good subject, upon which grounds, backed up by the prudent Coates, he succeeds in convincing the other to promise his aid.

He then communicates the signals and other arrangements for utilizing their promised help, and with a hearty good-bye is off on his way to negotiate other similar alliances. His footsteps had not long died away, when Mary, escorted by the doctor, arrived at the camp. But to find how they came to be there we must hark back a few minutes.

The fact is, that the abatement of fever cases at the hospital, and the quick recovery of the existing patients, had permitted Mary a few hours' much needed rest and quiet, which the doctor had himself prescribed for her, mindful as he ever was of her welfare, and pained at her apparent ill-health. Gentleman Jim had been reported cured, and had taken French leave a few days before, and with the absence of his unworthy rival the good fellow's hopes had again risen, and his face was wearing more of its old happy, easy-going look. So when the doctor in his old style ordered

"Her Majesty a few days' quiet," she looked smilingly at him, and with some of her old mischief; after a pretence of rebellion, complied with the order, asking for the escort, which he, of course, only too readily gave.

Now the doctor, like most male folk, did not know when he was well off, and tried to better his position. The inexplicable fascination of Gentleman Jim over his fair companion undoubtedly gained strength by the presence of the rascal, and was now fast fading away into the catalogue of the "Have Beens," but the recollection was still so present to the minds of both the doctor and herself that they could not regain their old footing at a bound. However, what with the doctor's rising spirits and Mary's determination to be gay *malgrè elle*, they managed to make considerable progress to the camp before they discovered the fact; then O'Donnoghue noticing that they had come out on to the silent plain, and that five minutes' further walking would bring them to their destination, made an heroic effort to disburden himself of thoughts which had always sent his heart pit-a-pit, and on this occasion caused a regular devil's tattoo to be performed within scarcely measurable distance of his fair companion's arm.

An awkward pause, which, like the calm preceding a storm, is generally portentous of unusual consequences, was brought to a close by a voice which, though it proceeded from the doctor's mouth, could scarcely be recognized by either Mary or himself as his property, so overcome was he with emotion. Mary naturally became somewhat startled, then to make matters worse, he became desperate and plunged *in medias res*.

"Miss Coates, I've had an offer made me by this morning's post, and as one wheel fits into another, I propose accipting this offer, if some one else accipts an offer of mine."

Here he paused awhile for a reply from Mary, who, however, maintained an inexorable silence.

"It's true," continued he, as though apologizing to some one who had advanced an objection, "that the two cases are not parallel, and the wheels don't quite fit in this case, for the offer made to me is one very advantageous to meself while the offer that some one else is to accept is more advantageous to the person offering."

Again a pause, but again Mary declined him all help, being in fact too embarrassed to frame any intelligible and sensible answer. The doctor's desperation increased, in three minutes more the camp would be reached and his opportunity gone till to-morrow, or for ever, who should say?

"The letter this morning was from the Colonial Secretary, proposing that I should become the successor of Doctor Baldwin at Pentridge Prison, at an increasing salary for the next few years, with liberty to take private patients, and the only answer I can give is, that if some one will share me home and me fortune, and enjoy all that devotion, love and homage can give her, I will write back yes—otherwise—but there can't be an otherwise, Miss Coates, Mary Mavourneen, say that it shall be a yes, ye don't say nay, ye don't flinch away; oh, tell me just that one little word."

Mary had, indeed, not drawn her arm or herself away, and her silence was almost acquiescent, her eyes were moist, and her lips quivering. Had he but said this a couple of months since, but eight short weeks ago, and how differently would she have received the words, how gladly, though shyly, would she have complied with the wish; but now, ah! there came in the difference, what then could she give in return for the devotion and homage of the generous-hearted Irishman. Her self-communing seemed an age of anxious hope to the doctor, a second's respite to the girl, before she replied with pale lips and face, her eyes now dry, and the expression of her face set as hard as nature would permit,—

"It cannot be, Doctor O'Donnoghue. It cannot be."

Then, as he seemed about to protest, she vehemently continued, "Spare me the pain of again denying to one whom I so much respect, that which he thinks so great a gift, but which, if he only knew it, is not worth his thoughts for a moment."

"I cannot believe that," almost shouted the other, "though ye tell it me yeself, I *will* not believe it; there is no question about the worth on your side, would that I had one-hundredth part as much worth to offer ye meself."

Mary smiled faintly at the poor fellow's exaggerated humility. "What do you take me for, doctor?" then, as she saw that her question led to an endless reply of platitudes and compliments, she hurriedly went on, "I am a piece of flesh and blood, like—well, like poor Susan Carter" (a poor degraded woman on the gold-fields who had caught the fever). "Ah, you may shake your head, but however hard it is to believe, we are both women, and both subject to temptations, trials, and sorrows: mine are, I sometimes think, harder to bear than those of her class, but if you will think of this sensibly and coolly, and just realize that you have only a woman to deal with whose love is not really worth the asking, unless she could give it freely and honestly, you may make my burden lighter as you will not persist in your suit."

She had become wonderfully cool and self-controlled now, as she realized that her obvious duty was to protect him from himself, even at the risk of overstating the case.

"Miss Mary, I have niver felt anything but the purest love of yeself, niver has it crossed my mind to think of ye but in affection, but I cannot stand near patiently and hear ye say hard things about yeself. If I am to be silent ye must shure be silent on this point too. I am fearfully in earnest, and every such word cuts me like—well, like a saw passing through the spinal marrow and every nerve in the body."

"Agreed then, doctor, if you will still call me your friend, believe me I will ever try to be worthy of your noble, unselfish character, and if you will let me call you as I used to think I might—my friend—"

"Be me hope of salvation, Miss Mary, say the slave of your wish, the lover of the very words that fall from your lips, one who would go through fire—but there, I won't boast, ye shall perhaps one day judge for yeself." Yes, soon, old friend, very soon!

"Then I may say that you are my friend, and believe me if I could call you so and only so, I would thank you every day, every hour, and every second of my life. It is my fault, and my fault alone, that this trouble has come upon you, and your truly unselfish character will help to make me feel my fault a little less, will it not? And you won't throw up the appointment, will you?"

"Your wish is as ever my command, as it has been from the beginning," said the doctor, with dignity "but before the opportunity goes, perhaps never more to return, tell me, is there no chance that if I wait you will give the question a 'yes,' not in a day, not perhaps in a year, some day, will be good news for me, and in anticipation I shall be merry in fact, not only in appearance."

Mary was silent, hurt that he should press a suit which she had so earnestly begged him to relinquish.

"If ye will say that ye have pledged yeself to another, I will let be, and ye shall not find a warmer friend to wish ye good health and long life and happiness with the other."

Now came a great temptation over the girl. To do what she thought right, she was prompted to do herself and the doctor a great wrong. She had but little time to debate the ethics of truth and falsehood, but she thought she saw the consequences, and grasped the opportunity. Now as ever for his sake, not to let him throw away such nobility and unselfishness, such generosity and devotion on one who could feel a passion for and listen to the entreaties of a man who was unworthy to unloose even the doctor's shoes. So she answered coldly and clearly, "I have," which was decidedly untrue, as my readers know.

This the doctor had never anticipated, her motives he could not fathom, her undisclosed scruples not divine, and though he had himself prepared the lure that led him over the precipice, he had always expected the precipice to be a mirage and imaginary only. The cold plunge into the abyss of realism woke him to a sense of the weird humour of his position, and with more self-control than he deemed he could have exerted, and some show of heartiness, he replied,—

"Then I wish ye both long life and happiness."

The camp was now only a few yards off, otherwise it had gone hard with Mary's scruples, as the good fellow's manly self-abnegation so completely turned the tables against her, that the strained sense of duty she had displayed would have rebounded by a species of natural elasticity and have led her into a complete surrender of her position.

"Hallo! you star-gazing pair," cried Coates, happy to see the two together, "come in here out of the gloom and behave like civilized nineteenth-century folk."

So they "came in" by approaching the fire and were heartily welcomed by their two friends. The greetings were returned in such a subdued tone by Mary, and with such forced merriment by the doctor, who winked alarmingly at the surveyor in a way to have caused him at another time to laugh outright but for the pathetic, worried look in the doctor's eyes, that the surveyor looked from one to the other inquiringly, as though awaiting some explanation which they had promised. Mary's conduct of hastening to her house with evident discomposure did not afford him much explanation, and his face fell when he regarded the doctor, who was bantering Jack with words in the old style but with manner of a new sort which ill-befitted the light-hearted fellow.

So suggesting that Jack should get some fresh wood for Mary's fire, hints of which sort Jack was always ready to take for "the Queen's" sake, Coates pounced upon the doctor and cross-questioned him rapidly.

"What in the name of fortune are you two people making yourselves so miserable about?" asked he. "Why can't you agree to settle down respectably and comfortably without such quibbles and tiffs as you must be having?"

"Few quibbles and tiffs are there, me bhoy, betwixt your sister and your humble servant. Why, what makes ye think that?" replied the doctor.

"Look at Mary and then look in the mirror that hangs in the tent," answered Coates, "and then you'll know the reason. Now come, I'm not a marrying man, you know, but it grieves me greatly to see two people misunderstanding one another like you and Mary. Why don't you put an end to the matter and propose, if you're really in earnest, and if I didn't think you were I should have given you right-about-turn long ago."

Then the doctor told his friend how he had just declared his earnestness, and, softening down Mary's brusquerie, how he was answered. Coates, jumping to conclusions, cried out,—

"My God! would that anything had happened than that she should have pledged her word to such a rascal as Gentleman Jim. Fool that I was to let her stay here, but I thought she had already fixed her affection on you and was doubly safe. Old fellow, I'm awfully sorry for you, I think you've been very badly used."

"Now look here, Coates," sternly says O'Donnoghue, "you're the lady's brother, and may enjoy many privileges which no one else can, among others that of saying of her what ye please, but don't let us risk our friendship on account of meself ever hearing such a remark from *you* again. I've been a born idiot to have thought of aspiring to such a woman, and have got less than full deserts for my vanity, and I cannot think that the rascal ye talk of has won her affection any more than I could that she would do anything unworthy of the Holy Virgin herself."

"All right, old fellow, perhaps you're right about my talking, but as a brother I feel very keenly and spoke hotly; now tell me, do you know that she and this fellow have been together?"

"Yes; I've often seen them; he exercises a sort of fascination over her; they're as handsome a pair as ye'd wish to see, but—I don't think—together. Do ye know it makes me sad to think of it, sadder than I would like to own, but this rascal is, I believe, no other than the robber, bushranger, and murderer, Black Jack."

"Good God! and you have let them be together, knowing this. Does she know it?"

"I don't think so, but I'm sure she knows he's not all that he seems, so honey-lipped and smooth-faced."

"But why didn't you tell her, me, or somebody?"

"I wasn't sure," replied the doctor, rather lamely, but loyal to the last not to disclose Mary's appeal to him on a recent occasion.

"Wasn't sure, my Colonial? Are you sure now?"

"No; not sure, only next door to it," replied the doctor.

"How's that?" rapidly queried Coates.

"Firstly, the man who shot at me as I hung on the gum-tree and when our claim was robbed, had only three fingers on his left hand, I could see him pull the trigger with his middle finger. The man in the hospital is without his first and second fingers on his left hand. Secondly, I hit the same man who shot at me in the right arm, and the bushranger's arm was dressed by me, while the man who lay in the hospital has an old bullet wound in his right elbow in about the same place. Thirdly, the voice of the bushranger, while he was talking to Mary after the coach had been bailed up, was soft and gentle for a second or two, like his voice in the hospital since he's been ill. Fourthly, the early part of his delirium discovered that he knew of a lot of villainies committed, though by the time Miss Coates came to nurse him he had quietened down and simply lay staring at her in silence."

"Well, but couldn't you swear to the man after all those resemblances?" urged Coates.

"Ye forget, me friend, that the bushranger's face was blackened, and the ivints of that one night went along rather like the Yankee's horse, too quick to note very carefully."

"But, just think, supposing for a moment that he isn't the rascal—and I could swear him to be on such evidence as that—was it fair to Mary and me to let her nurse him in ignorance of your suspicions."

"As soon as I found it was time to let her know I also found he was a rival, and I couldn't blacken him."

"Well, well," said Coates, impatiently, "you may carry those romantic ideas of yours too far, and I think you have this time. But the point is, what is to be done? You say you don't think she's in love with the fellow, but, as it were, fascinated, and yet she won't have you. Well, this decides me in going to Melbourne at once. I'll take her right away from the place and she'll forget about the man; then you pop in and take your opportunity."

"That, I'm afraid, may never be, at least, so she says," replied the doctor.

"Oh, don't believe her, she's worked up now, poor girl, to such a pitch that she doesn't mean anything she says. Why," continued this experienced person, "I've known plenty of similar cases where time worked wonders."

"Well, while there's life there's hope, is a good saying, and there's a good deal of life in me regard for your sister, old fellow; in fact I believe rather more noo that it's been a moment checked than before," said the doctor.

Coates then told him of his plans to start the next day but one if Mary were able to go away, that he will warn Inspector Cochrane of their suspicion about the handsome quondam invalid, and then bade him stay the night at the camp, which the doctor, tired out and excited as he was, was very glad to do—disappearing into the tent, where Jack, having arranged matters comfortably at Mary's house, had already preceded him. Hesitatingly Coates approached his sister's door and with some trepidation, unusual to him, laid his hand on the knocker, for this was a delicate and unaccustomed piece of business he was embarked upon, and the young lady had a will and way of her own, not withstanding her amiability and lovable disposition.

At his second knock he was admitted, and by the light of the feeble lamp sat down opposite Mary, beating round his subject with somewhat awkward circuitousness, until his sister, guessing his object, looked with pity on his perplexity and assisted him. Once started he found no difficulty in proceeding, and after a protracted interview of half an hour, which ended in his softening down all his hard words and becoming imbued with admiration for the self-sacrifice of the girl, who showed more than her usual courage and fortitude in loyalty to the doctor, whom she seemed to regard as infinitely above her, he gained her willing consent to accompany him to Melbourne, but was allowed to give no word of comfort to the doctor. She indirectly reassured him as to her relations with Gentleman Jim. He did not tell her the doctor's suspicions in all their bareness, remembering his promise, but he confirmed the thoughts of her calmer moments in a way that she might once have dreaded, but now that the patient was fading out of mind, she heard with scarcely any remorse.

In the morning, Coates was as good as his word, accompanying the doctor back to the hospital and so on to the barracks where, however, he failed to see Cochrane, who was still busily enlisting the help and sympathies of volunteers.

The Irish element was just then a strong one on the fields, and manifested itself according to the old story, "agin" the Government, whatever it might be, and so the numbers of those opposing the law were dangerously increasing. Coates saw the magistrate himself upon the matter, a stern old colonist—greatly differing from his corrupt predecessor—who was just then preparing to attend the preliminary examination of the prisoners captured in yesterday's conflict. To him he confided his suspicions, and, so far as he could, the magistrate promised to look into the matter.

Out of curiosity, Coates attended the court, where a strong posse of constables guarded against any chance of rescue. "Order! Order!" cried the constable-usher, preceding the magistrate; who, having disposed of the few assault and other cases of a light nature, called on the riot cases.

In the dock there stood the three unwounded worthies who had been captured the day before, side by side, the others having been too severely injured to appear; Ben was heavily chained and handcuffed, while Saltner had judiciously interposed the third prisoner between himself and the chained giant.

The case was called on, and the police evidence taken, Saltner being the whole while highly excited and nervous, Ben sullen and composed, and their colleague sarcastic and irritable by turns. A pause followed this evidence, during which the magistrate asked whether there was anything further, Saltner's agitation increasing the while. A constable approached the dock, opened it and let him out, locking up the dock again and escorting him past his comrades to the witness-box. His fellows were evidently unprepared for this move, for while Ben looked puzzled and smiled as though he anticipated the confusion of the magistrate at his comrade's ready wit, the other paled, muttered under his breath, and turning whispered to his remaining friend. Ben replied in no muffled sounds, "If he does, I'll break his back like a stick;" words which so disconcerted Saltner that he had to be assisted into the box and supplied with spirits. The constable who had the conduct of the case (lawyers had turned diggers and no one acted for the prosecution or defence) introduced the informer thus:—

"This man, though one of the prisoners, yer honour, is goin' to turn Queen's evidence, and tell yer honour all he knows about it."

"Do I want his evidence?" asked the magistrate.

"Well, yer honour, it's usual to have the police evidence substantiated if you can," replied the constable, "and Inspector Cochrane promised him that yer honour would deal leniently by him if he spoke the truth."

"Under those circumstances, I'll hear him," replied the magistrate.

But Ben here interposed with: "By God! you won't speak, Jacob, you cur, or I'll break every bone in your body."

"Be quiet, man!" sternly said the magistrate.

"That we won't if that man's going to swear away the life of a mate," replied Ben's colleague.

"Hold your tongue, both of you, and speak when it's your turn!" almost screamed the magistrate.

"Hold your tongue yourself!" shouted the prisoner; "don't you know it's a matter of life and death with us?"

The man is at once removed, and Ben threatened with the like treatment if he interrupts. But he has composure and doggedness to carry him through the ordeal, and stands out the evidence of his former associate without a word of comment except a grunt here and there.

"Committed for trial, all three," is the magistrate's decision; "and," nodding to Saltner, "your case will be specially recommended on account of the steps you have taken."

This speech was greeted with some expressions of disapproval from amongst the many sympathizers with the prisoners who were present, while the cheering which Ben and his more loyal colleague received, and the hissing and groans hurled at the head of Saltner, were a fair warning to the latter of the scant courtesy he would receive if he ever left the prison walls.

After order had been sternly enforced, Saltner's special petition to be imprisoned apart from the men whom he had betrayed was, in view of the circumstances of the case and the requirements of justice, granted, and the court was cleared for the day. The crowd dispersed into earnest knots of two or three, who discussed the action of the Government and the impending fate of the prisoners—or at least two of them—with grave, stern looks. Red tape has its advantages as well as its disadvantages, but in this case the latter were more apparent than the former. Had the usual forms of criminal trial been suspended and martial law been adopted at this juncture, or even earlier, there is little doubt that the rioters would have been overawed and the subsequent bloodshed averted. But the Fates were not, as it turned out, to be balked of their blood-stained path, and prevented reliable information from reaching the Governor's ready ears.

On leaving the court Coates became attracted by a large mob of men some way off listening to a speaker, who, perched on the shoulders of another, was holding forth in vehement style, to the evident satisfaction of his hearers. As it was no other than Robert Huxter, mounted on his inseparable and giant-like friend Jake, Coates went over to listen, and was somewhat shocked to hear the brusque but honest fellow urging upon the diggers armed resistance to the licence laws, and suggesting methods and plans worthy of more creditable undertakings. Huxter was especially bitter against the continued detention of the prisoners who had attacked the hotel, but his audience cheered more vehemently than ever when he touched on the attack and capture of the day before. Neither he nor his audience knew, except by name, the prisoners taken on this last occasion, but even had they possessed such a knowledge, yet it is unlikely they would have altered their opinion as to the merits of the case. One and all clamoured for the release of the prisoners, as many hundred years before a mob called for the release of a notorious robber. Principle was set against principles, right against reason. Incidentally the speaker touched on the expected reinforcements from Melbourne; how that very morning the "Commander-in-Chief"—by which name he referred to the self-constituted head of the rioters—had sent off a body of men to patrol the road to the capital and thus intercept the soldiers; how, to effect this purpose the easier, a stockade or encampment was to be built at Eureka Point, and how all loyal and faithful diggers should stand shoulder to shoulder in the cause. His vocabulary was astonishing; the length of his body was ill-proportioned to that of his words, but the diggers cheered him to the echo, hearing part, understanding less, but instinctively guessing his drift. When he suggested a round robin to be signed by all present demanding the release of the prisoners, his audience caught up the idea like wildfire, and jostled one another to reach the document drawn up then and there by a man of more education than usual for those parts—an ex-officer of a crack regiment, who had sold out for the purpose of "trying his luck at the fields," as the saying went.

By the aid of this worthy, most of those present subscribed or signed the document, which was then taken in charge by Huxter and his friend the ex-officer, who, together with Jackson and a large portion of the crowd, set off at once to the police-camp to interview the magistrate there. The rest, adopting Huxter's advice, sought Eureka Point, where they were soon busily at work under the "Commander's" orders entrenching a low mound with overturned waggons, furniture, and earthworks. This was the Eureka Stockade, so notorious in Australian history. Coates stepped forward, and button-holing Huxter held him for a few moments in conversation, disputing and arguing with him against the step he was thus taking. But Huxter was determined; he and his friends had had enough of the unsympathetic and unintelligent action of the Government, and brusquely, though in a friendly spirit, he turned away from the surveyor, refusing to listen any longer, although his interviewer happened to be the brother of the diggers' "Queen." Coates replied,—

"Well, you must do what you will, I suppose, if you won't let me help you, but this I will say that these riots have driven away the Queen of your hearts, as you call her, from amongst you."

"Ah! is she gone?" asked Huxter, lifting his hat the while as though in reverence to the girl's presence. "Well, I'm half glad and half sorry. I'm main glad that she's away from the row, but mortal sorry that she left us without a word of farewell."

"She hasn't actually gone yet. You may be sure she wouldn't have done that without letting her subjects know of it. She starts by the coach to-morrow morning, if it goes," replied Coates, "and I know would be glad to say 'good-bye' to you."

"So she shall, so she shall, bless her heart; and I'll be thinking she'll be coming back soon as the row's over, eh?"

"That I can't say, for she's not at all well. You've got to your destination now, so I'll leave you, if you really won't be convinced how fruitless it is for you to resist against the organized armed force of the Government."

"Not a bit! not a bit! Did ye see those chaps who were working at the stockade, digging and picking for dear life? D'ye know what they've got that the police and the sogers ain't? They've got their heart in their work, and I'd back them against all the organization, as you call it."

Fortunately for the other, Coates did not accept the wager, but followed him regretfully with his eyes as he, with his two friends, shabby and stained in attire and bushy-haired and unkempt to look at, strode up the hill, ushered by two constables through the police-camp to the magistrate's house, and leaving behind them a motley crowd of sympathizers and onlookers. They were soon admitted and granted an interview by the magistrate. They were nothing daunted by the stern, cold-blooded contempt which this official manifested for their wrongs, and the unmoved and inexorable way in which he repudiated their right to petition when so eloquently urged by the backwoods' orator, Huxter.

"The law must be carried out at all risks to the law-breakers," said he, rising as though to end the interview.

"Then," said Huxter, "those who carry it out against the wish of the people of the country will have the risk, and will have to answer for it!"

"Do you threaten, man?" thundered the magistrate, hoping to abash the irrepressible orator.

"I ain't deaf, thanks," said the other, as coolly as though talking to his comrade; "but since you say it, yes, I do—we do—we threaten confusion to the forces which are sent against us, sympathy of all the people with us, and the abolition of the licence laws."

"Who are *we*?" queried the official; "the handful of men who have put their names to this paper. Do you know I could put you three tattered rascals in prison for your threat—I have a great mind to do so—and that we have a force here ten times more than we want?"

This slight inaccuracy was doubtless excusable, but Huxter coolly replied,—

"If you'll come to this window and look at the 15,000 or 20,000 tents you see down the hillside and across the plain, you'll see the tents of men who are almost one and all determined to stop the licensing, and armed with pistols and other firearms into the bargain."

The sight was a somewhat startling one for the magistrate. The mob at the entrance to the police quarters had increased immensely in size, and was assuming a decidedly threatening aspect, the constabulary were turning out in force, and running down to support their comrades at the entrance, while the cries of the diggers came up the hill as the window was opened, and sounded clearly throughout the room—"Give 'em up, give 'em up," showing that their comrades thought that the three had, in putting their heads into the lion's mouth, been snapped up. Far away over the sunny plain, dotted usually with countless knots of one or two, was the ever-increasing crowd of diggers, whom the "deputashun" had just left, looking like a little army of sappers and miners at this distance. But the magistrate controlled his feelings, and replied,—

"Of those 15,000 or 20,000 diggers you boast, there are hundreds who have pledged their word to us, and who will help the Government, as all honest diggers should. But I do intend to bandy words with you; I arrest you all three for conspiracy and treason. Seize them, sergeant."

The order took all the occupants of the room by surprise; the sergeant looked extremely uncomfortable, and his subordinates eyed one another askance.

Huxter, recovering his senses, at once snatched at and crushed the round robin into his pocket, while Jake darted to the window, opened it, and shouted so that the mob at the foot could hear,—

"Mates, we are arrested for speaking the truth."

At these words, as though by one impulse, the threatening surges of the mob broke through the thin lines of the constabulary, notwithstanding the reinforcements these were receiving from the troops stationed hard by, and with hoarse cries the men charged up the hill towards the magistrate's house, waving revolvers and pistols, and brandishing sticks, picks, spades, knives, and all conceivable weapons as they came. The sergeant stepped forward and whispered a few words into the ear of the magistrate, who, pale with rage and mortification, stood unable to articulate for a minute or two. Then, by a great effort of self-control, he calmly gave the order—

"Let the rascals pass down."

"Rascals we are not," replied Huxter firmly, "though you have twice said it. We have asked you a civil question, and you have given us what you well educated people think a gentleman's answer, but which one of us would be ashamed to give a dog. As rascals we will not leave; so, before the mob attack the house, you'd better change the name."

In a harsh whisper, which whistled through his teeth, the officer replied, "Let the men go."

Only just in time did the three men regain the ground in front of the house, where Huxter prudently refused to give the men an account of what had passed within, and promised the pushing, surging mob that they should have a full history at the stockade. So thither they all marched, and from the hearty shouts and cheering and other expressions of emotion which came across in the evening air to the fort as the men marched away, the constabulary congratulated themselves that Huxter had been so discreet. Coates turned away, saddened at the thought of the inevitably foreshadowed contest, and booking three seats on the coach, returned to the camp.

In the meantime, Mary and Jack called upon Edith at the store, where they found matters rather disordered. The Ballarat Reform League, as the less scrupulous of the rioters called themselves, had commenced to issue notices to storekeepers to provide provisions and other articles to those of the members who chanced to require some, and poor Williams had come in for his full share of attention. He mournfully showed a number of dirty scraps of paper, upon which, in ill-written words, appeared such legends as, "Reseavd ov Muster Williams storkeeper Balaratt IV spades X shovels And terwenty picackses for Yours of balaratt Reform Leag," or again—"Bort of Williams Ballarat 4 pounds sugar, 2 sides bacon put down to League." Altogether they had to use their best endeavours to calm the poor man, who at one time inveighed against the rioters, at another against the police for allowing such steps, and again at Jeremiah for his continued absence. While they were at the door, one of the leaders of the mob, an Italian, entered, accompanied by three or four turbulent-looking rascals. He demanded, in broken English, some provisions and utensils for the use of the League, which Williams grumblingly gave him; but the man, growing insolent with success, challenged Jack as to his loyalty to the cause, and receiving no satisfactory answer, turned to his followers, remarking on the "cowdees of ze poltroon," which, fortunately for his own and Jack's safety, was not understood by the object of the insult. Turning to Mary, he cried out some coarse remark as to her beauty, which Jack overheard, and was for at once avenging on the miscreant's body, had not the girl herself stepped forward, and, with her usual calmness and dignity, reproved the man for his ignorance, and pitied him for his insolence to the diggers' queen.

"Diggars' queen," laughed he, in derision. "Yas, ze diggars hafe no queen in England, so zey git a queen here, Corpo di Baccho."

"Now then, you grinning jackanapes," called out Williams, "don't yer know 'nuff of the fields to know the queen of our hearts when yer boiled eyes catches sight on her?"

"So," said he, coming up close to her, "zes is ze diggars' queen; well let me tell, zat ze diggars don't go to care much soon for queen of zeir own choosing or ozers, an' I don't care whezer they do or no. Ze league is above ze diggars, and ze diggars are ze slaves."

With that he strutted out, followed by his companions, who appeared to think that he was a brave bird, and a cock after their own hearts, for his insolent speech. Jack tried to steal out, unobserved by Mary, as his fingers itched to thrash the fellow, but she was too quick for him, and prevented what might have been a catastrophe, for the diggers were of a time, as the Italian had said, literally slaves of their leaders' will.

Hastily arranging with Edith as to their departure on the morrow, in the arrangements for which the old storekeeper only too readily acquiesced, being somewhat anxious for his daughter in the troublous times, Mary and her companion returned to "the House," where they found the surveyor awaiting them with anxiety on his face. His sister, on hearing his story, was at once for stopping at the fields to nurse the wounded diggers and others, should there be occasion, but this was so evidently out of all reason, under the circumstances, that she was at last prevailed upon to carry out the original arrangement.

CHAPTER XII

BUSHRANGERS' MANNERISMS

ON the next morning, the day before the fateful 3rd of December, which was one of those delightful forenoons under Australia's blue skies, when the very air is champagne, existence in itself a paradise, Coates, his sister, and Jack, after an early breakfast, walked to the coach, calling for Mr. Williams and Edith *en route*. As they walked along they could see on the high road the stockade, which had assumed, under the hands of its laborious and numerous builders, definite shape, and now stood forth grim and bristling from the plain on the top of a knoll. But when they neared the main street another matter of excitement and surprise met their view in a small knot of men around the bank, whose doors at this unaccustomed hour were open, while a couple of constables were standing idly on the veranda. Inspector Cochrane came out of the bank as the passengers for the coach approached, and, singling out Coates, took him by the arm, while he told him under his breath, "Black Jack is loose again; there's some of his work in there," jerking his thumb towards the bank.

"What, bailed up?" asked Coates.

"Yes, and the manager and a clerk shot dead, and, what's worse for the force, the gang have rescued three of the prisoners who were sent for trial yesterday."

"Good God!" said Coates, "what is the meaning of it all?"

"Well, you see, the riots kept most of our men on the go yesterday, and so I suppose the guard wasn't so efficient as it might have been, besides there was a strong force patrolling down by the stockade to prevent a flank movement by the diggers."

"Where have they gone?" inquired Coates anxiously.

"Oh, clean away," replied the inspector.

Coates hurried on to join the others, concealing from them as best he could the bad news he had heard, but meeting the doctor at the coach-office took him into confidence.

The doctor, remembering his former experience, was for postponing Mary's journey for a time, but as Cochrane, who had joined them for a minute, gave it as his opinion that they would have gone up country, not down towards Melbourne, and that with the double obstacles of digger patrol and military reinforcements, the band would never venture along the high road, the two friends decided that the journey had better not be further postponed.

The coach was surrounded by the versatile Huxter and a select body of his friends, and the central "leader" was attracting a deal of attention from the onlookers; and well he might, for Huxter, determined, even amidst the turbulent and riotous atmosphere prevalent, to give the Queen of the Fields a fitting farewell, had during the night caused the horse to be shod with golden horseshoes, not mere gilt articles, but shoes of solid gold, as pure as was ever cradled out of paying gravel. The source from which he obtained the precious metal was the same as before—a public subscription—this time at the stockade, whence a few venturesome spirits had been prevailed upon to accompany him in the early morning to re-shoe the horse, and start the queen on her way with a huzza.

Mary, somewhat affected and much amused at this further instance of her rough "children's" goodwill, yet ignorant of the risk they ran, shakes hands gracefully with Huxter, Jake, and one or two others whose faces were familiar to her, passes through the some what embarrassing ordeal of saying good-bye to the doctor, with rising colour and downcast eyes, and mounts the coach, after laughingly imprinting a sisterly kiss on Jack's rough cheek, which, in anticipation, had been plentifully scrubbed that morning. Jack had, indeed, lost some sleep over the thought of a farewell greeting under the circumstances of Edith's possible jealousy. Edith is, however, this morning determined to be vexed at nothing, and, with a smile and glance of her eyes, collectively at the crowd and particularly at her betrothed lover, she waves adieux as the coach rolls off amid the huzzas of Huxter and company.

All is smiling and gay without, though various fears and anxieties fill the minds of almost all present, and to the knowledge of many, within a few yards lie the bodies of the bank clerk and manager—yesterday gay and full of that mysterious quality called "life."

Cochrane and the doctor walk back, the former to the barracks to report on the murder at the bank, the other to the hospital to make ready for the reception of the wounded patients, of whom he fears the riots will afford him only too many. Jack wanders listlessly to the claim, and commences but a poor day's work, feeling, indeed, most solitary, and right glad to accept the doctor's invitation to sup at the hospital. The affairs at the stockade are *in statu quo*, no sign having been made by one side or the other as to their intentions during the night.

I must, to keep the reader *au courant* with the details of the story, make a short tack against the wind, so as to fetch up the rest of the threads to date.

My excuse, if any readers deem me to require one, in introducing such horrors as were perpetrated under the light of the everlasting stars that night, must be that I am writing of gold-field life as it was in the early days, not as it is now, or, I hope, can ever be again.

Gentleman Jim and his gang had been somewhat disconcerted at the loss of three of their number in Ben and the other prisoners; but, nothing daunted, and much to the delight of the rest of his followers, who felt an *esprit de corps* worthy of a much better cause, their leader had determined to rescue Ben and his one associate, leaving Saltner to his fate. This he decided to do after the attack at the bank; and, having obtained, by the simple process of "eyeing," the necessary horses, and sent them, under the escort of one of his band, to a rendezvous near the police camp, within the fringe of the scrub, at midnight he and six others set off for the bank.

Their path, however, was not a bee-line, their leader deviating, with malicious intent, to the shaft where the luckless Miah had been lowered some five days before, and which, with some trouble, his two followers re-discovered. The occasional groans of the suffering man sounded dismal and ghostly in the stillness of the night; he had managed, after great exertion, to force the gag from his lips and the corks from his mouth, being somewhat assisted by his shrunken frame, the result of five days' starvation; but when he had done this he discovered that his trouble was lost, as his weakness did not permit of his using his voice above a hoarse whisper or a groan. So the lucky star which followed Gentleman Jim in most of his undertakings had not proved a false jade; even any stray digger who might occasionally stroll that way had not been apprised of Miah's predicament. I grieve to say that, under these circumstances, his scriptural texts stood him in little stead; it is not unusual for the self-constituted comforter of others to find for himself but empty consolation in "vacant chaff," whether or not "well meant for grain." Hence his thoughts—for being unable to speak he had become, in the words of the middle-country schoolmaster, "a oner to think"—were of a most lugubrious nature—hopeless, but unresigned. So when he heard the steps of Jim and his gang up above, his hopes can be more easily imagined than described, and low groans and hoarse guttural sounds in plenty issued out of the pit. The first words of the leader struck a cold chill through his frame, for he knew that his lot was as hopeless as before, if not worse.

"Hallo, Mr Spy, how d'ye get on down there?" cried the leader, with his usual cowardly cruelty. As only a slight groan answered, which showed that the man recognized his jailer, the other laughingly continued,—"We couldn't go, you know, without wishing you good-bye, and a comfortable ending, for we do love you so. No doubt you're in a jolly hurry to get up above howsomever, so I won't detain you. Lor', what a fine angel you'll make, won't you, light and airy, I s'pose, down there so long without vittals or drink. Well, I can't wait, except just to say that we're going to carry out that notion you heard us talk about, and, what's more, going to run away with two of the handsomest gals on the field. The diggers' queen—a slap-up gal she is, too, though she did once rescue her party, and gave me scare—and who d'ye think the other is? Can't guess, eh? Lor', I s'pose not. What d'ye say to Edith Williams? Ha! ha! ha! what a fine game, I say! Ta, ta! won't you wish me good luck? What a fool you are to stop down there when there's another fellow going to run off with your mistress! Can't think what you kin be about. Wal, here's good luck to you, an' if you go to the hot place by mistake, don't forget to take a berth for me. Ha! ha! ha!"

The ribald mirth of the rascal died away on the evening air, as he joined his comrades who had walked slowly on, while the wretched Jeremiah considered the terrible message thus brought him. His affection for Edith was strongly alloyed with jealousy, and all the keener for that reason did he feel the sword which was thus, Damocles-like, hanging over her head. To be abducted, perhaps with her own consent, by the man of all others whose attention to Edith he had during calmer moments feared, and whose cunning had thus outwitted him! Such thoughts inspired in him new life and for some time his voice acquired new strength and his shouts resounded in the pit, but unlucky wight that he was, no other foot stirred near him that night, and towards morning his voice and spirits failed, and intermittent groans alone disturbed the silence of the place.

Meanwhile the rascals approached the bank. Now the manager had permitted a young boy-clerk to sleep under the long counter that ran across the principal room, being, in fact, rather glad to relieve his sense of loneliness even by this little lad's presence, and the old servant-housekeeper had, according to custom, at sundown left the manager and the boy-clerk in the bank. Saltner had during his clerkship not only obtained the keys of the safes, but had managed unobserved to draw the screws from the iron bars which protected the little square pane in the kitchen, and the entrance to this room was gained in ease and in silence. The door leading into the bank itself checked them for a time, but by the skill of an "old hand" or convict the lock was soon picked, and the party gained admittance to the chief room. The order had been passed round that everything must be managed as quietly as possible to prevent disturbance by neighbours, and that any resistance must be met with a "quieting," a term significant and pregnant with meaning, as in addition to pistols the whole party were armed with knives ground into double blades.

The poor little lad had been dreaming that night, as he lay under the counter, of the fair home he had left at Wollongong, with its lowing cattle, its lush verdure, and its pleasant land and sea-scapes, and as he dreamt the tinkle of the cow-bell sounded louder and louder, so that he started from his sleep, to find himself opposed to the blackened face of Gentleman Jim, who had been the first to follow the old hand into the room. Startled at the sight, the poor lad uttered one cry and one only, for the cowardly hand of the leader fell upon his throat and choked all utterance and life. Even the members of his crew looked askance at one another at the cowardly deed, but necessity knows no laws, and having embarked upon this enterprise they could not hold or turn back. No more gentle gleams and sunny thoughts could fly through the poor little curly head which lay there, the face blue with suffocation, the limbs quivering with galvanic and muscular twitchings. But it was a time for action. The manager had heard the cry and had called out to know the reason from his bedroom; hastily getting up and striking a light as he did so. Out went their dark lantern. Down crouched the rascals behind the wooden part of the partition, just as the manager came out of his room with a lighted dip in his hand. He must have noticed something strange about the bank, either the open door of the kitchen or the head of some partly concealed member of the gang, for he turned round apparently to arm himself with his revolver; but before he had taken a stride, the watchful eye of Jim, fixed to a crevice in the partition, had noticed the act. Jumping to his feet and firing right through the glass which surmounted the wooden wainscot was the work of a moment, and as the man stumbled and fell right upon his lamp, the whole gang jumped up, broke the glass panel and were upon him. But *his* "quieting" was a *fait accompli*, so extinguishing the flames which the rolling candle had ignited, Jim turned about to the gang, not giving them time for reflection, handed them the keys of the safes, which he bade them open, and searched within the manager's room to see if there was anything of value there to lay his hands upon. But he was totally unsuccessful, though he overturned clothes and books, ransacked bedding and boxes, and finally searched the dead man himself. No keys or anything else of value could be found, so that it was fortunate he had planned the manufacture of the keys, otherwise they would have perhaps had their trouble for nothing. In the meanwhile the other miscreants had ransacked the safes, and placed in the bags and other receptacles they carried with them, the valuable contents, which were fortunately for them largely in bank-notes, though dust and nuggets formed a welcome and substantial addition to the booty. No neighbours appeared to have heard the disturbance, or if they had they paid no attention to it, a matter which was not cause for much surprise in such troublous times; so the gang got away without any opposition, and climbed the path to the police-camp, approaching it from the side nearest their horses, and furthest away from the infantry encampment. As they climbed they noticed many lights in front of the camp, and in the stillness of the night a few dropping shots were fired, which called for the attention of the watch to that quarter, a course even yet more favourable to their scheme. Up at the rear of the camp there appeared to be no guard, so Jim approached the snake fence which surrounded it there, and gave a short dingo-howl, the preconcerted signal between himself and one of the force recently enlisted, an old convict who had agreed to assist the gang on sharing their booty from the bank.

"Have you got the rhino?" whispered the man, approaching.

"Safe and sound on our saddles, and an extra quantity on a horse for you," replied Jim.

"This way then, you and three others had better come. I made friends with the turnkey of the prisoners' cells, and know where your friends are."

This was a part of the scheme Jim had not bargained for, that is, his active participation in the rescue, and though he could not back out under the circumstances, as he gave the order to three to accompany him, his knees knocked together and his teeth chattered as he said, "with the cold," though the warm summer night gave him the lie direct.

A few yards off stood the prisoners' cells, in a long stone building, at either end of which was a sentry, who patrolled half the building and then round the side. The five crept up under the building and separated, two to one end, three to the other, where each waited until the sentries had turned the corner from the front and were no longer visible to one another. Then each party pounced upon, gagged, and bound the sentries, it having been agreed with the constable that this more moderate though lengthier course should be adopted than the more expeditious one of quieting advocated by Gentleman Jim, who rarely stuck at such trifles, and held the lives of others very cheaply. The constable, with Jim, then approached the main door of the building, which was locked and bolted from within, guarded by one constable by way of turnkey. In all respects the riots helped the objects of the gang, and the result showed with what accurate judgment and foresight Jim had calculated, for the usual number of warders was three, often more, but the disturbances had withdrawn the members of the watch, and their places had not been supplied by others.

A knock by the constable and the password whispered to the turnkey gained him the opening of the door; and while he stood parleying for a moment with the other, the two fell upon the warder and gagged and bound him also. All this was so quietly done that Gentleman Jim took quite a pride in observing that it would not have disturbed a weasel close by. The keys hanging from the turnkey's girdle were fitted to the proper locks, and Ben and his colleague disturbed from sleep and assured of rescue. Dazed as they were, and unable to believe their senses, they had left the building before the fresh air had restored their wits, and with one accord they asked what had been done with Saltner.

"Left him behind, of course," said Jim. "We don't want such a sneak as that with us, for all that he helped us to bail the gold."

Though the mention of gold distracted the other's thoughts, Ben was not satisfied. His nature was now, as ever, revengeful, and though he had so far escaped, he was not content to leave Saltner to his fate. He refused to go any further until they had got Saltner with them, and so Jim was forced to give way, and fretting at the delay, for it was now nearly two o'clock, turned back with Ben and the constable, first, however, making Ben promise to do and say nothing to the wretched informer at or near the camp. So Saltner was also surprised in his cell, gagged to prevent the cries with which he would evidently have disturbed the neighbourhood, and was hurriedly walked off amongst the gang to their rendezvous, more dead than alive with fear. Mounting their horses, Ben taking care to tie Saltner on to his own in front of him, and for that purpose distributing his gold among the others, the gang rode off and disappeared towards Sandhurst, as indeed Cochrane afterwards surmised, nor did they draw rein until they had ridden twenty miles in a north-easterly direction, guided by the unerring instinct of an ex-shepherd, one of their gang. There they paused for a while at dawn while they ate a scanty meal out of the saddle-bags, which they might just then have wished fuller of a more digestible and comestible article than gold and bank-notes. The horses were hobbled and tied together to rest, their heaving flanks and distended nostrils showing too well the rough task they had accomplished. Then they held a council of war, in which the voice of Gentleman Jim was, as usual, the loudest and longest.

"The peelers will follow us up in this direction, boys, for a surety, and I'm for doubling back towards Melbourne, turning right round to the south of Ballarat along the sea-coast, and so into South Australia. What say you?"

"Why not turn back into Ballarat itself and help in the Eureka Stockade? We should never be found then," cried one of the others.

But this did not suit the book of two of their party, their leader and the constable, the former because he did not relish the task of fighting in such a determined, fair, open fashion, and foresaw the inevitable termination of the disturbance, and more than ever because he "had business" on the Melbourne road; the constable, because he feared to be recognized, tried by court-martial and shot, though he had taken care not to be imbured in any murder.

So the counsels of Jim prevailed, and right glad was he that it was so; only the day before he had heard that the "queen of the field" was going to start by the morning coach, and giving up all thought of Edith, he had determined to utilize the gang for the purpose of sticking up the coach and thus securing the treasures, human and otherwise, it might contain.

But here Ben broke upon the silence with an unaccustomed hoarseness of voice.

"Feller comrades," said he, with a lowering grin, "there's one here you haven't decided what to do with. Say what's to be done to a comrade who turns sneak."

The others are silent; they know what is coming, and the constable instinctively walks away and disappears into the forest. The gang smile at his scruples and tell Ben to "go on."

"I see one of us is afeared to think of what is to be done to a sneak, and don't like to see it."

Saltner has all this while been helpless and numbed with fear, and turns his eyes in supplication to the great giant who stands above him. But look not for pity to the revengeful, soured brute, poor wretch, nor to the leader or his crew, who gaze on curiously, as though awaiting the answer to a conundrum.

Roughly snatching the bandage from the unfortunate man's mouth, the burly giant asked him,—

"What have you got to say for yerself why judgment shouldn't be passed, as the beaks say?"

The terrified Saltner turned away to the rest of the gang, beseeching them in the most abject terms for life, and reminding them of the risks he had himself run for them to get the keys whereby they had robbed the bank, and assuring them how only under stress of great pressure (this was untrue) he had turned Queen's evidence.

Ben roughly interrupted,—

"What did I say," said he, turning to his other late fellow-prisoner, "that I'd do to him if he peached?"

"Break his back," replied the other, with a grunt.

"Did any of you ever know me fail to keep a promise?"

Silence reigned, broken only by the terrified exclamation of the helpless ex-clerk as the other held him across his knee as you or I do a twig.

Then was enacted such a horrible deed as the tongue and pen refuse to relate; such as even the lawless, hardened crew paled at, but which, without a pause or symptom of hesitation, the giant-like brute perpetrated.

The shrieks of the dying man echoed through the forest, and by a strange antithesis were re-echoed by the chattering of the jay, the screaming of the cockatoo, and the whistling of countless birds.

When all was quiet again, Jim, with a shudder at the form which lay distorted and quivering at the foot of the great gum, where they had halted, gave the signal to mount at once and leave the unhallowed spot, an order which was obeyed with alacrity by the other members of that grim gang, whose faces, in the morning sun, looked grey and ghastly with the traces of lamp-black which were still visible. Cooeing to the absent constable brought him soon to the path of the gang, where, in silence, he mounted the horse which had been led for him, starting and trembling in every nerve, for he guessed only too well what had been enacted since he left the sunny glade a few minutes ago. All but Gentleman Jim gave the giant a wide berth, a fact which the latter noticed, and which evoked an occasional burst of harsh laughter from his lips. The horses were rested, and the gang trotted along briskly, though the unwonted exertions of the leader soon told upon a frame somewhat enfeebled by long illness. He was, accordingly, glad to come out upon the coach-road, which he knew so well, at a point a few miles westward of the house kept by old Ned Manning, whither even then the coach was fast rolling. Riding down at a smart trot they espied the valiant old soldier at the bottom of the hill seated outside the veranda, apparently waiting for the coach, as fresh horses were patiently standing hard by, lazily flicking or biting at the impertinent though numerous flies which disturbed their repose.

CHAPTER XIII

A COACH IN BAIL

NO sooner did old Manning observe the band at the top of the hill than, fearing the worst, he caught the horses by their bridles and began to draw them towards the stables, then seeing that he would be too late after all, as the opposing band quickened their pace, he disappeared within, soon to reappear with his shot-gun and rifle; the latter he coolly placed between his knees, while he examined the loading of the other weapon, and congratulated himself that his daughter had left the day before to visit a friend in Melbourne. The coolness of the old man so impressed the bushrangers, for to this lawless pursuit they were now pledged, notwithstanding the remonstances of the half-hearted ex-constable, that they halted, and debating as to their mode of procedure, finally separated into two groups, the one disappearing into the bush by the side of the road, the other coming on slowly until the first had made its appointed circuit, and was advancing from the rear of the dwelling. The brave old soldier saw the plan, and without waiting for its inevitable result, knelt calmly down on the veranda as though aiming at kangaroos, fired at the oncoming band, and at his first shot brought down the horse of the ex-constable.

Repeating rifles, unfortunately for the brave old soldier, did not then exist, otherwise he might have held his position against the lot, for the man's coolness in the face of danger struck into their hearts a feeling akin to superstition. But, as it was, immediately he fired the band approached at a smart trot, Gentleman Jim alone bringing up the rear, and guarding the ex-constable, who showed unmistakable signs of having had enough of butchery, so that by the time the old man had reloaded, the gang were within a hundred yards of the hut, and carrying such impetus that each moment varied the chances.

Three revolvers flashed almost simultaneously as the duller firing of the rifle again rang out, and though the old man was sore hit, his pluck was unimpaired and the fall of one of the riders, Ben's colleague, told its own tale. Quickly seizing the shot-gun the old fellow aimed at the giant Ben himself, landing the contents of one barrel in the bushranger's face, and causing him to shout with the exquisite pain he suffered, while a dozen gouts of blood told how surely, in his own wounded state, the old soldier had marked his man. The horse of the wounded bushranger had started, himself cut by one or two stray shots, and was thundering back along the road up the hill, rushing as though for dear life, an example which the other two horses, one of whom was riderless, were not slow to follow, the riderless horse dragging along at the stirrup the fallen bushranger, and in his mad gallop crashing his late rider against log and stone, mud and tree-stump, impartially.

Even then, perhaps, the old man might have held his own until the coach arrived, had not the out-flanking body of three bushrangers dismounted and crept round the house, until coming to the side and marking their man unobserved, they discharged their weapons at such close quarters that his fate was sealed, and he who had with bravery and unscathed fought the campaign of Waterloo, and obtained the name among his Maori enemies of Pakeha Maia or, "The Brave One," was done to death, such was the irony of fate, by the ambushed treacherous hands of unworthy and murderous foes.

Gentleman Jim, after some pain, succeeded in stopping the riderless horse, while Ben and the other horseman managed to pull up their steeds in their headlong career, which indeed, as the career led them up a steep hill, the horses themselves were not sorry to stay. Ben's colleague would never trouble magistrate, judge, or hangman more, and with his usual affectation of *sang-froid* where others were concerned, the leader ordered the unwounded member of his portion of the gang to throw the body into the bush by the side of the road, and to follow him as fast as possible down the hill-side. The ex-constable had by this time mounted the dead man's horse, his own had staggered to its feet and wandered into the bush where it received its quietus from the leader, not from a merciful motive, as may be guessed, but from the policy of not allowing any disorder to manifest itself to the travellers of the on-coming coach, which was almost due. In this he succeeded, for a rough bush-road tells few tales of the evil deeds even lately enacted, and though the veranda was more obstinate, an old opossum rug and bed-linen judiciously flung over the boards concealed the damning spot from view.

The old soldier himself was thrown into the back room, while the bushrangers' horses were led to the stable, five being unsaddled and unharnessed. The five coach-horses for the fresh change had started off at the commencement of the attack, and were then in the bush; but their trailing harness hampered their movements, and they were soon brought back, just in time, in fact, to take their place at the veranda, and resume their passive resistance to the flies which again pestered them. All the bush-rangers, including the ex-constable, retreated out of sight into the house as the coach appeared through the trees at the top of the hill, and commenced its jolting, rumbling, heavy course downwards. Gentleman Jim had a few words with his new recruit, and taking the opinion of the other members of the gang, except Ben, who was too furious with pain to be consulted, intimated to the ex-constable that he must make up his mind to go through with them or—a significant handling of his knife spoke more than the general run of "ors" do, and decided the hapless man that a downward course cannot be stopped at pleasure.

It was now about midday and steaming hot to boot, and the occupants of the coach were all drowsily nodding their heads, and permitting themselves to be swayed from side to side in unison with the oscillation of the coach, lazily watching now the ascending clouds of vapour and dust, now a bright snake basking on the wayside and hastening away at the approach of man, now a wondering kangaroo who would skip out of the way with a few giant leaps, to watch in turn the curious unwieldy animal which moved so slowly and laboriously. The horses, though wet with their exertions, evidently knew that their journey would, for a time at least, end in rest, and that in the near future. They commenced at a sharp trot to descend the silent hill, between the gaunt rows of gums, whose scimitar-like grey-green leaves blistered in the heat, and, unmoved by breeze of any kind, afforded no shade to the coach or the hard-baked ground beneath them.

Of course, no suspicions were aroused of the real state of matters at Manning's hut, the driver indeed remarking that he supposed "Ned's gal hadn't gone to Melbourne, as she had said, but was having a washin' day, which was good for the leddies, as they could get a cup of tay or cawfy."

So the coach drew up at the door, and the driver patiently waited for Ned to come out and take the reins, and after shouting aloud, without, of course, obtaining any response, "supposed the old man was asleep," and handing the reins to Coates, clambered down, and went within to wake him up. Immediately he got into the comparatively darkened room, and before his eyes could become accustomed to the objects within, half a dozen hands had seized and gagged him, the bushrangers grinning at the success of their leader's plan. As the driver did not come out, one after the other of the men adjourned within, until Coates, his sister beside him, Edith, and one other inside, alone remained on the coach; the bushrangers' plan having, indeed, been successfully carried out, with one or two variations, with the other five passengers, who now lay within the hut gagged, disarmed, and overawed by the levelled revolvers of two of the gang, while two others were, to keep their hands in, busily searching their captives' pockets.

Though the gang were, doubtless, strong enough to have "bailed up" the coach, Jim had cautiously planned this method of attack, wishing to avoid bloodshed, in which the two girls might be concerned, as well as his own men. Spying through a crack the condition of the coach, he now, with another, walked boldly without, and demanded the surrender of the remaining passengers. Coates, with his hands engaged with the reins, and completely taken by surprise, could offer no resistance, for though instinctively his hand felt at his belt, before he could display his weapon the second bushranger had climbed the coach from the other side and thrown himself upon him. Even then he might have given some account of himself; but Mary was between him and the levelled pistol of the leader of the gang, and in the instant or two he had for thought, he feared to endanger her life, little reckoning of the worse fate he thus reserved for her.

The passenger within was unfortunately unarmed, and at this moment Ben, with his scarred and horribly disfigured face, came out upon the veranda, at sight of whom Coates was disconcerted, and in the twinkling of an eye disarmed; Mary turned pale and sick, and Edith fainted away. The man was truly an awful sight, while the passion of one eye—the other was torn and blinded—born of his morning's crime, and increased by his excruciating pain, betokened little mercy to all who might come in his way.

Having achieved his object, Jim caused the occupant to leave the coach, Coates and the other male passenger being at once pinioned and stationed with the rest, who were now brought out in a line, and placed in front of the house, while Edith was, through Mary's assiduous care, soon brought round, and lay, all her courage evaporated, clinging to the other frailer, gentler woman, upon the boards of the veranda. Ordering a couple of his men to keep their pistols fixed on the line of helpless passengers, and particularly on Coates, whose imperious air, never so imperious as when chafing at restriction of any sort, boded evil to his captors, and ordering others to saddle the fresh coach-horses, Gentleman Jim turned to the two girls and expressed his satisfaction at their good looks, thanking them for thus keeping their appointment with him, and promising them a happy future.

He could not, when thus talking, look directly at Mary, for even his impudent stare fell before the cool steady gaze of the poor horror-stricken girl, who thus found herself face to face with the man who had won her regard and almost secured her affection, a man whose hands were, if not to her knowledge, actually dyed with blood, yet who was ready, as she could see, to take the lives of others with impunity; as it were in a dream, she saw enacted that other scene with the bushrangers, and curiously noted how like in size, figure, and speech, the leader of that and the present gang seemed. The gang had, in the meantime, saddled the horses, and some in their plundering had come across the cupboard where the old soldier had kept his supply of spirits, which, of course, they were not slow in tasting and approving.

Hitherto the men had given the girls a wide berth, being, in fact, more concerned in taking life and plunder than aught else; but now, released from their more immediate *necessities*, they whispered together, and one approached Jim, who was standing rather sheepishly in the veranda, unable to make any good impression on either of the girls, and so fain to watch in silence Mary's gentle care for her companion.

It was a rough Irishman who was selected as spokesman.

"Captain, darlint, me mates and meself hey jest made up our minds that we ought to share some of the plunder of the coach, and as we've all got our share of the gold and other valybles, it's only fair we ought ter hev a share in the gals, an' as ye've bossed the concarn, an' very claverly, too, ye're to hey fust choice and the bhoys next."

The objects of these choice remarks heard the words only too distinctly. Mary, whose fears were now apparently soon to be realized, bent down to hide the deathly pallor of her face, while Edith clinging tightly to her friend, cried out, "Oh, save me from the wretches, save me! save me!" and then burst into a fit of weeping. Coates, unobserved by the members of the gang, who were interested in the events at the house, commenced, with the aid of one of the passengers, to slip the pinions from his elbows, a task rendered the easier by his having in his wrath swelled all his muscles and fibres to their utmost, and thus unconsciously practised the Davenport Brothers' trick.

The leader of the gang was now in a dilemma. Forced upon him by extraneous and extraordinary circumstances was the choice between the handsome, robust, petulant Edith, and the paler, sweeter Mary, and though comparisons are proverbially odious, it is fair to say that never was distracted *lover* in a worse predicament. Though he cared little about wounding the feelings of another, even *his* impudence was not proof against the thought of the feelings of the unchosen maiden abandoned, so to speak, to the ravening wolves, and he could not forget that he had toyed with the feelings of both apparently as an ardent admirer not long since. Had he then been able to gaze into Mary's mind he would have been surprised to find that she thought either fate equally horrible, to be saved or abandoned by the choice of the ruffian.

Edith, on the other hand, still ready to trust with child-like confidence the man who had once professed so much regard for her, while remembering with regret the absence of her plighted lover, only viewed the alternative of abandonment as abhorrent. But the spokesman was waiting.

"Well, mates," replied the leader, wishing to gain time for thought, "fair is fair, but I should have thought you would have been satisfied with your share of the gold, and leave the girls to me. I don't want any of the gold."

"What, Captain dear, ye can't commit bigamy, why"—this with a leer, which made the rascal's face look ape-like—"ye wouldn't go for to do anything agen the laws of the land. Fact is, Captain, we've made up our minds, and when ye've chosen, we're going to draw lots for the other gal for a wife. Ye see we're all quite respectable gents now, with about 800*l.* a piece to commence bisiness on."

Coates had by this time loosened one of his own arms, and was engaged upon the arm of his neighbour, who was a more difficult subject to tackle; he allowed the arm with the cord around it still to show prominently, to avoid attracting attention should any one look their way. Mary, who had exchanged quick glances with him, saw what he was doing, and to assist in diverting the attention of the bushrangers, nerved herself to the task, and stood forth, saying, with flashing eyes,—

"Before you discuss our fates any longer, just listen what *we* intend to do. I have here a revolver," drawing forth the weapon as she spoke, and making the rascals near her end of the veranda start with dismay, "and before we will let a man put his hand upon us, we will shoot ourselves."

As she said this, to show that the weapon was loaded, she discharged it at the coach, where the bullet struck a clean hole in the leather flap, and went careering away into the bush.

These words were uttered with such evident determination that the men and their leader were somewhat taken aback, and their utterance might have saved the girls, had not Edith imprudently discounted them.

"Yes, I'll shoot myself if any of you *men* dare to lay a hand on me," said she excitedly, and so evidently emphasizing the men, as distinguished from their leader, that Gentleman Jim took heart and said,—

"Well, boys, I think I'll choose Mr. Williams' daughter, and must leave you to settle who's to have the other."

Mary, thankful that his choice had at least not degraded her, smiled nervously, and thereby looked so graceful and sweet that the rascal had no sooner said his say than he regretted it.

Ben interposed at this juncture.

"Now look here, you fellers, just you drop these wimmen and make a clean pair of heels. I'm not going to chance being cotched by the beaks, if you are; besides, I want to get these darned shot out of my cheeks."

Mary, though dreading the man, yet, with her charitable instincts full upon her, at once offered to dress his face, hoping thus to gain precious time.

The ruffian, having at first surlily and curtly refused the offer, finally fetched a pail of water and submitted to her deft and careful bandaging, during which Jim, who was himself getting uneasy, had the horses brought up and himself examined their girths. As soon as the giant was duly bandaged he kicked the pail over the veranda, and, without a word of thanks, selected and mounted a horse, while the other rascals drew lots, as arranged, for the prize thus left to them by their leader, whom they praised for his "cuteness in pickin' out the handsome one."

Gentleman Jim approached the mounted bush-ranger, and whispering asked him to take Mary before him on his horse, which the other refused point blank to do, saying out loud with an oath that "the gal had fixed things for him, and she should go free."

The leader turned pale with anger, and, being still too weak to accomplish the task himself, singled out the ex-constable, to whom he entrusted the delicate task, and bidding another of the gang mount, ordered Edith to mount in front of him. But Edith, fast repenting her rash words, had again clung close to Mary, who still stood pale and resolute at the end of the veranda, her weapon in hand, though somewhat hampered by her companion's action.

Gentleman Jim, noticing this, rushed forward towards the two girls, hoping to take them by surprise, and motioned the ex-constable to do the same. Two reports and flashes, accompanied as by lightning by the fall of the leader, shot in the thigh, and a whistling bullet close to the head of the ex-constable, stopped at one and the same moment Mary from carrying out her threat in her dire extremity and the concerted action of the two worthies, while a shout from Ben, "Look up the hill! To horse, to horse!" announced that succour was at hand.

CHAPTER XIV

RESCUE

THE shots were those of Coates and his neighbour, who had completely loosed their bonds unobserved, and, at the instant when the attention of all was again drawn to the veranda, had sprung upon, pulled down, and disarmed two of the gang nearest them, and had thus changed the course of events. Partial success had followed the surveyor's shot, but his neighbour, nervous and unaccustomed to the revolver's kick, had fired too high. Ben's shout caused all who could to glance up the hill, where a horseman was observed rushing down at break-neck speed towards them. In the time that I am writing these words he had approached, and roaring out, "Rescue, rescue!" pulled himself up, firing at the leading bush-ranger as he spoke. His horse, its chest flecked with foam, nostrils bleeding, and its flanks heaving and distressed, stopped for an instant like a horse of marble, then crashed down, exhausted by the violence of its own exertions.

Fortune favoured the good doctor—for it was he—as usual, for a couple of bullets whizzing overhead as he fell with his steed would, but for this accident, have severely, if not fatally, wounded him. The *mêlée* now became general, the surveyor shouting to his friend, while engaged himself in aiming at the stricken Jim, who, to his horror, had rolled over and was preparing to shoot at the hapless girls, evidently determined, with devil-like consistency, that none but himself should "deserve the fair."

The odds were, of course, entirely in favour of the bushrangers, who were even now, including the ex-constable, six unwounded men. Their leader, it is true, was disabled, and the doctor's shot had hit one of the sentries of the passengers in the back, passing, in the doctor's excitement, unpleasantly close to the passengers themselves. But at this moment a loud cry up the hill caused the bushrangers to look hurriedly up to ascertain the cause, who, to their dismay, found the rescuing party were at hand. Ben had wheeled his horse towards the veranda and bade his leader roll towards him, but even through the other's agony and weakness ran his devilish intent, and, notwithstanding his wounded thigh, he had almost worked himself about for the purpose of firing when Ben, seeing that he would not come, sprang off his horse, notwithstanding the oaths and curses of the other, picked him up in his arms, and, knocking down with his bare weight the doctor, who had by this time rushed up and was about to prevent their escape, mounted his strong steed and disappeared in the thick scrub with his burden, whither three of the gang had already forced their way on horseback. Just then the rescuing party, headed by Jack Wainwright and Huxter, rode up, their horses almost as distressed and spent as the doctor's.

To find out how these good folk happened thus to arrive in the nick of time, I must go back a few hours in my narrative. Jack, who had been, as I have recorded, disinclined for work, and also somewhat distracted by the attitude of the diggers, had, when he left the doctor, gone for a stroll away up the plain towards the Canadian Gully. As chance would have it, he happened to pass along some spent claims and disused shafts, and, on examining them to see if there were any chances of success for him where others had failed, was surprised to hear a groan close by. Fancying that he must be deceived, he proceeded on his walk, but in a few moments more distinctly heard the groan proceeding from a shaft he was then approaching. Somewhat startled, he knelt down by the side of the shaft and there discovered the emaciated extended form of poor Jeremiah, starved and hollow-cheeked far beyond all recognition, seeming for all the world, as Jack afterwards said, like "death's head on a monument."

"How did you fall down there?" cried he, but no answer came except a groan, and he noticed, as his eyes became accustomed to the shade of the shaft, that the sunken, glazed eyes of the apparently dying man seemed to be trying to explain what his black, swollen dry lips and parched leathern tongue failed to do. To run to the nearest tent and return with a rope, a few stakes, and two sympathetic diggers he found there, was but the work of a quarter of an hour for Jack, though on his return he noticed that the man had ceased groaning and was staring fixedly upwards. Fixing a stake deep into the ground, the diggers lowered Jack into the shaft, and after some trouble succeeded in pulling up the insensible man with the rope fastened under his arm-pits. Then Jack was quickly pulled up himself, and while the two men carefully carried the emaciated form to their tent, he ran off and fetched the doctor to his new patient.

After applying the usual remedies, the doctor succeeded in restoring the suspended animation of the famished fellow, and by dint of gentle stimulative feeding every few minutes, managed to bring him back to consciousness and attempted articulation. His poor parched lips and tongue, moistened by the spirit, moved uneasily as though attempting speech, but no sound came forth until, what with the hot blankets and bricks which were constantly renewed, and the frequent doses of spirit, about nine in the morning; his whisperings gained definite shape. The doctor on one side of the couch, and Jack on the other, knelt down and heard, low but distinctly, the words, "Williams's—daughter—Queen-fields—bushrangers—bail up coach—break—bank before."

A long interval separated each word, so long that after he had finished they waited in breathless silence, thinking that more was coming; but as he became exhausted and closed his eyes, they waited in vain, looked up at one another, and started each to see the other's changed expression. Each guessed to the full extent the meaning of those disjointed words for the other almost more than for himself, and grasped the other's hand in sympathy over the form of the dying' man, whose flicker of life was fast telling on his emaciated form.

Leaving instructions with the sympathetic diggers what to do until he sent a nurse to alleviate the poor fellow's dying moments, the doctor went without into the sunshine, followed by Jack; but what a change in the sunshine, what a change in Jack, what a change in everything. The horror of the moment paralyzed the quick tact and ready brain of the doctor for a brief moment, then turning to his companion he said, through set teeth,—

"Old friend, the police can do nothing for us. They sent off as many as they could spare after the bush-rangers on a different track this morning: we must trust to our friends. Get Jake and Huxter, and whatever others you can find; I will go up and get horses and weapons and meet you on the Melbourne Road, at the one-tree hill, in half an hour at the most—every minute is precious."

Jack set off to the Eureka stockade, rightly guessing that he would most likely find his friend Jake and the others there, who, when he had shortly imparted his news, without being asked, at once volunteered to save "the queen" from her distress at the risk of their own lives, for being now known to be connected with the riotous diggers, for them to approach the camp or the high road was a dangerous adventure. It was a great sacrifice on the part of Huxter, as he had quite made up his mind to take a leading part in the ensuing action which he saw must be impending in the near future, but without a sign of the struggle which went on within him, he passed out with five others (getting the consent of the Commander-in-chief for that purpose), and with Jack strode hastily towards the one-tree hill. The doctor had been put to his wits' end to get the necessary horses, though Inspector Cochrane had at once lent him his own spare steed, a fresh, brisk little mare with plenty of go in her, that had been lately eating her head off on Government oats. But by dint of much persuading and bargaining he had got together as many as ten horses, which were soon cantering after him along the high road in the charge of two or three self-appointed ostlers. After seating and arming the whole of Jack's party, and taking two of the ostlers, who were only too ready "for the spree" which they anticipated, the doctor sent back the surplus horses and started at a smart trot to follow the coach, keeping well together, until one or two of the horses showed signs of fatigue. Then the doctor, who had taken the lead from the beginning, chose the fleetest horsemen out of the party, to the number of four, and with them pushed on, letting the others come on as quickly as they could.

When within a mile and a half of Manning's house, the report of Mary's revolver struck upon the ears of the advanced guard, and though they would have been more reassured had they known its origin, their suspicions and fears grew so that the doctor set spurs to his gallant little mare, followed by the rest of the party, who did their best to keep pace with him, but soon tailed off out of sight. He thundered along the road, round bend, down slope, across gully, ever on and on towards the hill at the foot of which he knew he could see—what? Jack, heavier of build, and not so well mounted, could not keep up with him, but shouting out "good luck, and that they would be close on his track," saw him pass round the corners and bends of the road in such hot haste that he feared the swerves and jerks might unseat him. But for the doctor there was no fear of unseating; never until lately had he felt the love he had for the girl who perhaps lay at the mercy of murderous brutes, never until this moment of doubt and expectancy had he realized his awful sense of helplessness towards one with whom moments were like ages. Right

gallantly did the tough little mare do her duty until, as we have seen, she
breasted the hill and commenced rattling down; once she had faltered and
well nigh fallen, but at a word of encouragement and the vigorous and
strong handling of the reins by her rider, she had pulled herself together,
and with a fresh inspiration, worthy of "Black Bess," had leapt from crack
to crack, rut to rut, carefully avoiding the slippery stumbling-blocks and
tree stumps in her way, until spent and fainting she had brought her rider
to his goal. Jack and the others pressed their horses hard after their leader
in order to lend him their ready support, being assisted thereto by the
firing which Coates had started as the doctor rode up, and they arrived
in time, as we have seen, to scare away the bushrangers from their prey of
a few minutes before.

The doctor, whom we left half stunned on the battle-field, scrambled
to his legs and hurried towards the two girls, who lay huddled together in
the corner, one above the other. Mary's fortitude, as she saw the fortune
of war changing to her own side, had, as is not unusual on such occasions,
given way, having no longer such need for existence as before, and she had
fainted; while poor Edith was incoherently muttering, "Oh, save me; oh,
save me," as fast as her white lips could form the words, her eyes fixed and
staring up to the shingled roof of the veranda. His first concern, of course,
was with Mary, and having after some trouble brought her to, and given
her a small dose of the neat spirit which remained in a little flask thrown
down by one of the retreating gang, at her weak though earnest request
he busied himself with Edith, whose affliction, however, he found himself
for the time, at any rate, unable to alleviate. After giving her a strong dose
of spirit, in the hope of its producing sleep and rest for her maddened
brain, he turned to greet Coates, but was shocked to find him, pale and
blood-stained, borne in the arms of Jack and another gentle brawny nurse
to the veranda, where they carefully laid him down. A film was over those
imperious eyes and a pallor over his cheek which made the doctor's heart
sob to see, but without showing the grief he felt, he knelt down by his
friend's side, and greeting him kindly, pulled and cut off with lightning
speed the clothes round the wound in his back, from which the bright
blood spurted upon the pressure of the clothes being removed with the
precision of the beats of a pulse. Rapidly the doctor ascertained, as well
as he could, the course the bullet had taken through the right lung from
behind, lodging against the breast-bone.

The surveyor's hours were numbered, and he knew it; a whisper, he said,—

"Tell me, old fellow, how long?"

"Perhaps three hours, perhaps nine," said the doctor, choking down a sob.

"Is Mary here?" asked the other.

"Don't speak more than you can help. I'll fetch her."

Poor Mary, who was lying down in the corner of the veranda, found new life imbued into her when the doctor informed her that her brother was thus wounded, and allowed herself to be carried to his side as he lay on the opossum rug, his head pillowed with a saddle, which the gentle girl tenderly replaced by her own lap. Then, in the face of the great calamity coming over her brother, which without the doctor's hints she could clearly foretell, she controlled her own emotions, rallied her scattered forces of character, and threw her whole self into the task of alleviating and cheering her brother's last moments.

The long hot afternoon passed, the surveyor getting weaker and weaker with his internal hemorrhage, which the doctor, although making a decoction of wattle or acacia-bark as a styptic, was unable to stop; the silence was hardly disturbed save by the incoherent murmurs of poor Edith, who lay flushed and feverish, tenderly though awkwardly watched over by the silent Jack.

The doctor had held a council of war with the rescue party, who had been reinforced by their rear-guard, and after clearing away the signs of the late struggle and laying out the dead bodies of two of the bushrangers side by side with their dead victim—poor old Ned—a party of five was made up to pursue the remaining members of the gang, though with small chance of meeting them at short notice, as the horses which the miscreants had left in exchange for those they had appropriated from the stable were almost as fatigued as the steeds of their pursuers. The doctor saw to the hurt of the wounded bushranger, who had been loosely bound and placed in the stables, and cared for the gallant mare which had brought him so well and with such success; though he found it hard work to save her life, he ultimately succeeded, and, I am glad to say, she lived to carry her former rider and then-owner for many years to come, and was patted by many a little hand, while the story of "Diana's" doughty deed was told.

Late in the afternoon Coates, who had looked anxious whenever the doctor was away from his side, turned his face towards him, and with something of his old energy, said,—

"What duffers you two are."

The doctor smiled, in spite of himself, and Mary coloured red, both understanding the drift of his thoughts.

A few moments elapsed and he said again, as though talking to himself,—

"I should like it so much, he is a man after my own heart, and loves her as she ought to be loved."

Then the doctor said,—

"Old fellow, ye know what I think about it. Ye know what I said one day about risking me life for her; and like a schoolboy I'm glad me words weren't merely empty claptrap and brag. If I had not saved Miss Mary alive I could not have faced an empty life, and if by doing this thing I am gratifying your wish, be sure I should be gratifying me own heart's desire more than ever I deserve or expect; but whatever I say is nothing unless the young lady herself speaks."

Mary, with her face the playground of many emotions, then said, lowly but distinctly,—

"Harry, my brother Harry, you don't know how hard it is for me to grant this request of yours. I who have let my life be marred by ever caring for such a wanton rascal as the chief of the bushrangers, how can I give my love to a man whom I respect with my whole heart?"

But her brother, with a coolness of judgment which had not even then forsaken him, replied,—

"Mary, you never marred your life, you only raised the life of that other a few degrees from the mud—the almost hopeless mire—into which it had been content to grovel. There has been gain to him, without loss to you; and though I can't wish the brute whose follower has given me my *coup de grace* much fortune, I could see as I stood there how your beauty of mind, your sweetness of disposition, and your purity of thought had raised in his conscience a pricking—a sure sign that he has the elements of improvement in him—and if given time and opportunity, might develop them."

Here he paused to take breath; the foregoing speech was painful and slow. After a bit he went on,—

"I find I must be careful of my words. See, my dear sister, a man who has already told you what he will do for you, and has carried out part—the hardest part, perhaps—that is, has ventured his own life to save yours. I believe him right through to be as sound as old English oak; don't you? Yes, you do. Now, knowing what I do of him, can you still say me nay and refuse his plighted troth for life until we meet again?"

Here the poor fellow gasped for breath; but the paroxysm over, he took her hand, and noticing it was not unwilling joined it to the doctor's.

The doctor raised the girl's hand to his lips in one long, loving, heartfelt pæan of thanks, and both of them were much affected.

"Now, doctor," said he, very weakly, but with his old mischievous spirit, "we ought to have some porridge and Kill-early cream, to celebrate this finding of *your* nugget."

But though the doctor feigned a smile, his Mark-Tapley spirit was not proof for this grief, and his heart, notwithstanding his recent ecstatic joy, was now heavy and sore.

In a few minutes more the dying man said,—

"Old man, do you mind what I told you of my first and only love? Will you tell her, if she asks—but not without, you know—how I felt that though I could never understand why she treated me so, I shall doubtless find it written in heaven, if I go there, for I really believe now that all her thoughts and actions had their mainsprings wound up above."

Although this was unintelligible to Mary, the doctor knew well what it meant, and replied,—

"It shall be as you ask; and right glad am I to find that ye can part company with that old sarcastic woman-hating self so easily."

"It never was a part of me, it was only assumed to drown the pain and regrets I had," murmured the other, and again was quiet.

After a bit he said,—"Did Jack come?"

"Yes, he swore to avenge you first and his sweetheart after," replied the doctor; and, louder, cried, "Jack, come over here for a minute."

"Jack," said the surveyor, attempting to raise his brawny, muscular arm and hand, but failing so utterly that Jack broke down and cried like a child, "I've asked you to come over and leave your poor sweetheart for a moment so as to tell you what I want you to do. The claim is yours, so far as I am concerned, right away. Mary will, of course, have all my share of the money in our banking account; and you'll not let the doctor defray all the cost of this rescue party of his, will you? As to the contracts for the road-making, I should like the money to be spent in helping to make better roads between Ballarat and Melbourne. And those allotments I bought near the Pioneer Hotel you'll divide with Mary too. All the rest of my property will of course be hers. Good bye, my boy. You've been a faithful chum to me through sunshine and cloud, through merriment and sadness, and poverty and wealth. Thank God, I can say that. It's a fine thing to know I've got so many good friends, though it seems hard to part with them just now."

This was the first, the only regret he allowed himself; thence, right through to the end, his voice getting weaker and weaker, his utterance often choked by coughs, which stained the doctor's handkerchief bright red, he spoke, but always encouraging them, and making now one now another arrangement, as though he were about to take a short journey away for a time. All through that silent night, unbroken but by the tread of the sentries who marched up and down in front, the little group watched by his side, allaying the fierce fever which consumed him as well as they could, and fearfully noting the grey look that stole over his face as the early morning hours went by and the pale moonlight looked in under the veranda full upon his face. They were about to shield him from its light, when he stayed them.

"Don't do that; I love to see the moon, I used to walk and drive with her by moonlight, and I seem to see her now, full in the glory of the moon, her sweet face looking sad but beautiful, her dark, bewitching eyes beckoning me to follow, her tresses—entwined—"

Then with one supreme effort he raised himself on his elbow, looked forth over the pathless forest up to the everlasting stars, and crying, "My love, I come, I come," fell back again into Mary's outstretched arms, overpowered by the sudden gush of heart's blood which escaped from his lips.

Tenderly but firmly the doctor took poor worn Mary in his arms and laid her down on the couch where Edith lay slumbering peacefully under Jack's never-tiring tender care.

"Is it over?" asked Jack, fearfully; and at the other's nod he placed his face in his hands and sobbed, his huge shoulders heaving like a child's.

"Hush, hush!" said the doctor, "for Mary's sake." But the soft-hearted giant could not restrain the grief he felt, and accordingly the doctor led him away and set him to put the veranda to rights, while he himself sought his old friend's body, and kneeling down by it, prayed then as he had not since he was a lad, for strength to carry through his duties and be worthy of the dead man's confidence and his sister's love.

Early in the morning the up-country coach arrived, and the wondering passengers were told so much of the events of the day before as the doctor thought fit; then hastily resuming their journey, with a shudder, they left behind them the little hut with its melancholy occupants, the driver taking a message of urgency to Williams. The news which they brought of the reinforcements under Major-General Meikle, then on the march from Melbourne, cheered the doctor, whose anxieties had not been determined by the disappearance of the bushrangers, for was it not possible for them to return and waylay the coach after all? But any fear on this score was set at rest by this welcome news, and with a lighter heart he discussed arrangements with the driver of the down going coach. This man, filled with the superstition of his class, was for refusing to convey the surveyor's body, though the doctor, with the ready aid of the friendly diggers, contrived a temporary receptacle for it. Some of the coach passengers, who now, with customary ingratitude, forgot the respect due to the dead man, supported the superstitious fellow in his contention, urging that the surveyor and his friends had been the Jonahs of the coach; but the rough and ready arguments of the friendly diggers, who overheard this discussion, proved more potent than the verbal logic and entreaties of the doctor, for they carried all before them by threatening to drive the coach themselves and turning off all who would not agree to the doctor's reasonable requests.

The good fellow himself worked with the untiring zeal and the energy of half a dozen, and by his efforts buried the poor old soldier in the bush close at hand, blazing the tree close by with the inscription, in hastily-cut letters, "Edward Manning, 1854, Decr. 1st. R.I.P."

The dead bushrangers were treated with less ceremony, though accorded the sepulchre which is frequently thought respectable if not essential for the welfare of the once clay-shackled spirit.

And before breakfast had come and gone the house was put in order, and little remained to show the fierce contest of the day before except a hole or two in the shingles and the dark stains on the veranda and the floor of the inner room.

Fortunately for Mary, exhausted nature had asserted itself, and she had slept heavily, and awoke somewhat refreshed. To distract her thoughts the doctor called her attention to Edith, whose incessant murmur, only broken by intervals of fitful slumber or dozing, betokened a mind unhinged by the fears and anxieties it had lately endured. When she awoke she repulsed poor Jack with evident aversion, and would at first only permit Mary to approach and tend her. The doctor quickly gained the poor girl's confidence, and by ready tact persuaded her, with Mary's help, to break her long fast, and subsequently to ride at full length in the interior of the coach. The shock which had bereaved her of mental strength had fortunately also deprived her of her physical force, which was, as it were, paralyzed, all her actions being weakly and requiring assistance.

Leaving one of the rescue party, a fearless, stout digger, at the house to assist the drivers of the coaches up and down, sadly the doctor gave the orders for the coach to start on its slow journey, and the rest of the party to fall in as escort. He himself rode one of the spare horses left by the bushrangers, leading the gallant little mare Diana by his side, and taking a farewell look at the hut where his short-lived but warm friend had breathed his last.

The journey to Melbourne was hot, dusty, and terribly tiring to the whole party, particularly to poor Mary, with her hands full of her fractious and captious patient, who to the petulance of her nature had added the caprices of a disordered brain. But somehow, what with her own spirit and sense of duty, and the loving aid and assiduous care of her betrothed, Mary accomplished her task most successfully, was able to heave a sigh of relief as on the Sunday they arrived at Melbourne, Edith was carried to a private hospital, and she herself was free for a time to rest and collect her own scattered thoughts.

To Jack the journey seemed but an episode in a dull, heavy nightmare. His despondency was one of the hardest of the many difficulties with which Mary and the doctor had to cope after they had settled down at their Melbourne hotel. His double bereavement in the loss of a friend whom he had loved as a dog does his master, and the mental affliction of a sweetheart whom he regarded with a boyish though warm affection, would, but for the support he derived from his two good friends, have led him to follies and excesses in order to drown his despair. But at the first symptoms, Mary's grave sisterly face, and the doctor's forced gaiety and lightness of heart had strengthened him against his weakness, and the discovery of his power of self-control thus aided, was the first step which led him by degrees away from the natural bent of his unbalanced mind.

When she thought Jack was strong enough to stand alone, Mary urged him to return to the claim, and carry out his comrade's dying wishes, and the dreadful news which shocked all Melbourne on Monday morning aided her purpose. The slaughter at the Eureka Stockade was called forth by the hawkers of newspapers, and special editions of the leading dailies came out at frequent intervals, as the press messengers on their heated, jaded horses arrived, one after the other, with fresh details.

It was then that news came of the brilliant and decisive attack made by the gallant Captain Thomas on the stockade, which they had seen only a couple of mornings back fortified and swarming with diggers armed with pikes and firearms, desperadoes and honest diggers resting and walking cheek by jowl, all bent on the same purposes from various motives. And then they, in common with all others, were electrified at the defeat of some 1400 desperate men by a small body of 300 or 400 troops and constabulary charging up a hill at an entrenched position. Then they thanked Providence that honest Huxter and Jake had been drawn away on a different quest, and had thus probably saved their lives. And then, above all things, when they heard that martial law was proclaimed from the ensuing Wednesday, and that comparative peace again reigned where anarchy, confusion, and lynch law had displayed their weird heads, Jack set out for the claim, and left the other two with mutual promises to write.

Though the Secretary of State, who had offered the place at Pentridge Gaol to the doctor, had now resigned his portfolio, still the offer held good, and the doctor was soon installed in his new post, with a full roll of patients on his hands. Melbourne was then, as she has been often since, a hotbed for typhoid fever, and cases were numerous and fatal. The new doctor soon proved that his office was no sinecure by looking after the drains and sanitary treatment of the convicts under his care, and earned the good words of the authorities, and even his patients, by his ready tact and good temper on all occasions.

CHAPTER XV

PURSUERS AND PURSUED

DECEMBER passed with its heated meetings, its inflammatory speeches, the masterly policy displayed by the new Governor, and the trial of some of the Eureka prisoners.

Christmas Day and the new year brought little change in the order of events. Edith was little better; Jack was busy at Ballarat, where things were quieting down, and martial had been replaced by civil law, while constant letters coming from Mary informed him of every hope and turn for the better in Edith, to which he painfully scrawled thanks after his hard day's work. And yet no news came of the bushrangers who had made good their escape on that fateful day from Manning's hut, nor even a word of their pursuers. The reason is not far to seek. The little band, though reduced in numbers, and hampered by their wounded leader, had a good start of Huxter and his party, and had, at Jim's instance, whose wits were sharpened by pain, made pursuit by unskilled whites practically hopeless by frequent doublings and false scents in the forests through which they had passed.

After three days, which Huxter spent chiefly in hanging on their rear by learning of their whereabouts from such sources as he could—passers-by, honest shepherds, and others—he had the good fortune to secure the services of a couple of natives who could follow the trail of the gang like deerhounds on the spoor of a stag. But by this time the gang had got far away towards the west of Victoria. News in those days travelled slowly, for telegraph wires and cross routes were few; but while the black trackers were slowly but surely tracking out the route made by the gang, news came that a gang of bushrangers had attacked a station near Fernshaw, in the Dandenory ranges, impudently near Melbourne. From their description Huxter made certain that this was the gang whom he had set himself to hunt down, and so set off across country with his black trackers and his party, all imbued with new life at the chance of action. He had not got beyond Kilmore before he was joined by Jack, for whom he had telegraphed, and who came up in hot haste to follow up the trail, and shortly after their numbers were increased by the arrival of a police party under Cochrane, whom the doctor had induced the Melbourne authorities to organize for the same purpose. These were glad to avail themselves of the assistance accorded by the sturdy band of diggers and their black *aides-de-camp*.

They soon came up with signs of violent deeds in the shape of a shepherd's hut containing a lifeless occupant, evidently killed while defending his master's flocks. Then a squatter had to tell a lugubrious tale how four ruffians, one of them of massive size and scarred, reddened face, had attacked the station and made off with their valuables, after helping themselves lavishly to meat, drink, and to the pick of his stable; and again, a travelling pedlar would tell how he had met five men, one riding with evident pain and many oaths in front of the burliest of the party, while a spare horse was led by another horseman.

Gentleman Jim had indeed by this time somewhat fallen from his high estate of leader. His plans, so successful at the commencement, had shown serious flaws in their further development, particularly at Manning's hut, and though his followers still had some of the booty they stole from the bank, having hidden the rest, *that* was of little use to them, for they could not use it openly, and had continually to disclose their presence on their quest for food.

The scars and seams on Ben's face, though healed up, had by no means added to the beauty of one who was by nature ugly to behold, but they caused him little pain, nay, rather, he deemed them an advantage, as his ferocity increased and developed itself in frightening all he came across, and even his own comrades, by his hideous gestures. But the wound in their leader's thigh was a more serious matter; the broken bone had little chance of setting properly, and though rough splints had served the purpose of reducing the pain and the jarring, and thereby induced a partial setting, the limb was practically useless, and the leader incapacitated. Nay, he had even to be cared for and carried *en pillion* by his fellows, a duty which they little liked and all but Ben shirked.

Very soon Ben had to take up the cudgels on behalf of their leader in earnest, for once, when he and his fellows had left him safely hidden, while they went marauding at a station, the men gave utterance to the thought, which had been long rankling within their heads, to rid themselves of their incumbrance by taking French leave of him and forgetting to return. The presence of Gentleman Jim, who was to their knowledge still as deadly and ready as ever with his pistols, had sealed their lips before, and a few rough words, uttered by Ben with curses and savage threats against any who turned traitors, crushed their discontent for a time.

Now Ben showed more foresight than friendship in the protection he thus afforded his lamed leader. He knew very well, as did the others, that had the wound been received by any of his fellows, Jim would, without the least hesitation, have cast off the wounded man to his fate; but he judged rightly that Jim constituted the brains, while he himself and the others were only the trunk and limbs of their body, and that without him they would never make good their escape. The original plan mooted by the leader, and adopted so unanimously by the gang, of doubling back towards South Australia and finding safety over the border, had necessarily been upset by the prompt action of the rescue party. Their next intention had been to cross the northern border and escape detection in the crowded gold-fields of New South Wales, their one idea being to get out of Victoria and the reach of the Victorian police; but while fixed in this determination, Jim had hesitated to risk the crossing of the Murray by the Echuca or Albury roads, rightly surmising that the authorities would be warned by the unfailing telegraph. He had indeed meditated the brilliant stroke of cutting the overland wires from Melbourne to the border, but, fortunately for the colony, was saved such reckless destruction by the reflection that *viâ* Sydney the border police would be notified before, in his maimed state, he could drag his party a dozen miles towards the border. Besides, they knew that the licence riots had caused an increased vigilance among the border police. So he decided to court the solitudes of Gipps Land, and was soon forcing his way up the grand valley of the Tambo, then hardly trodden by white men. Here he was within forty miles of the border, and, sore as was his wound, and low though the commissariat, yet with hopeful anticipations, curiously mingled though they were with oaths at his present pain and recent failures, he had revived among the gang some of that fellow-feeling which was essential to the success of their combination. Since they had ransacked the larder of a worthy squatter near Mount Wellington, two days before, the gang had not tasted solid food, though their leader had urged them to provide out of their abundance for the days of want. They had relied on shooting game in the huge forest through which they soon began to pass, a forest whose trees rose, like the Titan's pillars of olden times, to support the vaulted ceiling of heaven, their roots nestling in a tangled carpet of mosses, ferns, and grasses some four hundred feet below their tops. But here the gang soon began to regret their neglect of good advice, for of large game they saw none while their rifles blazed away without effect at the few parrots, parroquets and other birds whose cries at times disturbed the deep solitude of the primeval forest. Hunger was their only care. They felt themselves free from all risk of pursuit, which they considered they had long out-measured, and would have moved with more celerity and more unanimity had they known that the pursuing party were even then sympathizing with the poor old gentleman and his wife on the Mitchell River over the confusion and destruction lately wrought by the gang among the station live stock and chattels. The squatter's wife with shrill tones spoke of her overturned piano, with key-board damaged, ornaments and strings broken, her glass and china smashed and cracked in wanton mischief, her boxes and drawers ransacked. Her husband pointed out the while steers and sheep shot and stabbed out of pure devilry, and told how his particular filly had, with four other horses, been taken by the lawless gang in exchange for their own half-starved, overridden beasts, which were doubtless the property of some unfortunate squatter nearer Melbourne. The fervour of the old couple in assisting the pursuers with all the means in their power can therefore be readily imagined.

Thus the little body set off hard on a hot scent, with fresh horses and ample supplies for two or three days. Theirs was to be a forced march, and the squatter sent a couple of his best stockmen before them to the confines of his run, near the mouth of the valley. There, in a large grassy paddock, the next morning they rounded up a dozen strong horses which had been allowed for some months past to ramble free and unsaddled over the pastures, and had thus regained much of their ancestral fire and dash. So at sundown of the next day Jack, his friends, and the police found awaiting them a strong relay of spirited fresh horses, who chafed impatiently at their imprisonment in the yard by the slip-rails, and turned their eyes longingly towards the tawny, park-like plain, cooling water-holes, and dark forest-clad hills beyond, which the setting sun was even then splashing with gold, thereby throwing into splendid relief the intense blue of the shadows and the salmon tones of the sky. The black trackers, after careful search, reported that the gang had passed the previous night in that spot, leaving probably in the early morning, and so were at most thirty miles ahead.

"They haven't made thirty miles," said Cochrane to Jack, who had with some difficulty reined in his impatient horse. "Pushing on as hard as we can, we shan't do much more than fifteen miles before midnight, and, if I'm not much deceived, we shall have to come up with them by dawn, or shall miss them altogether, for there's a storm brewing somewhere."

"What?" asked Jack, "on such a quiet evening as this; why, there's hardly a cloud in the sky, except towards the east there, behind the mountains."

"That's just where we shall get it from. The wind is due west and hot, as you feel now, while that bank of clouds in the east has been braving the wind, and old Roland at the station yesterday told me his glass was falling fast. If they give us the slip to-night, or the moon sets behind those clouds before we catch them, we may say good-bye to them for ever, for we shall have to look to ourselves."

Trotting briskly along they had now come to the river Dargo, whose bed the horses crossed with dry feet, as the long drought had turned the running stream into a series of disconnected water-holes, though the wide bed of sand and high banks told plainly that the water would on occasion present an imposing spectacle of wild floods. Before them loomed up the Great Dividing Range, hard cut against the darkening sky, where the pale moon was already promptly taking up her "rule by night." The trail led them towards the valley whose western end, closed by a steep ridge, they took some time to enter. But on reaching the summit of the ridge their way was easier, for the bushrangers having had the advantage of daylight, had made for themselves an unmistakable track down the hillside, upon which the moon shone brightly. A clearing afforded them a view of the valley, and ever on the look-out for signs, while one of the trackers climbed a tree the rest scanned the valley with its silvery pools here and there embosomed among towering trees and pastures, its high hill-walls shutting in apparently on all sides, and its, grassy plain where kangaroos could be seen disporting themselves careless and ignorant of the presence of man. As no sign appeared, the inspector concluded that the men must be pushing on, and gave the orders to move ahead, and in single file they descended the hill, and marched along the valley.

"Now there's some fun in running in these fellows, ye know," said he to Jack; "there's rare cleverness in some one of the party, making for the border at this point, where they know none will be on the look-out for them."

Jack did not directly respond, but after a time said,—

"Do you think we shall meet them to-night?"

"Well, yes, I do," said the inspector. "I've seldom known black trackers much out in their calculation, and these fellows have had to force their way along, you see."

The evidences of a recent passage by horses or other large beasts were plain even to those unskilled in tracking, for with utter recklessness, born of assumed security, the bushrangers had not taken the least trouble to hide the traces of the path which they had torn through ferns and scrub, brushwood and jungle.

"Don't think me a coward," said Jack, after another pause, "but I can't help thinking, somehow, that I shall never pass this way again."

"Superstitious, my dear fellow, that's all; why, it's the moon, and the deep shadows, and the tall trees, and all that sort of thing, that makes ye feel so. I remember the time when I used to feel the same; but, bless ye, I've never had my quietus through it."

"Well, it may be, but I can't help feeling it, and if it does come true, I want you—"

"Oh, go to old Harry with your feelings and your wants, shure ye mustn't get in such a frame of mind, ye'll go and get shot on purpose," ejaculated the inspector.

"No I won't, I'll fight like the rest of you, I hope, but I've got a letter written here to Miss Coates, Mrs. O'Donnoghue as is to be, and another for Miss Williams, and I want you to promise to deliver them all right. They're not much—only good-byes."

"Oh, all right, av course I will, but there won't be any necessity."

"Thanks," replied the other, and seemed lighter spirited now that he had disposed of his will, which formed the contents of Mary's letter.

The bank of clouds still hung over the eastern horizon, and the inspector hoped that it would delay spreading over the sky, and obscuring the moon till dawn. They had ridden about twenty miles from their starting-point of the evening, and were rounding a bluff when the leading black tracker, who had disappeared round the bend some way on ahead, was seen coming back with emotion strongly depicted on his face and trembling with weird gestures.

"White fellows' horses hobbled, feedin' grass haf mill on—welly good," said he, gurgling and grunting out his pigeon English.

"Seen a fire, Wangaratta?" asked the inspector.

"No fire now, but smoke top him next mountain, welly good," replied the black, terminating with his usual click.

"Pass the word forward to keep close, hide all glitter, and make no noise," hoarsely whispered the inspector to the man in front of him. Then, turning to Jack, he said, "Now, me lad, ye shall have revenge on these scoundrels, for your sweetheart's sake."

Jack's eyes flashed, and his swarthy cheeks flushed in the moonlight with the rare emotion now so strongly permeating his frame. Noticing this the other said,—

"Whatever ye do, keep cool, and if ye have to fire, aim low, as those badly balanced pistols of yez will kick like buck-jumpers."

"Does that look like nervousness?" asked Jack, stretching out his brawny arm, steady and stiff as a branch of a tree.

"Go through like that, an' ye shall be in Melbourne safe and sound in three weeks," replied the inspector, wishing to counteract the other's presentiments.

"These devils are not expecting us, that's for certain, or their horses hadn't been down in the valley, and they making a fire. It'll be an aisy matter afther all."

Jack smiled in reply at his friend's sanguine description.

They had now passed round the bluff and emerged upon the open plain, which stretched far up to the end of the valley, where the black shadows of the frowning mountains stood out like silhouettes against the illuminated bank of clouds then slowly rising on the easterly breeze. Two or three rock wallabies, which had come down to their accustomed pastures for the night, started up suddenly on their left, calling forth a startled exclamation from one of the police, so great was the tension that even the man's trained nerves escaped control for a brief moment. Cochrane, fearing that any disturbance would awaken the bushrangers to a sense of their danger, and thus facilitate their escape among the neighbouring gorges and gullies, although feeling the same tension himself, sternly rebuked the man, and threatened to leave him behind or any one else who uttered a single syllable before the attack. To the little band, eager for the fray, this threat proved all powerful.

And now the bushrangers' horses were visible on the centre of the valley across the river Tambo, which here displayed its isolated, stagnant pools, cold and bright as bristling steel under the moon's rays. The clink, clink, of the horses' hobbles, which formed part of the plunder from the Mitchell river squatter, came sharp and clear in the warm, still air, which, undisturbed as yet, allowed the most insignificant sound to be heard far off. So the inspector confined his conversation to whispers, scarcely heard by Jack himself, their intended auditor.

"See that smoke curling against the sky? Shure Providence has just befuddled the fools entoirely. If they had camped this side of the bluff they could have seen us as we came down the end of the valley, a dozen miles off maybe. I s'pose they're afraid of catching cold."

Just then one of the bushrangers' horses whinnied, and in the twinkling of an eye was answered by the inspector's mare; it was evidently his comrade's voice which thus answered, for the first one again replied, moving towards the party across the valley slowly, and noisily shaking its metal hobbles. Cursing the accident under his breath, Cochrane, ready as ever, passed the order forward for the men to dismount at once and crouch down behind their horses, holding their reins low down the while. As soon ordered as done, for the men separated as they dismounted and thrust their horses' noses deep into the tall grasses, which helped them to conceal their presence and thus cause any observer to believe that he saw merely a mob of stray horses feeding. They had barely assumed this somewhat cramped attitude, when a grating noise of footsteps on the bluff above them, followed by the appearance on the rocky, precipitous cliff of the indistinct form of a man, with his moonlit face distinctly turned in their direction, apprised them how necessary was the manœuvre; and now that the rustle of the horses through the grass and brushwood had ceased, their strained ears caught the sound of conversation high up away on their left, in the neighbourhood of the sentry. It seemed like an age to them before he turned about and walked away leisurely into the shadow of the forest, evidently deceived by the inspector's ruse. The hobbled horse still neighed from time to time, and together with the oncoming freshening breeze and cloud-bank soaring to the zenith, caused Cochrane nervous apprehension, lest even in the very hour of success he might fail; but, fortunately for his plans, the sentry did not appear again, and a small patch of bush hard by, running from the mountain into the valley, lent its kindly shelter whilst they tethered their horses.

CHAPTER XVI

FIRE AND FLOOD

WHILE they are thus engaged, we will leave them and join the unconsciously-menaced gang of bushrangers.

The long and tiring journey of the day with the miserable outlook of a supperless sleep and a promise of a stormy night and wet skins, to be followed by a day or two, perhaps a week, of toil and famine, had again turned the bushrangers' thoughts to their hampered movements, and so out of very perversity, and in spite of the advice of their *soi-disant* leader, they had taken no trouble to hide their trail or to camp on the open side of the bluff commanding the entrance to the valley, as a precaution against possible though not probable pursuit and surprise. Physically powerless, Jim had to submit to the overruling of his fellows, arid there he sat gazing at the imprudently and unnecessarily lit fire, for it was a hot, muggy night, and as he cogitated on the mutiny of his followers with unexpressed but bitter curses for their folly, he planned to give them the slip as soon as he could and revenge himself, appropriating through agents in Victoria the whole of the hidden booty. Ben who, now as ever, backed up his friend in his plans, but thought him over nice to press such unnecessary precautions, leaned against a vast tree behind him, while the other three seated opposite (as it were intentionally forming a split in the camp) looked scowlingly at Jim and Ben and at each other.

At last, exasperated by a grim chuckle of the leader, one of the men called out in loud tones to an other,—

"This is a pretty fine piece of leading, to bring a party into this wilderness without any prog. Wot's the use of all this gold 'ere, I shed like to know?"

He kicked his saddle-bag viciously as he spoke.

"Zat is right, Corpo di Baccho," said another; "vot is a leader for but to manach effery zing?"

"Hold yer row, Bill Davis," replied Jim, conscious of his power in argument, and toying with the pistol which had never lately left his breast, its handle sticking out with significant protusion from his jersey pocket; "and, as for you, you grinning, chattering foreign monkey, shut up, do you understand? If it hadn't been for you we should have had plenty. I told you to lay in stores and you thought you knew better than me."

"Well, well, an' so we shall. I know where to get as fine a piece of beef as any man 'ud want, real 'ors beef, too," replied the unwashed Davis.

His comrades answered his grim chuckle with hoarse laughs; while Jim turned pale, and handled his revolver with ostentation. Ben gave no sign of having heard the conversation, he had been fortunate enough to appropriate a pipe and a small plug of tobacco of the squatter's at the last station, by smoking which he stayed his hunger for awhile; he had, with rough generosity, presented his leader with a small quid to chew and thus allay the fierce gnawing within. So these two were in a way provisioned; at any rate, free from pressing hunger.

"If you mean," said Jim, "that you want to shoot my horse, I'll tell you that the man who does that gets shot himself."

"Oh, if it comes to that, two can do that, we know; but then there are four of us, my cocky, and only one of you, you see, and four shots to one, though that one is a crack, 'll make a warm time for the one."

"Wot's the good of talking," interposed Ben. You know you can't do it. You ain't four to one, but three to three, for Jim's as good as any two of you, and you're blamed fools, by Gorm, to talk of quarellin' and shootin'."

"Oh, you're all right," responded Davis, "you earn your tucker, you do; but I guess Jim and you can jest ride one horse between you, as we're so near the border, as he says. 'Sides which I ain't in Van Denon's Land, and goin' to be cut up and eaten by other folks when there's 'osses running riot and doin' nothing."

At the horrible reference to Ben's Tasmanian reputation the giant gave a hoarse chuckle, grinning in ghastly wise, it was a joke he appreciated to the full; even Jim smiled, but with a shudder, for it was the nervous smile of fear rather than hilarity. Just then the neighing of one of their horses answered by the whinny of the inspector's mare away down in the valley struck on their ears.

"Run one of you to the point and see what that means, there's others besides us here."

Roused for a moment by a common danger to obedience, Davis made off for the top of the cliff, which jutted out bare and rocky on a level with their camp, but shaped so that none could approach it except by a devious path up the hill-side.

As we have just seen, he gazed at the troop of horses, and deceived by their scattered appearance, conceived them to be the troop which they had seen the day before wandering by the Dargo river; so, well pleased to find food to be procured so readily and without falling foul of Gentleman Jim, he walked back to the fire, where to the astonishment of his fellows, he explained what he had seen. Jim doubted whether such a large mob would have voluntarily followed them, but his suspicions were drowned in the acclamations of the others, two of whom at once equipped themselves to attack and kill one of the mob for supper. But Jim, whilst relieved from the immediate danger of discord, was yet burdened by a presentiment of evil, and persuaded Ben to keep a watch on the end of the cliff, which the giant proceeded to do.

However, by the time he had taken up his post there, the pursuers had entered the patch of scrub at the foot of the hill which concealed them from view.

Two or three hundred feet above their heads, and a quarter of a mile away, lay the camp they had to attack; but by the hazy light of the moon, which was now fast vanishing before a few light, fleecy clouds, spread over the heavens in skirmishing order, they rightly judged that they would have to make a circuit to effect their purpose. Deathly silence reigned in their midst as each tied up his horse to a tree, and buckling on his pistol, carbine, or other arms, left his steed with almost careless uncertainty whether he should live to return. The two blacks were by no means so stoical. The enterprise was a dangerous one, as they well knew; and having hunted their prey down, they thought that their duties were at an end. As an extra precaution, Cochrane ordered them to accompany the party, but their glistening eyes and chattering teeth well bespoke their fright of the encounter with the white men's death-barrels.

The forest grew denser and the trees loftier at each step, while the darkness perceptibly increased; but so carefully did they move that scarcely a rustle disturbed the silence of the glade through which they passed, while they caught the "wish, wish" of some animal ahead, which they at first took to be a wallaby fleeing at their approach. Nearer and nearer came the sounds, and caused them some uneasiness, for with the moon at their backs as they ascended the hill they could more easily be discerned than discern themselves. Suddenly a cry startled the solitude.

"Peelers, by the Lord Harry!" cried Davis, at the unexpected sight of nine men not more than a hundred yards ahead of him winding through the bush up the hill-side. A moment afterwards he could have bitten his tongue out, for he perceived he had disclosed his presence to the assailants. Attracted by his shout, Cochrane and one or two of his men levelled their regulation carbines at the spot whence the cry issued, though not till Davis, in his own defence raising his revolver, showed a glint of steel, were they certain where to fire. Then with one accord the two parties fired, the shots resembling rather a volley than a dropping fusillade, so simultaneous were they.

Cochrane's party, ignorant of the opposing numbers, yet nothing daunted by this fact or by the fall of one of their number, a black-tracker, charged up the hill. The two bushrangers, being themselves slightly wounded, and seeing the overwhelming odds against them, immediately fell back up the hill towards the camp, Cochrane and his party pursuing hard by the sound which the bushrangers made as they crushed through the brushwood. Cochrane's purpose was not to lose sight of the enemy, fearing thereby to imperil the safety of the rest of his party; but in this he failed, for as the pursuers naturally made slow progress over the unaccustomed ground, before they had stumbled many yards they found themselves at fault and wandering away from the bluff. Cochrane's face, by the uncertain and dimmed light of the moon, was pale with vexation.

The gang would now be fully aware of their presence, and might yet escape; the possibility of which event seemed emphasized by a flash far away in the east, followed by a low growl and reverberation of thunder. The gathering storm would soon bury all in Egyptian darkness, and then, *sauve qui peut*. So he pressed forward towards the bluff, which, he could feel by the incline of the ground rather than see, lay towards their left-hand, but soon stopped dead at an over-hanging wall of rock some twenty feet high, one of those many scarped cliffs which rise up so often in Australian mountain scenery, exasperating the traveller and defying bee-line tracks. As it seemed to run out and join the bluff in a wall of rock, they considered it hopeless to expect to find their way to the top in that direction, so, vexed and baffled, had to turn back and clamber along at the foot of the rock, seeking an accessible track. But a fresh danger arose as they turned about; a blaze of light and crackling shone some two or three hundred yards ahead of the which, while it showed the inspector he need no longer fear for want of light, led him to dread lest he was after all to be balked of his prisoners; nay, perhaps might turn out to be pursued himself by an all-devouring foe.

The bushrangers had fired the bush!

To those of my readers who have seen a burning forest in a temperate climate these words convey some slight idea of the terrific aspect and effects of a bush-fire after a dry and semi-tropical Australian summer. The fierce demon of fire, so useful a slave, so unruly a master, is truly in his element. He flings all his bonds and shackles aside, and with electrical speed he circles round massive tree-trunks, snapping up the twigs and the leathery resinous leaves as he climbs the highest gum, embracing each neighbouring tree in his fiery touch both alow and aloft in the twinkling of an eye. See, as one speaks, the great branches flame up, redden, and crash down, while the trunk itself half-eaten by the demon's savage and remorseless tooth, sways and falls, in hideous embrace bringing ruin around it. So, with astonishing swiftness, the flames run along the ground through dried bracken and brushwood, fallen log, and bark, crackling and triumphing as they pass, creating a very hell upon earth; while overhead the canopy of fire shoots up to join the clouds.

Between the nearer trunks and branches of trees, as through a vast black network, the fiery furnace could be seen wafted gently onwards by the breeze, which was freshening every moment.

"Curse it all," cried Cochrane, excusably excited at the turn matters had taken, "these devils have fired the bush, and are going not only to escape, but trap and burn us like rats in a ship."

"Where there's a will there's a way," cried Jack. "I'm not going to turn back; jump up, Huxter, on my shoulder, and let the inspector climb up on yours to the top of the rock."

"Bravely said," cried Cochrane. "Men, we must and will, for our own honour, capture these devils. What say you? Capture or death, that's the word."

The men and the diggers, who had paled at the unexpected sight of the bush-fire, the effects of which all knew either by experience or hearsay, took courage again at the brisk words of their commander and his prompt action. The rock wall here was only fifteen feet high, so placing his back to this Jack helped Huxter to his shoulders, and then stood firm and fixed as the rock itself, while the inspector, ever the first to face danger, clambered up the human ladder with the aid of friendly rocky projections and branches, and so reached the top, where one after the other in hot haste followed him. Once only did Jack tremble, as Jackson's muscular form bore down upon his shoulders; still, he stood bravely, and was finally assisted up himself by a rope of jackets knotted together which was lowered to him. Though his hands were bruised and terribly cut with the sharp points of rock, he uttered no word or sound of pain to Cochrane, who awaited him at the top, but hastened to join the others, who at once set off for the bush-rangers' camp, which could be seen by the increasing glare of the blazing fire but a hundred yards off; and almost on a level.

Hastily flinging the rope of jackets to Wangaratta, the black, who point blank refused to accompany them any further, and bidding him seek his wounded compatriot and take him down to the horses, Cochrane rushed after his men and reached the camp almost as soon as they. There he found all non-plussed at the absence of bushrangers, and gazing disconcertedly at the smouldering fire, which told that their foes had not long since left the camp; but whither? Here was another check; but here in turn Fortune favoured them.

Standing up in the shadow of the forest, with the rushing fire on their left and facing the valley, they chanced to catch sight of the glitter of steel in front of them. The moon again became obscured, but trusting to their first sight they fired a volley from the depth of the forest, and rushed through the fringe of the scrub on to the bluff, loading as they went. This time the howls and groans that followed, showed that they had taken their enemies by surprise who, in apparent security on the bluff, were watching with rocks poised in their hands for their assailants to pass beneath the cliff, never doubting that they would retreat that way before the fire. As the troopers rushed forward in the direction of the groans, one or two stumbled over an object which lay directly in their path. It was the body of Bill Davis shot through the back, and fallen at last under their united volley.

Pushing on, they soon had cause to regret their temerity, for on emerging into the comparatively bare plateau, the moon, by shining on them for a moment, favoured their enemies, who, by a galling fire, thinned their ranks to six; but they replied, and apparently with effect, as by the fierce flames which now mounted two hundred feet into the air, they could see another of the four black figures roll over and bite the dust. Then came the voice of Gentleman Jim, loud and clear—he had also been hit,—

"We surrender on one condition." But the hoarse tones of Ben were heard,—

"No surrender, no conditions, damn you, you cur, take that," and the others were horrified to see the great brute strike the other over the head with the butt end of his revolver. The third bushranger waited not to see the result of this curious contest, for with a parting shot at the inspector's party, which hit Huxter in the foot, he let himself over the edge of the cliff and commenced scrambling down its face, hanging by rock and crag, branch and tuft. Cochrane ran to the edge and threatened to shoot the man if he did not stop his descent at the first ledge, more than ten feet below him, but either from confusion, giddiness or accident, the bushranger slipped, and with a shriek of despair heard over the rending and roaring flames far down into the valley, pitched on to the ledge, and rebounding from rock to rock, crushed with a heavy thud on the tree-tops some four hundred feet below.

Cochrane could not help a shudder at the man's fate, but there was no time to lose, for the oncoming flames, fast fanned by the breeze, were an ever-increasing source of danger, and though the bluff was free from timber and scrub, yet the heat as of a furnace which could be already felt distinctly, warned them that their present position would soon be untenable.

"Surrender at once, or we shoot," cried he to the other pair, of whom Jim had alone been affected by the death of their comrade, Ben standing the while across his fallen leader, grim and ghastly, the reflexion of the fire bathing his face in blood-red hues.

"For God's sake, policemen, don't shoot," shrieked Jim, whose fears overcame all prudence, "we surrender, at least I do, and if you'll promise to take care of us, I'll split the whole affair."

"No fear," said Ben, "they say dead men tell no tales. Don't suppose you're going to get off better than Jacob Saltner."

With that he took up his comrade in his arms, and quickly ran to the cliff edge, bearing his shrieking, howling, praying burden as a featherweight; but not too quickly for Cochrane, who, wishing to incapacitate the men and carry them both prisoners to Melbourne, put a bullet through the giant's leg, which would have brought most other men to the ground in a second.

Yet staggering on, he hurled his traitorous leader over the cliff, and then turned like a bear at bay to face his antagonists. Firing his last shot with his revolver at Jack, who had imprudently rushed forward, he succeeded in stopping him for a second in his career, as the shot grazed his cheek; then hurling his revolver defiantly at his assailant, and with truer aim, hitting him full on the forehead, he rushed at him, and with desperate intent, locked the other in a vice-like grip. Jack, though at first stunned, was soon equal to the occasion, and, seeing the intentions of the other, put forth his whole strength to frustrate them. Like Samson of old, the grim giant was about to destroy his enemy, though the act involved his own destruction. The two men were fairly matched, for though the bushranger had the advantage of weight, Jack had youth and supple limbs on his side; so for a time the awful struggle, lit up by the vast torch blazing around, seemed in Jack's favour. The inspector and his party feared to shoot friend with foe, and the wrestling was so perilously near the edge, and so rapidly did the combatants sway about, that nothing could be done to aid their friend. Seeing that he was losing ground, Jack put forth his whole strength into one convulsive effort, releasing one of his arms, brought his clenched fist with marvellous force on his adversary's forehead, felling him to the ground; but, alas! that it should have to be told, the bushranger clung to his antagonist with the clutch of despair, and falling backwards, pulled the brave young fellow over the edge of the rock, and amid the startled exclamations of the on lookers, both instantly disappeared from view.

Rushing to the edge of the cliff, the inspector caught sight of the two men, still clinging together, and turning over and over as they descended; for a moment a jutting rock caught a loose leather belt round the waist of the younger man, and it seemed as though he would have been saved, but the grasp of the bushranger was fixed and inexorable, and the strain of the double weight broke the strap. However, their fall had been broken, and they rolled rather than fell for the next few feet, where a friendly ledge, not wider than a foot, again might have saved poor Jack, but for his antagonist's grip. Fate had ruled it otherwise, and from the strained gaze of the spectators, the pair rolling off disappeared over a prominent rock. In a few seconds, which seemed like hours to the inspector, came a crash on the tree-tops, and a sickening thud heard over the roaring flames.

With a sob which shook his frame, an expression of emotion experienced by all the rest of the party, to whom Jack had, despite his quiet, unobtrusive manners, endeared himself, Cochrane turned away, and hastily brushed his blurred eyes with the back of his hand. It was no time for tears; he could see that, for while these events had quickly happened, the scene had changed, and now that they stood victorious and alone on the bluff, they had to reckon with a more savage and relentless foe than the last—a foe whose very breath meant death, whose grasp destruction. Far up the hill the flames were roaring, as the wind had slightly shifted, and gathering strength, blew from across the valley, while to add to the horror of the scene, the thunder-clouds had spread across the sky, and reflected now the flashes of fire beneath, now the dazzling electric fluid above. The din of the roaring flames, crashing trunks and rising wind was so great, that Cochrane's shouted orders could scarcely be heard, and ever and anon were interrupted by the crashes of overhead thunder.

As the path they had taken up the hill was by this time completely cut off, their only chance of escape was in the other direction, and that speedily, as the fringe of scrub at the edge of the bluff was alight in several places, where pieces of burning bark and leaves borne on the wind, had dropped upon it, and the flames would soon be spreading across the neck of the bluff down the hillside.

Fortunately the fringe of trees at the foot of the cliff had not yet caught fire, for though the flames were steadily creeping down towards the valley, they were greatly checked by the force and direction of the fierce gusts bursting down the opposite mountains, bending mighty trees like saplings, and snapping off huge branches in their course across the valley. Thus, if Jack still chanced to be alive, Cochrane hoped to save him from the terrible death of fire.

A hasty examination of the bodies of the digger and constable, who had been shot at the commencement of the attack, showed him too surely that their vital spark had flown, but one of the bush-rangers still breathed, and in common humanity they must attempt to save him, though doubtless for the certain fate of the hangman's noose. So he gave orders to a couple of his men, who seized the bush-ranger by head and feet, whilst Jackson, with characteristic good-humour, bore along his wounded friend on his back. All this was arranged in the time that it takes me to write a couple of these lines. Then Cochrane rapidly tossed over the heavy saddle-bags in the contrary direction to the spot where Jack had fallen, and placing himself at the head of his party, plunged into the bush at the back of the bluff, where he expected to find a way down to open ground.

Skirting along the rocky prominences which here formed, as it were, the western, ramparts of the point, they came to a place where, by dint of great care, they managed to lower themselves and their burdens to a lower ledge or step, but not before they became aware of a fresh danger. Here, among the rocks, was the haunt of many snakes and vipers who, disturbed by the heat and smoke of the furious flames, were making the best of their way down the cliff and sides of the hill.

As it were by a powerful instinct, they appeared to realize that they were for once allies with these human intruders in the presence of a third more terrible and common foe, and offered the party no violence. So by dint of many a tumble and scramble, the party arrived at the foot of the cliff, and detaching the two men with the wounded bush-ranger, to find their comrade who had charge of the horses, and then seek shelter on the far side of the valley, Cochrane set off on the quest for Jack, alive or dead, accompanied by Jackson, who had gently deposited Huxter in a safe place, with instructions to fire his pistol should he need their help while they were gone.

Searching down below in the depths of the forest was not easy, and it was many minutes before, by the light of the flames now blazing away far down the hill towards them, they came across the insensible bodies of the two men, unloosed from each other's grasp by the force of the fall, but lying one on the top of the other, amidst a great heap of branches and *débris* brought down from the cliff side.

Fortunately Ben had fallen below the other, and though he had at last surrendered, who had so lately cried out no surrender, to the more inexorable demands of Death, Jack still breathed slightly. Lifting him between them, they marched with quick and more hopeful steps towards the fern-clad rock where Huxter lay, but before they had made any distance, groans and shrieks high up the cliff drew their attention in that direction.

Fearing lest, after all, one of their comrades had been mistaken for dead and left to his fate, they were relieved to find that the cries proceeded from a form they knew well, caught in mid-air by a patch of thick scrub, which grew on one of the many ledges of the cliff face; there, suspended 'twixt heaven and earth, though close to the tops of the trees below, in whose shade they themselves stood, was the leader of the gang, who, hurled from Ben's arms, had by some dispensation of Providence, lodged in a swinging soft cradle, little the worse for his fall, except for a stunning; he had now regained consciousness, and with it a keen appreciation that the flames would shortly reach him along the tree-tops.

"Nothing can save him," cried Cochrane; but he was wrong, and had to confess it the next minute. The man's struggles to be free from his fate, caused the bushes in which he was inextricably confined by his own weight, to lose their hold of the ground whence his fall had already loosened them, and as the two gazed they saw the whole bush sway and bend over, finally with a loud crack falling down the cliffs, and depositing him upon the tree-tops, through which the wretched man crashed with the tangled branches of the bush and tree, and tumbled to their feet.

Turning over the bush and heap of broken branches, they extricated his unconscious form, and placed him against a tree, while they hurried back to Huxter with poor Jack, returning for the other wounded man at once. Him they also carried to the rock, and then Jackson, carrying the unconscious form of Jack, and Cochrane assisting Huxter, they again set forth to join their comrades down below.

Gaining the valley, an unexpected diversion awaited them, for Wangaratta, who was on the look-out, with fleet foot approached and shouted, "Fellow horses gone away down river."

"Where white fellows carrying other white fellow?" yelled Cochrane back at him.

"Over dar by Tambo pool," answered the black.

"Here, take white fellow on back," shouted the inspector, transferring Huxter to the shoulders of the sturdy though unwilling black. Then turning to Jake he said, "Find out where the others are and get them to the far side of the river at once, up on the hill side in the shelter of the large rock opposite, the rain's coming down now like waterspouts, and before morning the river will have risen."

It was true; now that they were in the open plain they experienced the full force of the rain, which was hurled by the wind against their faces with incredible force, and half hid the flaming mountain from their view.

Darting back into the forest, Cochrane made for the rock where he had left the leader of the gang whom he found still unconscious and deathly pale. The exertions of the day and night were telling on the brave fellow, as with a violent effort he placed the body of the unconscious man across his back and tramped back into the wind and rain.

Already the rocky rivulets were hurling down the falling rain, already the ground was soaked and the cracks full of water, as with undaunted spirit he crossed the valley, and gaining the other side at last joined the rest of his party. Here the great panorama of fire was shut out from their view, except when an occasional pause in the fierce storms of rain and hail allowed a momentary glimpse of the glowing furnace with the great black background of the Dividing Range beyond. The indefatigable inspector searched for and found a small cave in the hill side, in the shade of which, after some trouble, he made a fire, and thither led the remnant of his party. Then he gazed around on his thinned numbers, and calling the roll missed Wangaratta and the other black tracker, as well as the man who had charge of the horses and the poor fellow who had been shot early in the fray. With the party thus reduced to six, all of whom were more or less wounded and busily engaged bandaging their wounds, provisions absent, and a chance of swollen rivers and flaming bush, the outlook was not promising.

As he sat pondering on his plans the warmth of the fire soon aroused the two wounded bushrangers, though Jim was evidently weak and dying. His lips moved inarticulately, and the inspector's sole fear was lest the man should pass away there in the dark without making some statement about himself which might disclose the whereabouts of the rest of the stolen booty and identify him with other and perhaps undiscovered criminals.

Then again how was the party to be kept from starving? Provisions were on the horses' backs, but where were the horses? Wangaratta had led him to believe that the animals had stampeded, a very natural result of the horrors of the night, and the trooper in charge was perhaps now far away at the lower end of the valley, altogether out of sight or hearing, or thrown from his horse and killed. Hoping against hope, he went out into the open, and firing all the barrels of his revolver in succession, waited to catch an answering sound or flash. The hurtling wind would carry the noise of his discharge, but would it bear back the answer? A second report, to his great delight, brought an answering flash and a dull sigh, which, had he not sharpened his ears, he would not have distinguished. Then, after flashing signals again and again, he was glad to welcome his follower, riding on one and leading two other of the truant steeds, all heated and flecked with foam.

The man's story was told in a few words. At the first sight of the reflected fire the horses had grown uneasy, and, although he had tightened girths and reins and had, ready for any emergency, seated himself on his own horse, the increasing flames and the on-coming thunder and lightning so frightened them that one and all commenced to kick and plunge; then, suddenly, notwithstanding his best efforts, they had, with one accord, wrenched themselves loose and stampeded through the bush and down the valley. The trooper had managed to separate his own horse and two others from the rest, after vainly trying to round them up, and on turning back had chanced to see the inspector's signal.

While the trooper had been telling his story, the others had not been idle, for at the inspector's orders they had opened up the saddle-bags of the three horses and brought out the provisions which they found there. In one of the saddle-bags there was, fortunately, a large flask of brandy almost full, and with this as his only medicine, by the light of the flickering, unsteady fire he had lit, the inspector managed to inspire life into the unconscious form of Jack, and to strengthen the other wounded men.

The injuries of young Wainwright were terrible, both thighs fractured to splinters and one arm broken at the shoulder, while the other had sustained a compound fracture at the wrist, both bones being forced through the skin; minor hurts consisted of broken collar-bones, immense bruises covering the back, his limbs and trunk, and some internal injury, which, as the spark of life revived, was noticeable by spasmodic contractions of the body. His head and face seemed saved as by a miracle, and it was a wonder to all who witnessed his fall that, notwithstanding his great strength and vigour, even the smallest spark of life remained. It was evident he had escaped the fate of his antagonist, partly by his comparative lightness of weight and partly by falling uppermost. But his condition was most deplorable, and it was not till morning broke grey and grim, with the clouds still hurling down their contents on the mountain and valley, that he gave any signs of returning consciousness. The pallor underlying the swarthy sunburnt hue of his face was intense, and seemed to the inspector's rough and ready bush surgery to betoken signs of great shock and loss of blood. At more frequent intervals Cochrane fed him with the weak brandy and water, for which the wounded man expressively looked his gratitude, and when the light had gathered force, though still grey and blurred by the falling sheets of rain, the flickering spark seemed to expand rapidly, and for the first time the poor fellow became aware of his utter helplessness.

"What's up?" whispered he, looking inquiringly, now at the black roof of the cave, now at the flickering light of the fire, and back again at Cochrane.

Cochrane heaved a sigh of relief that, at any rate, he could speak, and replied, "You've had a little tumble and jarred yourself; don't try to move for a bit."

"As I can't move a muscle I shan't try," replied Jack. "Now I remember; what's become of the ranger?"

"You fell above him, and crushed him," returned Cochrane.

"Crushed myself, too, so't seems," muttered Jack.

In reply to the natural question how he felt, he answered that he felt nothing whatever: every sense of feeling seemed numbed as with cold, except in his head, where he felt Cochrane's cool hands pressing his throbbing temples.

Instinctively the rough, hard men around him knew that his end must be near, but partly consoled themselves with the thought that it would be painless.

With quiet pertinacity, after having scanned the faces of the bystanders and read their thoughts, he hoarsely whispered,—

"See, Cochrane, how surely my presentiments have come true!"

"Nonsense, man," said Cochrane, with as light a heart as he could assume. "We're not out of the wood yet, it's true, but you'll be down in Melbourne very soon, never fear."

"Perhaps so, but not as you think," replied Jack, though what he meant the others could not divine. "Cochrane," said he to the inspector, "do you know why I felt sure I shouldn't return last night. I didn't tell you at the time, for I thought it might scare you. I saw Harry—you know Harry Coates, that was killed last month;—he was standing in the path as we went up the ridge, and laid his hands smilingly on my reins. At home, in Warwickshire, there's an old saying that—

'A spirit's hand on a horse's rein
Betokens death by grievous pain.'

That's all."

The group of men who had come around wore awe-struck faces, such as only the simple-hearted superstitious can wear, and the silence which followed was painful; even Cochrane could find no words to counteract the depressing effect of the country jargon, which sounded so small and flat in the presence of the impending calamity.

But in the silence Gentleman Jim, lying prone on his back at the far end of the cave, had caught the sound of Warwickshire, and cried out,—

"Who's there who hails from Warwickshire?"

The inspector bade him hold his tongue, but he continued,—

"If there's a countryman from there, let me see him before I pass in my checks, for there's little enough comfort where I'm going to, I guess."

At Jack's request, the wounded bushranger was brought near his fallen foe, and there, raised in the arms of one of the diggers, he gazed at the face of the fallen giant.

"What's your name, mate?" said he; "why we shall be company it seems."

Jack said, "My name is Jack Wainwright, and I was born near Leamington."

"Who are you?" the bushranger shrieked, "coming to torment me with thoughts of her! Good God! Hasn't she been dead and cold in my heart ever since she died? Haven't I had enough cursed ill-luck ever since she found out that I had deceived her and broken her and her pious old father's heart? Haven't I lived a hell of a life ever since, but you must be here at my death to kick me down to the other hell?"

Here his excitement overcame him, and he subsided, fainting, in the digger's arms, while Jack's face grew strangely perturbed as he said to Cochrane,—

"Ask him if his name is James Whitehead. If it is, the wretch is only paying for his crime against the purest girl on earth."

After a time the bushranger came to, but was weaker than before, and apparently forgetful of the recent conversation. When sufficiently recovered, the inspector questioned him at length about his career, his recent crime, and the place where he had deposited the gold, and whether he had any other accomplices. Finally he asked him to tell his true name, which the other refused, saying, with a ribald jest, that—

"Gentleman Jim or Black Jack was quite good enough for any one."

"Is it James Whitehead?" asked the inspector, according to his instructions.

"Curse it, how do you know that? Are you a devil or a conjuror?"

"Neither," hoarsely whispered Jack. "You stole away the girl who had all but promised to be my wife, back there in the old country, and yet you are here; how is that? Did she die?"

"Curse her, yes," replied the rascal. "Her soft eyes were always soaked in tears, until I wished she would go, and the wish came true." Then, as he saw Jack's fierce, eager look of horror, and the threatening gestures of the diggers around him, he added hastily, "No, no, I didn't do it: she died in childbed—both died—and she thanked God that she went. I remember how she prayed to the last that I might be saved. Yes, I was saved from death, and have been saved over and over again since then, and shan't die now. Saved—turned from wickedness, she used to say. What is wickedness? I was clever, and I used my wits; why shouldn't I? Is the merchant who raises the price of flour, and starves people so as to make money by his wits, wicked? Is the lawyer who takes up a hopeless case of murder? Is the priest who humbugs the common folk wicked? All's wickedness say I, and as soon as I can move about I'll show you how to prosper. Prosper, yes, you grinning ape, I say prosper! Curse you! why do you look like that? Haven't I prospered? Haven't I made money out of other's folly? Haven't I—Curse you!—I tell you I'll live—I won't give in—"

The death-rattle was in his throat as he raved, and with a shudder the digger laid him down, while the others stared at one another, more moved than they would have liked to own by the death scene of this rascal, caught red-handed; and thus hastened into eternity, hardened to the last.

"Cochrane," said Jack, after a long silence, "you've been very good to me."

"No, no, I haven't," said the other; then sharply he addressed himself, "Darn ye, Cochrane, can't ye help being a snivelling idiot?"

Then, after having entrusted Cochrane with a few messages to his friends in Melbourne, thoughts for home folk, and last but not least his letter to Edith, he said,—

"D'you know anything about the world to come?"

The inspector shook his head sadly. "No, me lad, I haven't had much thought for it. I always left that to the praest."

"I should like to see Coates and—and Ellen again—wonder if I shall? Why, surely yes!"

These words uttered so gently that only Cochrane caught them, were his last coherent words. Once or twice he muttered names, chiefly that of his sweetheart and that of his old friend Coates, and then his mind evidently wandered back from the turbulent scene and the wild valley to the soft, undulating pastures of his boyhood's home. For many hours they watched and waited while the tempest lulled and fell, and his breathing came weaker and weaker, then sank to silence, and about noon, as the blue sky showed in patches through the driving clouds, the quiet, honest, brave spirit crossed in Charon's boat the dark river-boundary of the Great Unknown, while the river in the valley, swelled to overflowing, sang his lullaby.

Fortunately for Cochrane and his followers, no time could be spared in mourning the loss of their comrade; grief found a ready antidote in the necessity for prompt action, and after dividing up his little party and sending some to find the horses, others to bury the dead, and one to search for game or find provisions should the searchers return without the horses, he set himself to reconnoitre his position, which the mist soon lifting enabled him to do.

Then was presented to his gaze such a sight as he could not have credited but for the intimate knowledge he had of fire and flood; the flames had before the heavy rain quenched them, blackened the whole of the opposite range of mountains for a breadth of five miles, spreading havoc and destruction over even a wider area, and where but yesterday the vasty gum-tree reared its proud head, and the fern-tree rose thirty feet in its shade, tenanted by birds of gay plumage and marsupials of fleet foot, was but a huge steaming heap of charcoal, from which occasional isolated bursts of smoke showed that even then in many spots the demon was only slumbering under the influence of an opiate, the effects of which would soon vanish and leave him free to commit fresh havoc.

The valley itself was changed from a tawny plain dotted with timber and seamed by cracks to a muddy marsh, down the centre of which yesterday's dry river-bed carried a roaring torrent impassable as a cataract.

This he knew he would have to cross before he could regain the western end of the valley and the Mitchell River Station, though even after emerging from the valley he had the unpleasant outlook of having to ford the Dargo and the Mitchell, both of which would by this time probably be impassable.

For a moment he thought of making his way out of the valley along the southern bank of the river, and thus into the untrodden tracts of country that lay between the mountains and the seaboard; but the thought was almost as soon dismissed as entertained, for to pass into such a country would mean starvation and untried perils of various kinds. There was no time to lose for more reasons than one; not only might dangers of flood and fire increase, but his commissariat was low and means of replenishment uncertain. His party were somewhat rested by their enforced quiet of the last few hours, and everything was put in order so that at evening when the various members of his force returned from their several errands, the stray horses had been captured, the bushrangers' steeds discovered across the river, the two dead bushrangers had been unceremoniously buried in a hole close by, and he was himself ready to render the last sad office to his deceased companion and friend, and then start off as rapidly as possible.

He had dismissed as impracticable the thought of carrying the remains of his friend to Melbourne, as the heat of the weather and the difficulty of transport would alone be sufficient obstacles to his doing so; therefore he had selected a site for the grave, which was dug on a small mound or knoll, bare of trees, overlooking the valley and commanding the entrance by which the dead man had entered the fateful spot.

There in silence they deposited the remains of the brave fellow upon green branches torn from the neighbouring scrub, and as one by one those rough men looked in and dropped or gently tossed down a few leaves, branches, or fern fronds, the bower of greenery rose around and above, soft and gentle as a bed of down; no words passed their lips, but emotions strange and deep were depicted on the face of each in none more than in Cochrane, who felt, more than ever at this juncture, the loss of his true, sturdy friend.

Upon the mound of earth above the grave they set up two roughly-hewn pieces of wood, tied together with withies, in the shape of a cross, which they hoped at no distant date to replace with a more fitting monument, and as they regretfully left the vicinity, the sun gliding to the west, peeped from behind a bank of clouds, and gilded the whole mound and rustic tombstone with its favouring splendour. They made great progress that night, for though the sun went down, the moon promptly shed her lustre across the valley, and guided their footsteps from the treacherous quagmires and swamps brought down by yesterday's rain. The wounded bushranger was slung between two horses in an improvised palanquin, while Huxter was strapped upon a horse led by his friend.

As they journeyed up to the end of the valley to ford the river, the mountain-side began to glow with countless red-hot eyes like a thousand furnaces, and but for the severe soaking of yesterday the blazes of flame which shot up here and there fitfully would have once more fired the whole range. They forded the Tambo, where the torrent allowed them, then returning along the northern bank of the river, passed close to the smouldering mountain. Here evidences of the destruction of life caused by the fire and flood were numerous. Kangaroos, wallabies, bandicoots, sloths, parrots, and birds of countless species, besides reptiles and smaller animals, lay around on every side, either suffocated by smoke or drowned by the flood. Here they found the hobbled horses which had so lately carried the bushrangers, and turned them loose in the valley after an ineffectual attempt to drive them before.

When opposite the bluff they could see that all around was blackened and burnt, even the rocks were discoloured by the heat of the fire, and though the herbage at the foot was still unscathed, Cochrane had no time to look after the giant bushranger who lay there, but hastily sought and found the saddle-bags, which, heavy with their precious contents, had fallen together where he had dropped them. Loading one of the share horses with these and another with a few of the half-roasted birds as possibly necessary provender, he pressed on his way.

By dawn, after surmounting many dangers and obstacles, such as swollen torrents, swamps, and landslips, which had not existed the previous day, he gained the western end of the valley and mounted towards the ridge or saddle there; the southerly wind which had brought such havoc the night before, had long dropped, and the prevalent north-easterly breeze which had set in was freshening slightly as they neared the ridge, and fanning the huge bonfires, assisting them to shake off the thraldom of water and burst back into life and freedom.

By the time they reached the summit, Cochrane congratulated himself on his prompt action, for already smoke and flames were blowing down the mountain and obscuring the track they had made, and unless more rain fell, the whole valley bid fair to be very soon a blazing furnace; the sky was clear and starlit, and there seemed but little chance of rain, for the eastern morning was opening fair and cloudless as they made for the Mitchell River Station. Then his followers took heart again, but their troubles were not over, for their provisions soon gave out, and they were glad to subsist on the inspector's cockatoos, at which they had before turned up their noses as at vermin.

The Dargo river proved impassable at the usual ford, and at great risk the inspector tried another and yet another spot, until success crowned his untiring energy, but though he exercised great care he could not prevent an accident which happened to the wounded bushranger's litter and horses, all of which, together with the wounded man, were washed away and drowned, the rider of the foremost horse narrowly escaping with his life.

On the banks of the Mitchell river the squatter had sent men to meet him, who having found out a fresh ford, had lit a huge bonfire to attract the inspector's attention. Weary and travel-stained, the party reached the station after three days' hard toil, where one and all experienced such care and kindness at the hands of the worthy man and his gude-wife, that they soon forgot all the perils of their adventurous journey and set off for Melbourne, leaving Huxter, who was still incapacitated, behind them, with Jake as his body-guard.

These two were gladly retained by the squatter, short of hands as he was by the superior attraction of the gold-fields, and were duly enrolled as storekeeper and stockman, in which characters I may anticipate this simple history by saying that they long prospered, until the death of the squatter left Huxter and his friend joint managers of the station for the widow's benefit. Huxter and his friend had long before this been pardoned for their share of the gold-field riots at the instance and entreaty of Cochrane, who bore ample testimony to their endurance and courage in the pursuit of the bushrangers; and not long after the squatter's death, his widow, wishing to live at the capital, sold out to the two men on very reasonable terms, so that they became wealthy landed proprietors, owning over 100,000 sheep, and lastly, but not least, forgot their radical doctrines in conservative opulence.

CHAPTER XVII

HYPNOTISM

THE inspector arrived back at head-quarters early in February, and reported himself to his superior officer, received compliments for the complete extinction of the gang, and after a night's rest set off in search of the doctor. He found his friend snugly housed in his official residence attached to the gaol, and as hearty and cheerful as ever.

"Well, ould fellow, right glad am I to see ye back safe and soun', but where's Jack, the rascal? sore I suppose from his riding. Did ye wipe them clean out, as ye say?"

"Wipe them out it is you're asking," said the inspector, "you shall judge."

Then he narrated the story of the attack much as I have told it, omitting all mention of Jack's death, and as the narrative progressed, the doctor's face lengthened, when, with consideration, the inspector finally remarked,—

"So you see we had to leave some of our number at the Mitchell Station; Wainwright was too bad to be moved."

"I know what ye mean," replied the doctor sadly. "It was thrue after all. Edith, I beg pardon, I mean his betrothed after all was right; and so the brave, good-hearted fellow is gone."

"Well, there's no use denying it, I see you can guess it, you can't imagine how we all suffered when he died, and we were real sorry to leave his body up in the valley. He had such a funeral ceremony as is given to few; for three days after we left, the flames and smoke rolled over from the valley, showing that the whole place was alight; it must have been even a grander spectacle than we witnessed ourselves; but what do you mean by his sweetheart being right, how could she have known it, you're the only one besides myself and my men who knew any thing about it in Melbourne, though, by evening, doubtless all the papers will be having specials about the matter?"

"I'll answer your question by asking another. When did the brave fellow breathe his last?"

"Monday last about noon."

"Yes, that was the time that she began to mend. Ye must know that his betrothed, Miss Edith Williams, was frightened out of her seven senses by the bushrangers when they attacked the coach, and has been at a private hospital at Collingwood ever since, under the care of a tender-hearted but firm medico, whom I know very well. Miss Coates has been visiting her ever since she was afflicted, and on the Monday ye mention, both she and I were sent for early in the morning, and learnt that the patient had been taken seriously ill about midnight. Miss Coates found her lying hot and feverish on her bed, muttering to herself not as before—'save me, save me,' which was her heartrending and incessant note, but a new cry had seized her, 'save him, save my lover, save my lover,' and as she spoke her eyes acquired a new—a saner light, and then dulled over into semi-conscious apathy.

"Dr. Price—that's my friend—could offer no explanation; on inquiry he found no one had had any conversation with her the day before, but he imagined that by some inexplicable tether her mind had been so bound up with her lover's, that she was excited with thoughts of him, a hopeful sign, as it showed that the spark of her sanity was rekindling.

"However that may be, her ramblings became more coherent, her cries came quicker, and her eyes resting on Mary—I mean Miss Coates—for a second, appeared to recognize her. Then Miss Coates, laying her soothing hand upon her forehead, asked her if she wished to see her lover, Jack, and to the astonishment of all, she replied, 'He is over there, in a dark cave, lying by the side of the bushranger. He is there, yes, and oh! so pale; oh! save him, the bushranger will hurt him.'

"She pointed to a corner of the room as she spoke, shrouded with darkness, for the sun-blinds were down outside, and the venetian blinds within, and altogether she was so realistic, that Miss Coates, though firm and free from fear, turned somewhat pale, and Price standing behind her bed, looked grave, and pointing to his own forehead meaningly, shrugged his shoulders. But she left us no time for consideration. Her description of the cave became more vivid, her pitiful cries after her lover more and more frequent, until about noon she cried out, 'Oh! my God, my God, he's dead, and they've killed him,' then fell back in a swooning sleep, from which she awoke hours afterwards, refreshed and quiet, uttering a pleasant word of recognition to her gentle friend, who still watched her. What it all meant none of us knew, though Mary, who's a good girl and reads her Bible, conceived that this was a case of the evil spirit coming out of the poor girl, as they used to say in days of old; but now it seems to be only too apparent, in the loosely-hinged state of her mind, by some occult tie, which we can only whisper about and cannot divine, her mind was bound to the stronger mind of her lover; who, in dying, gave back to her her own identity."

The doctor paced up and down, grave and silent and in deep thought, while Cochrane, who was much moved, waited in silence for his friend to speak further. After a time the doctor said,—

"Ye look incredulous, you cannot believe that this mystery is anything but a coincidence, but let me assure you that in my professional experience I have come across several instances of mental contact, not certainly so extraordinary as this, but in each case there has been no actual contact of the two or more persons involved, and in several the persons have been far apart. Dr. Price has had even greater experience of such cases as this than I. He, was telling me that he was called to attend an old gintleman in the town some months ago, who was suffering from severe mental shock. It appeared that as he was reading the paper at the breakfast-table he suddenly cried out aloud, 'Why, Davidson, what are you doing here?' and a few seconds after fell down in a fit. After infinite care and good nursing they got him round, though he was never the same man. As he had lived a fast life as a youngster, Price ascribed his non-recovery to natural causes, but the old fellow disburdened his mind to his doctor one day, by telling him that at the moment he exclaimed he had seen what he took to be the spirit of an old friend. This man had been a sceptic and a boon-companion of his in the old country in former days, and on parting had exchanged and exacted a light-hearted promise that each should, on dying, notify the other if there were a future state. He averred that his sceptical friend appeared older in appearance but recognizable, and in sad tones informed him in answer to his appeal, that he had found out too late that there was a future state, but that he himself was doomed to annihilation. This might all have been a pure creation of a sick man's imagination, but with the next mail came a letter from his friend's widow, announcing her husband's death at the day and hour when Price's patient maintained he saw him.

"If this was coincidence, then coincidence is nearly allied to psychology. Besides these there are many other cases of inexplicable though evident mental contact, which defy discovery and elucidation by scientists and others. So ye see that me explanation may be a right one; but it would be as well not to mention it to Miss Coates, or even Miss Williams herself when she grows well enough to listen, should ye meet her."

Soon after this the inspector took his leave, but the doctor paced the room, his brow contracted with sorrow, his hands behind his head, and his mind revolving the double loss he had thus sustained.

Fearing that any version of the matter might reach Mary through the evening papers, he set off to the private hotel where she was staying, and finding her in, broke the news gently. Though she was deeply moved for the brotherly, amiable man whose dog-like affection she had thus lost, she felt more than ever for his betrothed who, with daily-increasing strength of mind and body, looked forward hopefully to her lover's return, and joyfully exchanged confidences with her friend.

It was agreed that she could not yet be told the blow she had sustained; fortunately the vision of the cave and her dying lover had become completely effaced from her memory, as though it had been an unremembered dream, and to Mary was set the hard task of weaning her thoughts to resignation in the abstract for unknown but possible ills. Always difficult of perfect, always easy of apparent accomplishment, the task seemed in Edith's case too suspiciously easy from the outset, for she was only too glad to acquiesce in what she considered wise remarks which had no application to herself, radiant as she was with hopes of expected happiness.

All papers were kept from her with the greatest care, and all attendants and friends likely to converse on such matters were cautioned, while her father, who had long ago sold out and come to Melbourne exhausted his ingenuity to distract her attention.

CHAPTER XVIII

AND THEY WERE HAPPY EVER AFTER

ONE day, when convalescent and almost well, as fate would have it, Edith received some article of apparel from her milliner, enclosed in many wrappers, amongst which was a portion of an old *Argus* newspaper. The paper she with avidity, after long isolation, was glad to read, and there they found her, hours afterwards, prone and ashy-pale, shivering in every limb. The poor girl had read an account of the gang, and the gallant conduct and grievous death of her lover, and for weeks afterwards suffered a serious relapse; but this time the disease was one with which the medical attendants could grapple more easily, and finally conquered it.

She was a different woman when she rose from this, her second bed of sickness within six months; for her old flashy levity had departed, or was rather subdued into affability, her thoughtlessness had been replaced by consideration for others, and her loquaciousness by attention to her father and friends, so that Mary would smilingly say to herself that it was the case of ill-wind blowing somebody good again. Mary herself quietly aided this strange development, for it could be called little else, of the girl into womanhood; often sacrificing her inclinations and her time to accompany her friend on the rides and walks which the convalescent took; never but once did they talk of the dead man, and that was when Mary came blushingly to announce to her friend that her wedding-day was fixed. It was to be the 20th of May, the day of all others, when the doctor and his co-partners had turned the corner to wealth. Edith timidly asked if she might officiate as bridesmaid, much to Mary's astonishment and delight, who had, of course, refrained from asking her for fear of giving pain.

Then, as Edith reclined in the wicker lounge on the veranda of the little bungalow at Hawthorne, which Williams had purchased for his daughter's occupation, she added these words,—

"I think it would have pleased him so—he loved you almost as much, if not more than me."

The other woman kneeled by her side, put her arm round Edith's neck, and cried, as of course she was out of sympathy and in duty bound to do. After a few minutes they exchanged smiles through their tears, and Mary said,—

"No, no, dear, he worshipped the ground you walked on; he loved you as much as a man can, aye, and perhaps more, for he was a bit of a boy, and, for all his beard and muscles, a bit of a woman too."

"How have they decorated the valley?" asked Edith.

"We couldn't do anything until your choice was asked; at present, we believe the rough wooden cross Mr. Cochrane put up is still there. What would you like?"

"I shouldn't care for one of those gaudy monuments with angels crying over them, and so on, but a plain white marble cross, just as simple as you could get one, with the words, 'Australia expects every man to do his duty' as a motto."

"So it shall be," replied Mary.

"And so you've been merciful to Doctor O'Donnoghue at last?" said Edith, more cheerfully, turning the conversation.

"Yes, he's been so patient and good, and you know never once broaching the subject, although I could see he was only deferring to my wishes, that I thought it better to let him have his way at last, and the 20th of May is to be the day."

Then the pair wandered off into a delightful discussion of what should be worn and who were to be invited, the last point being somewhat easier to settle than the first, for the wedding was, for obvious reasons, to be very quiet. The doctor had had by no means so easy a task as in her remarks to Edith his fiancée seemed to imply. For, on his referring to the delicate subject with true Hibernian tenderness and gallantry, Mary had burst into a storm of tears, reproaching herself with the death of her brother and Edith's lover, and when the astonished doctor required an explanation, reverted to the afternoon at the hospital when the doctor was about to commit the bushranger to the inspector's tender care, and she had intervened. Then the doctor, grasping the situation at once, and understanding the meaning of her pale, subdued looks ever since the fateful December morning, resolved to tell a deliberate untruth, justifying the means by the end. With ready tact and well-feigned surprise, he denied that he was bringing the inspector to the bed of the sick bush-ranger, and in his enthusiastic desire to place Mary at her ease and cure her of her morbid thoughts, went still further, and denied all recognition of the man. He knew well that it was worse than useless for him to fence the truth, and attempt to persuade her that even had he and she known the man, and thus given him to justice, her brother might still have been the victim of his fellows, so he adopted the only available alternative, and told the lie. Doubtless pure-minded people will be shocked when they read of such a rough-and-ready method of dealing with the difficulty, and they might have themselves treated it to a touch of *finesse*; but, as subsequent events proved, he was quite justified in his calculations and in the course he took.

This is the only secret he has ever had from his wife during the whole of their long and happy union. To such as ask with fashionable languor or cynical sneer, "Is marriage a failure?" I would say, when in Melbourne, go to "Nugget Lodge," Toorak, near the St. John's Church of well-deserved fame. With a letter of introduction in your pocket you will gain welcome admittance within the handsome iron gates, with their brass plate announcement (for the doctor still practises more from the need of occupation than necessity), and the park-like railings which environ the verdure-clad grounds, themselves bright with countless semi-tropical flowers and shrubs. There, within the handsome modern building, with its great spreading eaves, low roof, and broad verandas, half hidden with graceful festoons of creepers, is a family party, young men and women, boys and girls, a regular Noah's ark, as the doctor laughingly declares, brimming over with love and respect for their young-hearted father and mother, who thus enjoy again all the pleasures of youth. The rooms are handsomely-furnished, displaying taste in combination with wealth, pictures from old-country exhibitions hang around the walls, furniture from Regent Street warehouses beautify the great reception-rooms, which open in suites one out of the other.

As we look a young girl with flushed face and sparkling eyes, and tennis bat in hand, bounds up to the French window of a sunlit room, and stands there, a bright picture, framed in a fitting frame of flowering climbers.

"Come along!" says sweet but imperious sixteen, "lazy papa, nodding there to mother as though you were acting Darby and Joan. Come along! the queen of your heart commands you to play with us."

"Ah!" says Mary, whose locks show "but the veriest streaks of grey," "I'm to be deposed altogether, am I, from my royal throne, deprived of my sceptre because my head is getting white and I old is that it?"

"Nonsense, mother, you know better than that; whatever we call ourselves, you'll always be the queen of our hearts, and papa's, and everybody's."

"That's rather too wide a sway, I fear," says Mary, laughing, "for me to rule my subjects as they ought to be ruled; but, come, I'll commence with you—Why have you left your Aunt Edith to come in by herself like that?"

"Aunt Edith? so it is," cries out the impetuous maiden, and, crying out, "Here's Auntie Edith!" she scurries along the lawn to meet a stately, handsome, white-haired lady, more like a duchess than a store-keeper's daughter, who has just come within the iron gates.

Tennis is forgotten; a superior attraction engrosses all present, for the elder children love the gentle, tender lady, while the personal admiration of the younger ones is not lessened by the prospect of "lollies," and other substantial favours, always accompanying their "aunt's" presence. A favourite with young and old, a benefactress of the sick, and an active member of women's guilds, servants' institutes, and the like, is Miss Williams, whose success with children is a proverb, whose gentle but firm voice is never heard without commanding respect and attention, and whose many charitable and self-denying deeds, unknown by even her intimate friends at "Nugget Lodge," form so many jewels to the plain betrothed ring she still wears on her finger.

As she enters the sitting-room, and the doctor and his wife greet her, the former says,—

"Our Annie here was just aiming as you came in to fill her mother's place as queen of our hearts. What think ye? will she make a good queen?"

"She bids fair to make as handsome a queen, but to make as good a queen would be difficult, even for bright, clever, tender Annie."

"There, me dear; now Miss Williams wants ye to subscribe to that Mechanics' Institute at Warnambool, which she is getting up, or the Servants' Home at Williamstown is in low wather perhaps."

Then mischievously he looks at the new-comer.

"Never mind papa, Aunt Edith," cries Annie, "he'll give you much more than mamma, I know, for I saw him give a blind flower-girl half a crown the other day, and all for a sixpenny flower, when mother had already paid for it."

The elders laugh at the girl's defence of her father. Very soon Harry, the eldest son, appears on the scene, home from the counting-house of Williams, O'Donnoghue and Co., in Elizabeth Street, bringing with him two white-headed old men, who call themselves "the long and short of it." They are none other than Huxter and Jackson, inseparable as before, and on a holiday visit to Melbourne club-land.

"See, father, whom I've brought home to dinner from the club—two old friends of yours, who'll talk to your heart's content of the good old times," cries Harry.

After dinner the whole party are seated in the veranda, watching the rosy western clouds dissolving into dew, when the conversation turns to Huxter's old prospects of reform. The doctor laughingly jokes him about his radical notions of former times, when separation from the mother-country would scarce have satisfied him, and more gravely adds,—

"How little do we carry out that we propose to do! Here are ye both respectable, wealthy, good-hearted land-owners, who were thirty years ago all for Communism and Socialism; me two old friends and partners, who were going to do such wonders with the wealth which they barely touched, and which unfolded after their death, are—well, they are, I should think, possessed of wealth untold and view wonders unheard of; while I, who set out with the patriotic intention of restoring Ireland to the Home Rule party—well, perhaps I have altered my plans the least, for here I am, married and domesticated."

"What shall be done to him, gracious queen?" queries bright little Annie of her mother.

"Then Miss Williams, whose ideas when I knew her had got no further than dress, good looks, and flirthing, why I blush to say how she has surpassed me expectation, and completely upset me preconceived notions."

"And the queen of our hearts—"

"Aye, aye!" chorussed Huxter and Jackson; "what of her?"

"Well," said the doctor, gazing round at his audience smilingly, but with his bright eyes glistening, "she has even a wider sway than when a thousand diggers were cheering her for her acts of bravery, for she is the

queen and idol of her children, her friends, and—notwithstanding the
Home Rule subjection I mentioned—of her husband."

THE END

ALSO AVAILABLE FROM NONSUCH PUBLISHING

Reflecting the enormous changes wrought by the Industrial Revolution, John Halifax is a poor orphan who raises himself up from his humble beginnings, triumphing over his poverty-stricken start in life to become a respectable member of 'society'.
448 pages
ISBN: 1-84588-027-7
£6

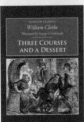

Bitingly satirical and richly illustrated in a style familiar to readers of *Oliver Twist*, this collection of humorous short stories is sure to delight a modern audience able to see in its allegories and allusions plenty that is still relevant to the social and political scene of today.
448 pages
ISBN: 1-84588-072-2
£6

Forced to conceal his identity and forego his inheritance, Rufus Dawes is unjustly implicated in his father's murder, convicted of theft and sentenced to be transported to Australia, where he encounters the brutality of the penal system.
544 pages
ISBN: 1-84588-082-X
£6

Sam Slick, the Clockmaker of the title, is the embodiment of straight-talking. Witty and irreverent, often satirical and sometimes downright scandalous, Sam's shrewd observations on 'human natur' mark him out as one of literature's greatest comic sages.
576 pages in 3 volumes
ISBN: 1-84588-050-1
£10

For sales information please see our website:
www.nonsuch-publishing.com